Joan Shirley-Davies

ALYONA'S VOICE

Limited Special Edition. No. 4 of 25 Paperbacks

To Meg, with love
from Mum
✗

Joan Shirley-Davies
✗

Joan finds inspiration from the many beautiful and interesting places in her home county of Shropshire, especially the meres, near her village. She is also inspired by people and loves to create characters, giving them life, feelings, emotions and a voice. *'Alyona's Voice'* is the second in a trilogy and follows *'Money Is Easy'*.

For my family.
And for all those wonderful people who plant daffodils.

Joan Shirley-Davies

ALYONA'S VOICE

AUSTIN MACAULEY PUBLISHERS™

LONDON · CAMBRIDGE · NEW YORK · SHARJAH

A CIP catalogue record for this title is available from the British Library.

ISBN 9781528934831 (Paperback)
ISBN 9781528968034 (ePub e-book)

www.austinmacauley.com

First Published (2019)
Austin Macauley Publishers Ltd
25 Canada Square
Canary Wharf
London
E14 5LQ

My grateful thanks go to Meg Cooke, Luke Dowdy, Debbie Lloyd, Ismay Evans and Nicola Tildesley, for your much-valued support, encouragement and for tolerating my many questions about your specialist knowledge.

Chapter One

It was just a knock at the door like any other. It might have been a package delivery or a neighbour, but when Claudia saw who was standing there, her heart and soul chilled to the core. This caller was bad news.

The tall, lean, sophisticated woman raised one neat eyebrow. 'Hello Claudie,' she said with an arrogant, authoritative tone in her voice.

'Don't call me that!' Claudia returned unemotionally, having long since learned the folly of revealing her feelings to this person. 'Those days are gone, and so is Claudie.' She noted a familiar twitch of the woman's mouth, not the kind that might turn into a smile and bring some light into those cold, grey eyes, but one that demonstrated her displeasure at being opposed so firmly. 'How did you find me?' Claudia challenged, her own reactions still well hidden. 'More to the point, why?'

'Don't be difficult, Claudie.' The woman tilted her finely coiffured head and added, 'We have something to discuss, don't we?'

Claudia stepped out onto the doorstep. 'I can't think what.'

'Try!' The word fled from the woman's lips, sharp and swift. 'I've flown over especially to see you.'

'Flown?'

The woman scoffed. 'My word, we are out of date aren't we? I moved my office to LA three years ago.'

'I can't imagine how you conned them out of a green card.'

'The obvious way,' the woman said coldly, 'you marry somebody. I kept my own name though. I've worked too damn hard and long on my business to change it now.'

Claudia continued to keep her reactions hidden and her voice steady despite old scores, coming back from the past, to torment her. 'So the Elsa Hamilton Agency is still out there, still selling hungry actors down the river, finding lots of work for little baby pageant princesses…?'

'Don't be so petty.'

'So, where's my father?'

'He bought a straw hat, picked up his paint box and moved to Cornwall—to find himself.'

'All he needed to do was look under your foot.'

Elsa's cool, classy veneer slipped, her marble-like eyes narrowed. 'Stop this nonsense, Claudie,' she said, as if Claudia was still five years old and being very difficult. 'You know why I'm here.'

'It's sure to be something for your benefit, Mother, and not mine.'

Elsa's lips tightened as she snatched a piece of paper from her huge, expensive bag and waved it in front of Claudia's face. 'You owe me an explanation, my girl.'

Claudia swatted it away as if it was an irritating fly. 'I owe you nothing.' She was accustomed to her mother's tactics and knew that she would change up into another gear and become more forceful.

Just as Claudia predicted, her mother reached for the door. 'This is so undignified. I refuse to stay outside, haggling with you.'

Claudia gripped the letterbox behind her back and pulled it until the Yale lock clicked. 'You have no business here. So go back to LA and take that useless piece of paper with you.'

Elsa was astounded. Her eyes widened, her brow lifted, and several creases formed across her forehead. 'She cut me out! But then you know that, don't you?'

Only then did Claudia let her feelings show. She glowered at her mother. 'Why should she consider you? You never gave her a thought. Not even a call, a flower or a card on Mother's Day. What right have you to stand there waving your greedy hands in my face?'

Elsa closed in on Claudia and glared. 'I didn't come all this way to listen to your sentimental angle on it. I want those diaries!'

Claudia, once again, became unemotional and hid her true reactions. She could almost feel the cold emanating from the woman's soul, but she stood her ground. 'No chance! They're mine—legally and morally.' It wasn't easy for Claudia to appear calm when talking about her grandmother, who died only a few months ago. Elsa's abrasive words were a cruel reminder. 'You never gave a toss for the diaries before.'

'Well, I do now, and I won't leave until I have them.'

'You're wasting your time. I promised Grannie I'd protect them, make sure they weren't misused in any way.'

'Promised what?' Elsa scoffed, 'to hide them in a cupboard like she did?'

'Alyona's diaries aren't going to be shut in a cupboard anymore. I'm going to write her story.'

Elsa sniggered. 'You couldn't handle a gutsy plot like that. All the raw emotion, the passion, the—'

'Scandal?' Claudia interjected. 'You're too concerned about the sketchy account that's been handed down. The real story, the truth, is in the diaries and Richard's letters.'

Elsa sucked in a breath through her teeth and said, 'You might just manage to cobble a cheesy, sentimental little novella, and then what? It's still going to end up in a cupboard. My husband's a publisher. A proper novel, with the right promotion, would be worth a fortune. There's even a film deal in it.'

'In your hands there wouldn't be anything *proper* about it. You'd slash Alyona's life into bits of trash, just to make a cheap movie. The real scandal, back then, was the way Richard's family treated her, bullied and threatened her, tormented her with demands to disappear from Richard's life. She was muted by her fear of them, never had a chance to speak up.' Claudia threw her a determined look and added, 'But she's going to get one now. I'm going to give my great-grandaunt a voice at last.'

'Over my—'

'I won't let that amazing woman be used to make you a quick buck.'

Elsa fixed a piercing look right into her daughter's eyes. 'You, of all people, must know that I won't walk away from this.'

'Yes, I know.' It was clear, to Claudia, that this was the beginning of a very bitter conflict. It threatened to be a one-sided one, for she wouldn't play her mother's vicious game. How to settle this and keep her dignity and self-respect was something she couldn't yet imagine, let alone accomplish. People's weaknesses were Elsa's strength, and her talent for exploiting them was immense. She would use them by turning on increased pressure, like some kind of emotional thumbscrew. The more her demands were refused, the more she coldly and callously turned it, and it was impossible to anticipate her next move. Dirty tricks were a stroll in the park for Elsa, and she played them with such callous precision, and then covered her tracks so nobody suspected what she had done.

Elsa pointed her long, slender forefinger like a weapon aimed to back up her words. 'I'll have the diaries and the letters. And don't think for one minute that I've forgotten the jewellery.'

Then, in that moment of dreadful conflict and bitterness, just like a glimmer of sun through a dark raincloud, Claudia laughed at her mother's ridiculous notion. So when she spoke, there was still a hint of laughter in her voice. 'What jewellery?'

'Don't be cute. I know there's a valuable piece hidden somewhere, a necklace... worth a fortune.' She raised her brow and said, 'Unless, of course, you've sold it already.'

'Not all white *émigré* escaped with gems and Fabergé eggs hidden in their muffs. If they did, Zara and Alyona would have parted with them long before they managed to reach Paris.'

Elsa drew a long breath as if she was going to issue an ultimatum. And then there it was, the characteristic calling card of a malicious, manipulative woman. 'Well, everybody has a weak spot,' she said with a smug look on her face, as if she'd won the day already. 'It's just a matter of finding out what your particular weakness is these days.'

'I assumed it would come to that.' Claudia faced her mother, with a cold stare. 'I'm 33 years old. I'm not your cute, curly-haired little property anymore. Threatening to take away my pet bunny or my kitten or even my horse isn't going to work.'

'Something will,' Elsa said with a smirk on her tight lips. Then she turned the thumbscrew a little more. 'You must have a boyfriend or a husband by now. Maybe he has a weakness. A little smutty skeleton tucked away in his cupboard...hmm?'

Claudia shook her head and said, 'I'll never give in to you.'

Elsa's smirk twitched into a brief, sly smile. 'We'll see.' She stared at Claudia's eyes, as if to burn the threat into her mind. 'It's going to be a bit of a scrap, isn't it? Are you ready for that, Claudie?'

Claudia knew this wasn't an empty threat. There had always been something her mother could find to twist her arm. 'My whole life with you has been a scrap,' she said with a sharp edge to her voice. 'And the only reason I've never settled it—once and for all—is because I won't lower myself to behave like you do.'

Elsa sniggered. 'Settle it? You have nothing on me. How will you do that?'

Claudia thought of her mother's one weakness. It was the only thing that would break through the armour of self-assured power that Elsa Hamilton exercised over those who opposed her. Yet, there was just one weak spot in that cold, cast iron woman that would enable Claudia to bring her down. But then, she would have to deliver one dirty, low-down trick for another. She wasn't prepared to lower herself, deny her integrity and risk becoming a woman no better than her mother. 'Go home to Mr Green-Card,' Claudia said. 'We're done here. And to use a term from your world…I think that's a wrap, don't you?'

*****

Although Claudia fought her corner, she knew that the visit changed everything. Her mother would never give up or cave in. Claudia was caught between a promise made to her grandmother, and the threat from her lifelong bane—Elsa Hamilton.

Claudia needed time to think, to work out how to deal with this in a dignified way. To that end, she decided that it was necessary to go away for a few weeks—take Alyona's diaries with her to keep them safe. It wouldn't be easy, life was very settled in London.

She made a plan, it included her car, a map and a pin. At the very last minute, her agent found her a commission, 150 miles away. Tapestry restoration wasn't her favourite work, she much preferred to restore finer textiles, but it was a relief to get something so quickly so she wouldn't have to use her savings to live. The client, Tony Franklyn, had been looking for somebody for a long time, consequently the money was insane. It felt too good to be true, and Claudia looked for the catch, imagined that it would be the job from hell in some dark, Dickensian Manor, where a dour housekeeper walked around with a chatelaine jingling on her belt.

Mr Sharpe, Claudia's neighbour, an elderly ex-serviceman with old-fashioned manners and integrity, said he would keep an eye on the house. Confident in the knowledge that he would never betray her trust, she gave him the keys and her new mobile number.

The speed with which Claudia rolled up her life in London, and laid it out in a small town called Merevale, was a feat of sheer gutsy determination. The only accommodation immediately available, within a ten-mile radius of her new commission, was Heather Brow Cottage. Part of Heather Brow Farm, it stood in a very beautiful but remote spot. It was approached via a steep, gritty track. Her small car could only complete it in first gear, with the accelerator pedal pressed firmly down to the floor, and the engine roaring loudly. However, the journey downwards needed no gear at all, just the clutch, brakes and steering wheel. It was a big change and way out of Claudia's comfort zone. Now she woke up to the sound of cows and sheep instead of cars and motorbikes. However, she felt blessed to have found a landlady, like Molly, a true guardian angel who helped her settle in this new environment.

Monday seemed a good day to venture into the unknown and find Scary Manor. She arrived at Merevale, far too early, and to kill a little time pulled in to take a look at the beautiful lake. All manner of wildfowl jostled over the bird food tossed by people, old and young alike, sitting on the nearby benches. Ducks dabbled at the water's edge. Some were on the lake, heads immersed, feet and tails up. Swans glided majestically as if they hadn't a worry in the world. There was a picturesque parade of shops, white buildings, standing in an arc, with a paved courtyard that was adorned with large planters bursting with colourful, summer blooms. There was an art gallery, jewellery designer, florist and a boutique. A small wooden sign told her that it was the Lakeside Centre. It was a truly beautiful sight, and she felt fortunate in that her brief exile, from London, had brought her to this lovely place. Phase one of her plan was complete, and she felt proud of herself.

She asked a man for directions.

'Larchwood House?' He smiled and pointed across the lake to an elegant Georgian property. 'You can swim across to it, walk around the lake to it or take the next turn left, another left after half a mile and then look out for the wrought iron gates.'

The gates, to Larchwood House, were open. The ten miles per hour speed limit gave Claudia a chance to glance around. It was like a park. She passed through an arbour where dashes of yellow sunlight flickered and danced over the windscreen. Once through, it was as if a curtain was raised to reveal yet another beautiful scene. This was a very well-maintained property. The grass was short, and the gardens were bursting with colour in the June sunshine. The house was big enough to be impressive but most definitely not a huge, dark, scary Dickensian manor. Several other vehicles were parked by the house, so Claudia pulled in at the end of the row and made her way across the gravel forecourt to the four curved steps, leading to the main entrance. By the side of the door, an ornate bell push invited her to press. So she did and then turned back again to look around. The lake was just as beautiful from this side as it was from the road. She could now see more of the woodland to the left of it, its reflection seemingly a mysterious extra dimension existing beneath the surface of the water. A marquee had been erected on the grass, and people were moving in and out of it. Claudia smiled and thought it a fabulous location for a wedding. Lucky girl, whoever she was, about to be a beautiful bride. She would sit by her guy as he made his romantic speech. Then she'd become a girl again and dance with her father. Her bouquet would fly through the air while her friends laughed and jostled to catch it. Claudia thought that independence was all well and good, but a husband's company going through life would be nice, a hug on a bad day, a kiss for no particular reason, nights in somebody's arms and perhaps even a tiff now and then to make it realistic.

The door opened. A man's voice startled her and brought her out of her daydream. 'Hello there! Can I help you?'

Claudia turned and smiled. 'I'm here to see Tony Franklin, about the…' Shock hit her abdomen, like a blow from a huge fist. She feared her body would sway, but she pressed her hand to the wall and then fixed her wide, staring eyes on the man who stood by the open door. Her voice was mute, but a loud cry inside her head screamed out, 'Fraser…Oh, my God, no! Not Fraser!'

Chapter Two

Locked in the grip of disbelief, Claudia stared at the man she thought to be well and truly fixed in her back-story, a time when her life's course suddenly twisted out of shape and left her heart in shreds.

Fraser's arms were extended, one hand gripped the edge of the door, the other rested on the frame. His brow was furrowed as he uttered, 'Claudia?' His voice was hoarse and hardly audible. 'Claudia, what...?'

Elsa Hamilton had trained and prepared Claudia—from childhood—to face many challenging situations, but this one wasn't in the manual. It was like a chilling nightmare. If only it was, she wouldn't have to think what to say, what to do. She would wake up, go downstairs as usual and make coffee—just for one. Words failed her despite searching her muddled brain for the right ones. All she could do was softly say, 'Hello Fraser.'

Fraser's throat twitched above the knot in his tie, and a look of complete bewilderment lingered on his face. But bitterness lurked in his deep blue irises. 'Hello Fraser?' he challenged. 'Hello Fraser? Isn't that a bit casual after all this time?'

Claudia's body was trembling as her mind frantically searched for a way out of this. Should she walk away from him? She did that once, it was harrowing, but she thought it was for good. Her brain teetered on the brink of decision, whether to leave, stick that pin in the map and find work elsewhere or stay and deal with the implications of this cruel and untimely coincidence. Fraser seemed taller where he stood in the doorway, like some mythical gatekeeper, waiting for her to say the right words so she could enter. She didn't have them, but a lucrative commission, a solution to her problem, lay beyond that threshold, this was no time to be a coward, giving up at the first obstacle. 'I didn't know what else to say,' she told him. 'I'm here to do some restoration work on a tapestry.'

They seemed to be the magic words because Fraser gestured for her to enter.

As Claudia walked past him, she recalled the last time she saw him, the heart-twisting pain, the isolation, and then the vow she made to free herself from the powerful grip of an unrequited love for man she could never have. She stood in the entrance hall and waited, fearful that the feelings would return. This was to be her haven while she thought through the disastrous situation with her mother, but she had gone headlong into another potential crisis.

'You look as though you need to sit down,' Fraser spoke politely but with a cool edge to his tone. The good manners she already knew, but the cold hint in his attitude was not something she had experienced before.

'I'm fine. Just a bit tired.' Claudia searched her mind for an excuse. 'I moved house a few days ago, it's been very stressful.'

'Yes,' Fraser agreed, 'one of the major ones I believe.'

If he'd changed in some way, it might have been easier to deal with. He still had thick, dark hair, eyebrows that lifted in a slight arc towards his temple, and his nose straight and noble but with a slight bump on the bridge. His mouth curled upwards slightly at the corners, which, even when he was serious, looked like a very faint smile. Everything was just as always, save for that cold look in his eyes, something else she hadn't seen before.

Fraser made no attempt to move on. 'I didn't know you did wall-hangings,' he said. 'What brings you, so far out of London, to do this one?'

'I had to...' Claudia faltered for a moment and then spoke more convincingly. 'I normally do finer work, but my agent told me about this.' Fraser frowned and didn't seem convinced, so she bluffed a cheery answer. 'I felt like a change, so here I am.'

'Yes,' he returned bluntly, 'here you are. I didn't know Tony had found somebody. I only arrived here last night.'

Job or no job, Claudia still wanted to run, but at least it seemed Fraser was only visiting. He was being a gentleman, but she could see that he was still rather cold towards her. Did he honestly think it was her fault entirely? 'You're not very pleased to see me here, are you?'

Fraser scowled. 'Two years ago, I would have been delighted.'

'It's not…' she hesitated. 'It's not quite two.'

'You look pale.' It sounded more like an accusation than an observation. 'Can I get you something, some tea, water?'

Claudia shook her head. 'I was told to ask for Tony Franklyn. Do you know where I can find him?'

'This time of the day, he'll be with his children. He likes to spend time with them before he starts work.'

'Don't let me keep you. I'm very early. I'll just wait.'

'I have a meeting in the marquee, and then some business with Tony. Excuse me…' He walked towards the door. Claudia recognised the easy, athletic, gross motor action of his limbs. His business suit was immaculate. Her soul sighed twice, once with admiration and the other with relief to see him leaving. Yet, both made her heart ache.

Fraser reached the door, paused a moment and then turned back as if a question burned in his mind and needed to be asked. 'So you're just going to carry on?' he challenged. 'No explanation, no excuses?'

Claudia was taken aback. 'Explain what?'

The gentlemanly tone in Fraser's voice suddenly lapsed, the volume raised and echoed around the entrance hall. 'What the hell happened to you?'

Claudia glanced around, wary of the echo but suddenly feeling more positive. 'I didn't come here to see you. I came to work.'

Fraser's expression softened. 'You're quite right, I'm sorry.' A sudden glimmer of sincerity sneaked through his bitterness as he said, 'I missed you,' almost in a whisper.

Claudia feared the careful seams, that once mended her broken heart, wouldn't hold. 'You clearly see yourself as the injured party.'

'How else would I see it? You fall off the planet and then turn up, almost two years later, in my cousin's house?'

'I didn't even know you had a cousin.'

'Otherwise you wouldn't have come?'

'No, I… I wouldn't.'

Fraser expelled a sigh of frustration. 'What on earth possessed you to just…?' He seemed to check his frustration.

Then he paused a few moments and said, 'We were friends, for goodness sake, such good friends...the best.'

Fraser's gestures of frustration were completely out of character. She felt cornered but made an effort to keep her voice stable. 'Friends, yes, but that's all we were.'

'All we were?' Fraser challenged.

'It was very casual,' Claudia returned. 'We weren't a couple. There was no Claudia and Fraser, no double dating with friends. Did we ever go out to dinner or the theatre...?' She paused awhile waiting for him to speak, but he didn't react. She had spoken the truth, but it seemed he hadn't considered it that way. 'You'd turn up at my apartment now and then, after a bad day at the office. Sometimes you wanted me to help you celebrate some good news—usually when everybody else was out. Often we cooked, talked about books, movies, art, but never family or anything else real. I settled for that. It was a great friendship. No strings, just strictly here and now, right?'

Fraser nodded solemnly. 'A person can miss a friend like that.'

'I did...desperately,' Claudia murmured. Her eyes became watery. This was impossible. Her coping mechanism was already seriously challenged. One little chink now would start a cathartic flood of tears. It would be so embarrassing. 'Losing touch with people isn't a crime, Fraser.'

He looked at her face for several seconds. Eventually, he said, 'I didn't recognise you at first.'

'Have I changed so much in a couple of years?'

'No. Just your hair.'

Claudia grasped it and pushed it back from her face. 'What's wrong with it?'

A faint smile momentarily twitched at Fraser's lips. 'It's almost fair. You've obviously been out in the sun.' He reached out and gently touched her head as if she was a stray puppy liable to run. His voice mellowed as he ran his fingers slowly down to where her hair fell past her shoulders.

Claudia's neck tingled at the illusive touch. 'I walk a lot.'

'But it was so short back then,' Fraser continued. 'Short, light-brown hair...like Peter Pan.'

She was a little insulted by the reference to a boy, but it helped to keep the old reactions at bay. 'Peter Pan?'

19

Fraser frowned, paused a moment and then said, 'Where did you go?'

'Well, I couldn't fly anywhere, I was fresh out of magic fairy dust.'

Fraser shook his head. 'Well, the last two years haven't mellowed your sharp tongue, that's for sure.'

A voice from upstairs echoed around the entrance hall. 'Fraser!' A woman looked down from the landing, her hands rested on the shining bannister that was supported by white, bulbous balusters that skirted the curve of the landing around the hall. She walked, barefoot, to the top of the sweeping staircase. A man's dressing gown was wrapped around her tall, slender body, long, blonde, tousled hair fell about her face and shoulders. 'Darling, I wondered where you'd gone. Your half of the bed was cold when I woke up.' She began to step down the blue-carpeted treads, like a movie star entering the scene.

Fraser looked at Claudia, nodded politely and said, 'Excuse me.'

He went to meet the woman as she stepped down onto the tiled floor. 'Natalie, I'm working this morning. I did tell you, darling.'

'I know, but...' she shrugged, as if she expected him to understand what she meant.

'I'll catch up with you at lunchtime.'

Natalie's eyes darted to Claudia, and then returned to Fraser as she pulled open his jacket, threaded her arms inside it and hugged him.

Claudia turned around. There was way too much information flowing in her direction, but she mentally thanked Natalie for her timely appearance. There was a very large mirror on the wall, so she didn't escape the interaction altogether. If only she hadn't arrived so early, then maybe Fraser would be long gone to his business appointments. She went to look at the beautiful, rich, flower arrangement on the round table that stood in the centre of the hall, but there was no escaping the conversation.

'I have to work, Natalie,' Fraser said, 'you know that.'

'Can I come with you? If you hold on a minute or two, Hon, I can get ready.'

Fraser chuckled and said, 'A minute or two? You couldn't get ready in that time. You'd be hard-pressed to make it in an hour or two.'

Natalie pulled her tall body closer against him and pressed a kiss on his mouth. He stepped back and said, 'This isn't appropriate. We're guests here, it's a family home, there are children in the house. I'll see you later.'

Natalie groaned. 'Do you have to? Can't we go somewhere?'

Fraser's voice was firm. 'Yes, at lunchtime. You can amuse yourself until then, can't you?'

'So these meetings are more important than me?'

'You can't compare your boredom with the difficulties that the people, of Wainford, are facing right now. These meetings are very important. You can find something to do. You haven't seen the place yet. There's a pool and a gym. The gardens are lovely. You can go for a walk.'

'Walk?' Natalie made it sound like a barefoot trip across hot coals.

'Then go shopping, in Bowbury. Take my car. I'll get Joe to bring it around to the front. I know this is tedious for you, but before you know it, we'll be in Tuscany. We'll have time together then—lots of it.'

Natalie expelled a loud sigh, akin to that of a teenager being told to tidy her room, and went back upstairs.

Fraser left the house. Claudia's whole body and mind sighed with relief.

'Miss Hamilton...Claudia?'

A woman, about Claudia's own age, approached. She was dressed in jeans and a blouse. Her shining, chestnut hair fell to her shoulders. A warm smile lit her face. 'Hi! I'm Lizzy. Sorry, have you been waiting long?'

'Not long, I was really early.'

'We're so relieved you're here. Tony's been trying to find somebody for ages. The tapestry's in the banqueting room. I'll show you.'

In total contrast to the high specification of the décor in the house, the banqueting room was not so fine. It was a cavernous place approached by double doors that were already open, and a smaller door at the other end. There were four huge windows along one wall, and on the opposite side, a fireplace with a mantelpiece, that was way above Claudia's head. A chaise longue was by one of the windows, two odd dining chairs by another. A beautiful, shining, Regency banqueting table, long enough to need five tripod pedestal supports, stood in contrast to the gallery of old, cracked, sombre portraits around the walls.

'Spooky, aren't they?' Lizzy said as she looked around. 'They're the last relics of the Franklyn Estate.'

'So this is Tony's family home?'

'In a way, his father didn't inherit, his uncle did, let it get into a terrible state. Tony bought him out before it crumbled to the ground. Anything that could be moved had been sold.'

Claudia smiled. 'But not that fabulous table.'

'No, thank goodness. The chairs went and any portraits of pretty, young ladies in beautiful gowns.'

'And you're left with the grumpy old men in black coats.'

Lizzy's face lit up, and her eyes shone. 'But I'm going to put beautiful gowns back into it. It's going to be my new showroom and studio. I'm already running my business from here. It was meant to be a temporary measure while the children were small, but I'm going to make it permanent. I like working from home. So, the tapestry and the ancestors will be moved on.'

'You're an inspiration. Running a business and still being there for your children. How old are they?'

'Stephanie's almost three, and Eddy's nine months.' She sighed and pressed her hands to her chest. 'It's so hard leaving your babies, no matter how good the carers are. But it's equally hard to turn your back on your dream. I did once, to help my sister, it took so long to get back on track. This way my babies will thrive, and so will the Lizzy Yardley label.'

'You're Lizzy Yardley?' Claudia beamed a smile. 'I'm sorry, I should have known that.'

'Why would you?'

'I've seen your work recently. I restored some embroidered silk cushions for a very stylish, traditional drawing room. The client's daughter was getting married at home. I was invited. Her dress was stunning...the beadwork...' She shook her head, unable to find words fit enough to describe it, and then she simply added, 'Beautiful, just beautiful.'

Lizzy laughed. 'We were on the same team and didn't know it. We should do that more often. Tell you what...when I first moved into Larchwood, I found some fabulous textiles, packed away in the linen room. Could you look at them sometime, and let me know if any of them can be restored? Of course, I'll wait until you can fit it in.'

Claudia felt warmed by Lizzy's presence. It was like meeting a sister who appreciated the same things, such a comfort after the shock of meeting Fraser. 'That sounds great. I'd love to.'

Lizzy grimaced and indicated to the tapestry. 'But I think his needs are more pressing than our passion for fine textiles.'

Claudia scanned her eyes over the tapestry. It featured a knight, but he had suffered a great deal of damage and appeared to be headless. 'I guess you'd call it distressed.'

Lizzy laughed. 'Well, *he* is that's for sure.'

'It must have taken a whole army of moths to do that.'

'Or a bunch of young guys in fancy officer's uniforms, playing jousting games after dinner.'

'Don't worry, I can certainly improve it.'

'Thank goodness. Tony will be so pleased. You have *carte blanche.* We'll get you whatever you want. Just ask. You'll probably need a worktable. I'll get somebody to sort that out. There's going to be a lot of activity in here. People will be packing the portraits and cleaning the walls. I hope it won't be too much of a hassle.'

'Don't worry about me. I'll just get on with it. I need my equipment from the car.'

'I'll get Joe to help you. He's in charge of security, and he's a chauffeur. The guy looks pretty fierce because he's huge, and he keeps his hair really short, but he's our gentle giant...takes care of us. There's so much going on, inside and out.'

'I noticed the marquee.'

'At least that'll be over by Friday. I hope it doesn't rain, the forecast isn't too good.' She sighed and shook her head. 'I suppose it would have been much better in the hotel, but Fraser was adamant it had to be here... He's Tony's cousin.'

'Yes, we met in the hall.'

'I've never seen him make such a fuss. Everything's got to be perfect, invitations, catering, flowers etcetera.' She smiled and said, 'I must go and get back to the children so Tony can leave. Will you be OK?'

'Yes, there's plenty I can do here.'

Lizzy walked towards the double doors, turned back and pointed to the wall above the fireplace. 'That sour-looking guy is Silas Franklyn.' A dour-face, surrounded by a hefty gold leaf frame looked down. 'The maintenance crew swear at him. I hope that won't bother you.'

Claudia was less bothered by Silas Franklyn's face than she was by Fraser's cold eyes. 'Thanks for the warning, but I can cope.'

Claudia strolled to the window and looked at the marquee. A sharp pain hauled itself from the past and gripped her heart when she put the clues together, invitations, catering, flowers, everything perfect. This was obviously Fraser's wedding. It didn't seem possible. Somebody, at last, had persuaded him to change his negative attitude towards matrimony. But then that particular person looked fantastic, even when she'd just rolled out of bed.

Claudia had been a good friend to Fraser, but she had to deny that she was hopelessly in love with him. With practice, her ability to bluff in his presence became second nature. She wore her pretence like a theatrical costume, a motley for a fool with an aching heart.

Once more she considered leaving but then gave herself a good talking to. It was just the shock of meeting the past, head on at the front door. It'll pass. You could never have him. You were his friend, he needed that from you and nothing more. You got over him, so stay that way. Don't hang around to see Natalie, looking fabulous, or Fraser in his morning suit and cravat. Just stay the hell out of it, wait until after the wedding, and then they'll be off on a long, hot honeymoon in Tuscany. By the time they get back, you'll be done here.

A young man strutted into the banqueting room. He was dressed in jeans and a scant vest top that enhanced a body that could only be achieved by many hours of slog and sweat at the gym and a strict diet of chicken and broccoli. He was very good-looking and possessed an added layer of expensive grooming, tanning, trendy hairstyling and cosmetic dentistry.

'Hi!' he called, 'I'm Todd.'

'Claudia.'

Todd moved closer, 'I won't shake hands, they're grimy—mine that is. I've been in the attic, sorting out some old frames for Eliot.'

'Eliot?'

'Eliot Gallier, Tony's cousin.'

'Another cousin?'

'Yes, they're more like brothers though—very close. Eliot's an architect, with a passion for rescuing dilapidated buildings. He's overseeing the makeover, but he won't be here until Wednesday.'

'You work here?'

Todd shrugged his toned shoulders and said, 'It's a temporary job—preparation work before the decorators move in. I'm doing that recess at the moment.' He indicated to the end of the banqueting room. 'Around there.' Then his cheerful disposition dropped, along with his shoulders, and he groaned. 'God, it's so boring.' He laboured on the word boring and made it last for several beats. 'And all I've got for company is a bloody great picture of dead pheasants and rabbits—not very inspiring. Are you part of the interior design team?'

'I'm a textile restorer. I'm here to help the knight get his head together.'

'Textile restorer,' Todd echoed, 'I've never met one of those before.' He struck a dramatic pose and said, 'I'm an actor.'

'Well, I've met plenty of those.'

Todd was suddenly very interested. 'Anybody we know?'

'Not anymore. It was a long time ago.'

Todd lost a little of his enthusiasm. 'This job's just to keep me ticking over until my career gets going.' He beamed with pride and said, 'Got my equity card now.'

'Congratulations, that's quite an achievement.'

'Ain't that the truth? I had to go on a gruelling tour to get it. Eight weeks in Turkey—gyrating in a white sailor suit. That is, in it and out of it. The only thing I didn't fling on the floor was my hat.'

Claudia laughed. 'Well, you needed something to protect your dignity. So, now you can look for a job with more dialogue.'

Todd rolled his eyes. 'Looking is all I get to do. It's a minefield. Got an audition tomorrow though, "Othello", I'm reading for Iago. I'll be late in.' He performed a sweeping bow and delivered a dramatic quote, 'We cannot all be masters. Nor all masters cannot be truly followed.'

Claudia gave him a moment's genteel applause. 'Bravo! I'd give you a job.'

'Yeah right!' He made his exit into the recess.

Todd's friendly company, his hopes, ambitions and his obvious efforts to prepare for his career were so positive. Until recently, Claudia's ambition burned brightly, but now Alyona and Zara's amazing escape from St Petersburg, their work in Ballet Russes, along with Alyona's passionate, controversial love for her English gentleman, were all still locked in the diaries. Writing the story was a dream that had now plummeted to the bottom of Claudia's to-do list, and Alyona's voice remained silent.

*****

Tony was driving. He looked ahead at the road as he said, 'So, after today, we should have a better idea of how to pitch the conference. It's fragile, but if we handle it carefully…' He lifted his voice a little. 'Fraser, are you listening to me?'

Fraser turned his head. 'Yes, I'm listening.'

'It's not apparent. What the hell's the matter with you?' Fraser's mind was elsewhere, turning up memories. 'It was a big surprise to see Claudia this morning—a shock even.'

'You know her?'

'Yes, in London. I haven't seen her for nearly two years and suddenly out of the blue she turns up at Larchwood… incredible coincidence.'

'Life's full of those,' Tony said. 'But you seem to be more than just surprised. Is it going to be complicated, an ex in the house while Natalie's there?'

It seemed odd to Fraser to hear Claudia being referred to in that way. 'She isn't an ex. We were friends.' He was silent for a few moments, his fingers drummed on the arm of the car seat. 'Good friends, very special, but we lost touch.'

'Well, as the cliché goes, that was bloody careless.'

Fraser felt restless talking over this part of his past. He drew a long steadying breath. 'She just faded away without a word. It was as if she was kidnapped and never came back. I missed her.

God, how I missed her! It totally threw me off kilter. You think friends will always be there, don't you?'

'I suppose good friends expect that of each other. Did you look for her?'

'Yes, as soon as…' Another troubling memory crashed into his head, and he stopped talking. He was silent for a while and then continued to explain. 'She moved house, her phone numbers were a dead end. Short of putting a PI onto it, there was no more I could do. I'd be arrested for stalking. I presumed she was in a relationship and moved on with her life.'

'Without saying goodbye or explaining?'

'That's what grates. It doesn't make sense.'

'Couldn't you ask her friends?'

'I didn't know her friends.'

'So what did you know about her?'

'Not much.' His voice softened. 'I knew her favourite Champagne—it's the same as mine. She liked pine cones and absolutely loved daffodils.'

'Cristal Champagne, pinecones and daffodils? If you knew so little about her, what was there to miss?'

Fraser's mouth twitched into a faint smile. 'Her,' he said softly. 'I missed her. I wasn't curious about who she was, I just liked to spend time with her.'

Tony shook his head. He didn't appear to sympathise. 'When it suited you,' he suggested, 'but not all the time I suspect.'

'I guess I'm guilty of that. I needed her friendship, and I was gutted when it was gone.'

'You never mentioned her before.'

'Didn't I?'

Tony shook his head.

Fraser discarded his nostalgic thoughts and prepared himself for a morning of business. 'She made her choices. I just wish this had come at another time. I've got enough changes to deal with.'

'Are you getting cold feet?'

'Course not. I'm totally committed. It's the best thing I've ever done in my life.'

Chapter Three

Fraser quietly closed the door of the guest suite and approached the staircase. He had no need of the bannisters because his feet had trodden these stairs many times. As a boy, staying during the holidays, he had occasionally found the shiny, polished oak too tempting and had managed to slide down to the hall before Tony's grandfather, more generally known as Grandpa Franklyn, saw him.

Fraser smiled at the memory and made his way to the kitchen, a place of comfort to the family. There was a wood burner set in the old fireplace. In Grandpa Franklyn's day, it was an open fire where logs, from the estate, crackled and spat. When the flames died, and the embers glowed hot and red, it became a fine place for toasting bread, marshmallows, as well as drying socks and gloves after tobogganing and making snowmen. These were old-fashioned pastimes, because Grandpa Franklyn was old-fashioned, but they were fun and comforting and still held precious memories.

The kitchen table—so big it could seat everybody no matter who turned up—was laid for breakfast. Fraser smiled at Stella, the family treasure, she had been at Larchwood as long as he could remember. She kept them in line when they were boys and still spoke her mind now they were grown up.

'Morning, Stella,' he said as he poured a glass of orange juice. 'It's very quiet, where is everybody?'

'There's a new baby elephant at the zoo. Tony and Lizzy have taken the children to see it.'

Fraser drank down the juice in one go and then strolled over to the window. The sight of the marquee made him feel tense, this next move was going to change his life beyond recognition. It had to work, promises had been made, and he was determined to deliver. But what of the things beyond his control, the quirks of fate, the unexpected twists in life's plot, such as finding Claudia on the doorstep yesterday? The situation was far too distracting. He was drawn to her, wanted her friendship back, yet he couldn't find forgiveness in his heart for the way she just suddenly dropped out of his life.

Stella called across the kitchen. 'You're like Tony, looking out of that window in the morning, as if the answer to everything was hovering over the lake.'

'If only,' Fraser said with his eyes fixed on the marquee. 'What makes you think I'm looking for answers?'

'Your fingers are drumming on the wood. You always had twitchy fingers when something was on your mind.' She approached him and handed him a cup of coffee. 'Why don't you stop looking at the marquee, it only makes you edgy?'

'It's an important step, and it's not just about me, is it? It's a partnership. We have to make it work.' He smiled. 'That's enough to make a guy's fingers twitch at least.'

'Tony asked if you'd look in on Claudia. Make sure she's got what she needs. Eliot gets here tomorrow. He can take over then.'

Fraser expelled a gentle laugh of affection. 'He's never as happy as when he's working on this place.'

Stella chuckled. 'Even when he was just a boy, he was the house-builder, hedgehog shelters, bird boxes...' she shook her head and smiled as if to enjoy the thought. 'Tony was the inventor.'

'And the patriarchal one,' Fraser added.

'Grandpa Franklyn used to say he was born to run Larchwood, and it was a pity he wouldn't inherit it. I hope the old man can see him now.' She opened the drawer at the end of the table, pulled out her daybook and took her reading glasses from her apron pocket. 'Grace, bless her, tended your wounds and kept the peace between you.' She looked at Fraser over her glasses. 'But you...'

Fraser raised his brow and stared at her. 'What about me?'

'You were the big mystery, couldn't find a vocation that really inspired you.'

Fraser frowned and shook his head. 'I was more than happy to join Dad's business.'

Stella continued to talk even though she was writing in her daybook. 'And you've made a huge success of it, but did you really want it? Or were you just being loyal?' She glanced up from her task. 'Are you in for dinner tonight?'

'Yes, but not lunch.' He looked at his watch. 'What time is Claudia expected?'

'She's already here, had coffee with Lizzy. They're soul mates already, talking about working together. You'd think they'd known each other for years. I suppose it's because they have a common interest.'

'They're both good with people too. I guess they can fast track into friendships. Where is she staying?'

'I understand that she's got a place up on Heather Brow, by the farm.'

'I'll go and see if she needs anything.'

'Be careful now, those shiny, brown eyes of hers would fetch the ducks off the lake.'

'Then I'd better not look—had I? Maybe she's got a jealous partner up there on Heather Brow.'

*****

Claudia was doing some stabilising work at the top of the tapestry. Todd was away at his audition, so she was alone. She could almost feel a pair of eyes on her back as she worked.

'It's no good glowering at me, Silas Franklyn,' she called out. 'I didn't give the poor knight a hole in the head.'

'You're coming very close to making one in mine,' Fraser called back from the doorway.

Claudia's body jerked in surprise. She automatically donned her old motley, it would still serve the same purpose and allow her to communicate with him unemotionally. 'Fraser! Don't creep up on me like that.'

'What the hell are you doing up there?'

'Up here needs fixing,' Claudia answered and returned her attention to her work. 'I have to stabilise it.'

'Not on that contraption, you don't.' Frasers's voice was sharp and authoritative.

Claudia sighed, but she willed herself to keep her cool. Hang in there, Claudia, he'll be gone by Saturday. She turned and looked down at him. 'It's not a contraption,' she said evenly, 'it's a beautiful set of library steps.'

'And when Queen Victoria was on the throne, it would have been a very suitable workstation—for a librarian. How on earth did you get it in here?'

Claudia pointed her finger down to the floor. 'It's got wheels. That's what it does, it moves from room to room so you can reach…high places.'

'Don't be sarcastic,' Fraser chided.

'Then don't push my buttons when I'm trying to work,' she returned. 'This isn't the Sistine Chapel, Fraser, I'm only a few feet off the floor.'

'High enough to break your neck if you fall off it,' he said. 'Say nothing of the chances of stabbing yourself with that enormous needle you're using. You can't work pivoting on that.'

'I can pivot on whatever I choose.' Claudia's tolerance was wearing thin. This was her job, and she wasn't about to be told how to do it. 'I have handrails on each side, very deep treads and a perfectly adequate platform. Apart from that, I'm here on a freelance basis, responsible for my own safety and insurance. But I'm not sure I'm covered for people who burst in and yell at me.'

'I'd forgotten how sharp you can be,' Fraser said. Then he softened his voice and held up his hands as if to accept responsibility for his action. 'I apologise for the sudden intrusion, but will you please get off that thing?'

Claudia suddenly felt a sense of power as she looked down at him. 'Haven't ever used it?'

'Yes, I have, when I was about six. And I was in big trouble.'

'Claudia laughed as she pictured him, as a small boy, being ticked off. 'What am I, six? You got told off, so now you lay this learned behaviour on me?' She noted Fraser's clothes, smart, pale grey slacks and a fine black sweater. Such men might call it casual wear, but Claudia felt that it was way too expensive for chilling. It suggested that he would be going out with Natalie, possibly for a few hours. She was relieved, but Fraser stared at her as if to say that he wouldn't leave until she had her feet on the floor. She sighed and stepped down, and he offered his hand to help her as if she couldn't manage the last two steps. 'So kind, Mr Knightley,' she said, like a lady vacating a barouche.

'You can be as cynical as you wish, but I still prefer to see your feet on these floorboards.'

'I respect your concern, but I need this job, and I'm not likely to risk my neck?' Claudia paused a moment and then spoke more formally. 'Will you please report back to Tony that I'm preparing the tapestry, so it can be taken down without causing any more damage to it? Then the rest of the work will be done down here on a frame…nice and close to the floorboards.'

'Frame?'

'I've only done this kind of thing in a museum, and they had their own equipment. I'm trying to find out if I can hire one, but I've had no luck so far.'

Fraser scowled, 'Nobody expects you to do this alone, Claudia. You should say if you need anything. I'm sure Tony's told you that already. What kind of frame are you talking about? Can you describe it?'

Claudia went to her worktable. 'Here, I'll show you.' She began to make a rough sketch to explain. It wasn't easy, Fraser leaned so close to her as she worked. She didn't love him, but he still had the same potent, sex appeal. Her hand was unsteady, she was afraid he would notice, but at least he couldn't hear her inner voice begging her cheeks not to blush.

'So you don't want a solid top?' Fraser said, peering at the drawing.

'No. I need access through it.'

Then Fraser seemed to understand. 'Ah! I see now. You roll it onto one pole, complete a piece and then roll it on to the next part. Like a scroll.'

Claudia smiled and nodded, it was good to be understood, and for a moment, they were in harmony.

'This is a job for Tony. He can design something. I'm sure the maintenance people can build it.' He tore the page from the sketchpad.

Claudia protested. 'But it's a very rough sketch. I should do…'

Fraser ignored her protest. 'He'll understand it. He's the gadget man.'

Claudia was thankful to get one of her minor hassles sorted out, and that Fraser would now leave, but he hovered. This wasn't what her plan was all about. It was meant to get her mother out of her life, not to get Fraser back into it. She drew a long breath, and a look of resignation lingered on her face as she said, 'You're going to ask me again, aren't you?'

'Yes.'

'You think I can explain it all in a few seconds? Settle it to fit in with your busy schedule, make it neat and tidy in time for Friday?'

'That isn't what...' Fraser snapped, as if she'd touched a nerve. Then he checked his tone. 'But there must be something you can tell me.'

Claudia hated her slip of the tongue about his wedding plans, but couldn't retract it now. She paused a moment and then said, 'I moved in with my grandmother. She was becoming frail and needed support.'

'Why couldn't you have told me that before?'

Claudia failed to prevent a gasp of impatience. 'Of course I wanted to tell you. I had to change my phone number. What could I do if you wouldn't answer yours?' She could sense that he wasn't convinced.

'Didn't you try my office?'

Claudia was even more exasperated. 'Oh! Why didn't I think of that?'

'Now you're being cynical again. What's wrong with straight-forward honesty?'

'Honesty?' she echoed. 'I can do honesty.' She scowled at him and said, 'Have you any idea how difficult it is to get hold of you in your London office? You're either abroad, in a meeting, interviewing, out to lunch or just plain not available.' She found herself suppressing a wave of anger to see that he had no idea what he'd done, how he'd hurt her. And now she had to put up with him, drifting in and out her day looking for answers. She closed in on him and stared into his eyes, suddenly unmoved by the hint of bitterness in them. 'I'd heard enough excuses, Fraser.' She spoke boldly and deliberately. 'I got the message. OK?'

'There was no message,' Fraser protested strongly.

Claudia was standing up to him, but she wanted this to stop, yet the confrontation wasn't over. 'Whatever you think of me, I dealt with it the best way I could. I'd like you to understand that and remember it.'

'That's a tall order.'

'Then you weren't the friend I believed you were.' Her words seemed to strike a blow. It silenced him. He turned from her and strolled to a window. Claudia remained on the spot and called across to him. 'What we had…' Her voice seemed to echo around the cavernous space. 'What we had has gone.' She drew in a shuddering breath. History was about to be repeated. He would walk away with a beautiful woman, and she would be left to get on with her single life. But this time, she wasn't going to suffer, she was determined about that. 'There's no trust between us anymore, but now isn't the time to settle it. When people are about to get married, they shouldn't drag up the past like this.'

Fraser turned from the window and stared as he approached her. His face was grim. 'You're in a relationship?'

'Me?'

'You're getting married?'

Claudia frowned. 'What? I'm not getting married.'

Fraser looked totally confused, 'Then what are you talking about?'

'The marquee…your wedding?'

Fraser was suddenly very amused. His laughter rang around the banqueting room.

'It's not funny,' Claudia protested.

'It is,' he said. 'I'm not getting married.'

Claudia's surprise rendered her speechless. Her mind refused to form a coherent response. She looked at Fraser's face, but all she could say was, 'Oh…! I see.'

'You look shocked,' Fraser said.

Claudia managed to side step her reaction. 'No, I just feel stupid for making assumptions. So, who's getting married?'

'Nobody, unless you count Tony and me, we're forming a business partnership.'

Claudia listened as Fraser told her that they would be hosting a conference, next week, at the hotel. The marquee was for a welcoming party on Friday evening.

'There's a factory, in a small town called Wainford, a few miles away,' he explained. 'It used to be a very prestigious company, the biggest employer in the region for generations, but now it's gone into receivership. Jobs in bigger towns aren't an option because of the cost of travel and the extra childcare they'd need. This is going to jeopardise a thriving community.'

Claudia watched as his eyes lit up and a smile lingered on his face as he talked. This was clearly very important to him. She had listened to his business talk many times, but never once saw that light in his eyes.

He looked at Claudia and smiled. 'We've joined forces to float the factory again, find investors, backers, etcetera.'

Claudia's heart pounded. In the old days, she would have hugged him, told him how proud she was. But this was just a few moments respite from the conflict, and gushing terms of praise would seem out of place. 'Can you do it?'

'The Wainford people are a bit suspicious, rumours of fracking and great industrial projects are going around. But we'll dispel those at the conference. We have to reassure the local people that the idea is to restore what was there before and not use it as an opportunity for personal growth. Neither do we want to come across as a couple of patronising do-gooders. It's a fine line but yes, we'll do it.'

'That's amazing,' Claudia said, sincerely.

'Tony's the real patriarch. This region means a lot to him. Have you seen the Lakeside Centre?'

'Yes, I stopped to look around on the way here. It's beautiful.'

'Tony built that. It's for artistic, creative people with special talents. A place to live, work and market their products. He believes that their excellence will enhance the town.' He smiled, but a hint of uncertainty lingered about him. 'This is a big change for me. I've never been in manufacturing, that's Tony's field. But I'm so inspired by it. It's more important than anything else I've ever done. When I first found out about Wainford, I seized the opportunity to do something that will keep on giving—way into the future.'

Claudia smiled at him. 'That's so generous.'

Suddenly, a cold haze came back into Fraser's eyes as he stared at her, a hint of bitterness returned to his voice. 'It wasn't my idea,' he said, 'it was yours.'

'I don't understand.'

'I'll leave you to try and remember for yourself. Excuse me.'

Claudia watched Fraser leave the room. No marriage meant no honeymoon or dashing off to a new life, with Natalie, on Friday. This changed everything. The situation had suddenly become even more difficult than before. He and Natalie talked of a holiday, but the fact that he was working with Tony indicated that he would return to Larchwood. She didn't want the old feelings to return, to have to pretend all over again that she wasn't in love with him. But at that moment, she knew she couldn't guarantee that. She looked at the tapestry, it was too late to bail now. There was no choice but to stay and thrash this out once and for all. Stop Fraser's barrage of questions every time they bumped into each other. Yet now wasn't the time for personal discussions, she would wait until the conference was over.

To Claudia's relief, Fraser didn't return that morning. By mid-afternoon, no more could be done until Eliot arrived tomorrow, so she decided to call it a day.

A very quiet Todd arrived.

Claudia called to him, 'How was it?'

'Don't bloody ask!' Todd threw up his hands in frustration. 'I thought that once I got my equity card, everything would start to happen, doors would open.'

'Didn't you get any feedback?'

'They said to give them a call nearer Christmas, there would definitely be something for me.'

'That's a positive—right?'

'Yes, it positively means one thing.' He performed a brief tap dance. His trainers padded and squeaked out the rhythm on the wooden floor. He ended with a clap, a slap across his thigh and a loud cry of, 'Ta dah!'

'Pantomime?'

'I nailed that audition,' he said. 'I really nailed it. I can do Iago. And they offer me the dame... Widow bloody Twankey. All that work on my abs, just to drag-up in a frilly frock and poufy mob cap.' He slapped his hands on his chest. 'I didn't develop these pecks to push out a padded bra.'

Claudia tried to be encouraging. 'Maybe they'll consider recasting you, as Ebanaza, he's just as devious as Iago. You'd get to crack a big whip and have a swordfight.'

'A bunfight, more like.' Todd sighed. 'They can keep their damned panto.'

'I'm sorry, Todd.'

He shrugged, 'Well, back to scrubbing the skirting board. I suppose it'll make a good anecdote for chat shows when I'm famous.'

'I'm off now, Todd, see you tomorrow.'

'Not if I get a re-call for Iago.'

*****

Natalie padded around the bedroom, her scant underwear covered but a small percentage of her lightly tanned flesh. 'Must we stay in? Can't we go out to dinner?'

'Sorry darling, it's too late,' Fraser said, absent-mindedly, as he looked out of the bedroom window. 'I told Stella this morning. I assumed, as we were having lunch out, you might like to stay in this evening.'

'You could cancel it, couldn't you?'

He turned swiftly, his brow creased. 'No, of course not, Stella's probably preparing it already.'

'All right, all right.' Natalie closed in on him and put her arms around his neck. 'You're so on edge. I'm just not used it. If you ask me, you're a bit wrapped up in your Claudia.'

'She's not my Claudia. I was just surprised to see her here.'

'You're still wound up about her, I can tell. How do you know her?'

Fraser was irritated by Natalie's curiosity. This was something new. His friendship with Claudia had never collided with his love life before. Now he was being questioned about it. 'I haven't seen her for a couple of years. People move on. Find new relationships. For goodness sake, Natalie, stop quizzing me and get dressed.'

Natalie sauntered off towards the wardrobe. 'Don't be so touchy.'

Fraser turned back to the window and looked down at the marquee. By next week, his life would be unrecognisable. Work would be focused on Wainford. He wondered about Claudia's plans, how long she would take to complete the tapestry. What she would do then. Would she disappear again? They were never in each other's pockets, but that was the beauty of it, the unconditional relationship, the simplicity of being able to meet up now and then without it becoming complicated. It was always so easy. From the moment they first met, in St James's Park.

It was during the flat, empty period after Christmas. Fraser had been tied up in a conference for what seemed like hours, and the bright, crisp day had lured him to the park. When he saw Claudia, something special happened. It wasn't one of those explosive, erotic moments that guys talked about when they saw a woman and described her as gorgeous, sensational or hot. This was easy, calm, fascinating, and he was mesmerised. She wore a light blue, button-up coat, a bulky scarf wound around her neck, and a ridiculous woollen hat trimmed with a bunch of little pompoms, like cherries, that danced about as she moved. Her breath made visible clouds in the frosty air as she searched the ground beneath a tree. He wondered if she'd lost something and was about to offer to help. But she took off her glove and bent to pick up a pinecone, then ran her fingers over the tightly shut surface of it, smiling at it as if it was made of gold. He felt cheated of his chance to speak to her. He moved on very slowly as if he'd seen a rare bird and didn't want to scare it away. Then he saw that she rested the pinecone on her cheek before slipping it into her pocket. What was so special about it he would never know, but it pleased him to witness her pleasure in something so simple. They acknowledged each other with a smile, and reluctantly he moved on, afraid that if he lingered it would look sinister. A couple of weeks later, he saw her again. They graduated to a brief interaction regarding the weather. But after that, their visits obviously didn't coincide, and she just became a pleasant memory.

It was a happy surprise when he next saw her. Daffodils were blooming in great carpets all around the park, the weather was cool but pleasant. She was sitting on the grass, leaning against a tree, the ridiculous hat had been discarded, revealing her short, light brown, boyish hair. Dressed in light blue jeans and a very arty sort of chunky sweater, arms linked around her knees, she gazed around.

'Haven't seen you for a while,' he said casually, it never occurred to him to use a chat-up line or flirt with her.

38

She smiled up at him. 'I was in Scotland, working.' She chuckled and added, 'Too far away to spend my lunch breaks here.'

'Mind if I join you?'

'Not in that suit, surely, I'll come to the bench.'

Something compelled him to sit with her, right there, leaning against the tree, surrounded by daffodils. 'You look very comfortable, I'd rather join you.' He sat by her side and offered his hand. 'Fraser,' he said.

'I'm Claudia.'

Fraser then had a closer view of her face. Her brown eyes seemed to shine. But she turned away and stared ahead, she wasn't flirting either—or speaking. The amazing thing was that they sat in silence. It surprised him because it was so comfortable.

After a long pause, Claudia sighed and said, 'I love it when the daffodils come out everywhere, don't you?'

'Er...sure, they're lovely,' he agreed.

'Summer flowers are beautiful, but daffodils are so...' Her hand waved about as she searched for a word then, as if she plucked one from mid-air, she added, '...Giving. That's what they are, they give so much pleasure.'

Fraser had never considered them to be any more remarkable than other flowers. They were yellow, arrived in great numbers and then left, other flowers bloomed in their place. He didn't want to contradict her, so he said, 'Giving? That's an interesting angle.'

She smiled, her eyes lit up again. 'Every year, they come back.'

'I've noticed that.'

Her brow puckered a little. 'Oh, the gender divide,' she sighed ruefully. 'You're not on my wavelength are you? Am I boring you?'

'No...God, no,' the words flew from his mouth without first consulting his brain.

'I'll try and explain myself.' She drew a long breath and then said, 'Each year they all come back. We've already agreed that, right?'

'Absolutely! We're on the same page so far.'

'It's like a bequest, only it's given to us over and over again…year after year. Makes you think, doesn't it?'

Her question confused him, but he wanted so much to understand. Very carefully, he said, 'What does it make you think about?'

'How a magnificent display like this came to be here.'

Another thing he'd never considered, but he was glad to make a contribution to the discussion. 'It's simple, bulbs, soil manpower, rain, time…'

She looked at him and expelled a gentle laugh. 'Well, that's the mathematical way of looking at it. You're a businessman, right?'

Fraser laughed. 'You guessed.'

She wrinkled her nose. 'We're not very alike, are we?' She commented with honesty that shattered his belief that they were comfortable together.

He frowned. 'Don't say that. Give a guy another chance to understand your theory.'

She laughed. 'Theory?' She gestured to the daffodils. 'OK, here's my…theory. You mentioned bulbs, soil, manpower rain…but you missed something out.'

He smiled and said, 'That was careless. What did I miss?'

'This proverbial host of golden daffodils didn't just sprout through the grass. Somebody had the vision to make it happen, to bring together the bulbs, the soil, the rain etcetera. Over time, it grows into something spectacular, that's enjoyed by so many people year after year…an ongoing festival.' She smiled and said, 'What if nobody bothered to plant them?'

'Good point,' Fraser said with a nod.

'Do you employ a lot of people?' Claudia said, seemingly changing the subject.

'Yes I do.'

'Did you start the business?'

'No, my father did.'

'And it thrived?'

'Yes, it's very successful.'

'So thanks to your father, who did the original spadework, planted the daffodils, so to speak, you can afford to sit on the ground in a very expensive suit.'

Fraser chuckled at her blunt honesty. 'What you mean is that there are pathfinders whose actions are fertile and go on giving long after the original deed was done.'

'Yes,' she said and sank back against the tree with a sigh, as if she reaped some kind of contentment to have been understood. 'I've never beaten a path anywhere. I'm not sure what a textile restorer could do to make a difference. I don't do anything new, I just patch up the old.' She expelled a brief laugh. 'I'm sorry. I've been rambling, haven't I? It's just that I love this time of year so much. I didn't mean to bore you.'

'I'm not in the least bit bored,' he had told her. But he had failed to convince her because she smiled, got up and moved on.

'Fraser!' Natalie's voice was sharp.

He turned. 'Hmm?'

'What is it with you guys and windows?'

'What are you talking about?'

'You and Tony, you're always standing by a window.' She spread her arms wide and turned about. 'Will I do?'

Fraser smiled. 'Yes, darling, you look very beautiful.'

Chapter Four

The next morning, Fraser was keyed up the instant his eyes opened. His mind was racing around, considering the possible pitfalls of the next few months. He'd taken business losses before, but if this failed, then the people of Wainford would be the losers, and for them it would be for a second time. He could always try it again with another plan, but would they trust him again? He wasn't sure he'd gained their confidence even now, it all hinged on the conference.

As he showered, he mentally thought through his morning schedule. His head was well and truly fixed on work, so it was a surprise to find Natalie standing there when he turned off the water. As beautiful as she was, he felt invaded. Natalie wasn't normally with him on a workday. His life was carefully structured into two definite times, business and private. Natalie belonged in the latter when she could expect his undivided attention. He would never take phone calls or talk about work when they were together. This cosying up in the shower was strictly a leisure time thing.

Natalie circled his rib cage with her arms. 'Want some company, Hon?' she said seductively.

'It's a lovely idea, darling, but I really need to keep my mind on my work this morning.'

Natalie's arms dropped. 'Sure you do.'

'I thought you were asleep.' Fraser stepped out of the shower, snatched up a towel and wrapped it around his waist. He used another one to dry his shoulders.

'What's wrong with you?' Natalie complained as she put on a bathrobe.

'Who said there was something wrong?' Fraser said and returned to the bedroom.

Natalie followed him. 'Nobody said it, but you've been showing me since we got here. I know something's wrong with you. Or is something suddenly wrong with me?'

'Natalie, don't exaggerate. I'm just the same as usual.'

'Is that right? So when did you ever wear pyjamas?'

'I always do if I'm a guest in somebody else's home,' Fraser answered.

'Is that why we don't make love, because we're in your cousin's house?'

'For goodness sake, do you keep a log on our sex life?' He rubbed his hair with the towel, then combed it with his fingers.

'You're going off me,' Natalie insisted. 'I know you are. Is that how long a relationship lasts with you...six months?' She returned to the bathroom.

Fraser continued to dress. Now his work schedule had gone from his head in favour of Natalie's need for attention. They were good together. Until recently, they wanted the same things from a relationship. Now it seemed Natalie had a new set of priorities that involved a bigger commitment than Fraser could make. He had feelings for Natalie, but he had never felt that powerful, consuming love that Tony felt for Lizzy. But then it seemed that all Franklyn men were destined to be smitten that way.

Natalie emerged, snatched up some clothes and returned to the bathroom as if to deliberately deny him the sight of her body. It was some time before she came back into the bedroom. She was dressed, her hair and makeup perfect. He could see that she was watching him adjust his tie.

'It's perfect,' she snapped. 'For Christ's sake, leave it alone.' She sighed and said, 'This trip is turning out to be a disaster.'

'Natalie, when you decided to come here for the whole week, I explained how it would be. I have people arriving at the hotel this morning. I need to be there. I can't change the schedule arranged for over a hundred delegates, just to please you.'

Natalie moved about the room, talking to nobody in particular, blaming her own actions for the rift, muttering about pushing him into a corner.

Fraser scowled. 'What are you talking about?'

'You've never been the same since I made that stupid proposal.'

43

'It wasn't stupid,' he reassured her.

'But it isn't what you want.'

'It isn't what you wanted either. All you asked was that we had fun, and I didn't cheat on you. It never occurred to me to be unfaithful, and you have to admit we've had a great time. Now you've changed the rules, you want something I can't give you. Look at us, we can't even spend a few days together, let alone a lifetime. We'd be divorced in no time at all.'

'Everybody takes that risk.'

'It's not supposed to be a risk. You can't make marriage vows with your fingers crossed behind your back, just in case it doesn't work out.'

'Are we breaking up?'

'No, why do you think that?' Fraser went to her. 'I'm perilously close to being 39 years old. It's high time I was thinking about marriage, I know, but I'm not. I'm really sorry.'

'No, you're not. I don't want to be on my own again today. Being in the country freaks me out.'

'Being on your own, anywhere, freaks you out.'

'I'm going to London. I'll come back on Friday, for the party. I'll get my things together.'

'Take your time, it's early yet. I'll arrange some transport for you.'

'A lift to the station will do. I'd rather go on the train. That is if you have trains around here.'

'Of course we do, if you don't mind the soot and the steam.'

'I suppose I asked for that.'

'Country living isn't primitive, Natalie, just different from the city.' He put his arms around her and gave her a hug. 'I'll get Joe to take you.'

When Natalie got into the car, part of him was saddened by it, yet he felt relieved because she hadn't enjoyed being at Larchwood. What she would do after the party, he couldn't guess, maybe she'd just go back home again until the conference was over. He watched as the vehicle moved through the arbour, and then he returned to the house. One thing was certain, compromises would have to be made if the relationship was to last any longer.

As he made his way to the kitchen, in search of coffee, he felt bereft. It should have been because Natalie had left, but it was Claudia who had suddenly invaded his thoughts and made him think of the old days. He would have gone to see her. It's what he did when life was out of sync, and she was always there to listen, sympathise and often chastise him—very often. Above all, she let him drone on about his frustrations long enough to set things right again. But the Claudia from his past was gone now, and this new person was in her place. He drew a long breath and sighed it out, all too aware that part of him was still missing. He then began to question if it was really all her fault that they lost touch. His phone had been switched off most of the time back then, when his private profile became way too high for comfort—one of the drawbacks of dating a hot Latino movie star. It was all very thrilling and good for morale, but it came at a price, his privacy being the bigger part of it. He shook his head and muttered, 'Paloma Cardini? Not your finest hour, Fraser.'

He stopped as he suddenly wondered if that was the time Claudia drifted away, when he was preoccupied and foolishly infatuated. She was always well grounded, had probably lost patience with him and decided to move on. Thinking about it made him even more restless. He called his London office and spoke to his PA. Asked if she could remember anything about that time when the press were troubling him.

'But that was a couple years ago, Fraser, I'm not sure—'

'I need some feedback on this,' Fraser scotched her negative response. 'Find your notes, ask around. Just try and remember something, anything, and get back to me. I'm going to be at the hotel all day.'

*****

Lizzy, and her close friend, Jenny, met for tea and cake at the Merevale Hotel, every Wednesday afternoon. Claudia had been invited to join them. She was concerned about her workload, but thought it would be ill mannered to refuse. Besides, she loved Lizzy's company, and it sounded fun. She tied her hair back neatly and was happy that her jeans and top were presentable.

The hotel was bustling with guests, and the restaurant was busy, but the hum of conversation over afternoon tea was not so noisy as to drown the genteel chink of china.

Lizzy smiled and waved to her from a table by the window. 'Brilliant!' she said as if Claudia had done something special. 'You made it.' She introduced her friend, 'Jenny has the florist studio at the Lakeside Centre. She's like a doctor or a lawyer, she probably knows more about the private lives of people in this community than anybody.'

'Yes,' Jenny confirmed. 'Birthdays, anniversaries, new babies, whose had a row with his wife…'

'But she never tells,' Lizzy reassured her.

'This is great,' Jenny said with a beaming smile on her face, 'another member for our tea and cake club, our weekly fix of gossip and comfort food.'

Claudia glanced about. 'How many members do you have?'

'Altogether, including you, that's three.'

Claudia smiled. 'I'm very honoured. You did well to get a table here, it's really busy.'

'It's not luck,' Jenny said. A hint of mischief glinted in her eyes as she leaned forward to whisper, 'It's Lizzy, she's having this long-term, steamy affair with the owner. They're crazy in love. He'll do anything for her, picks up the tab—every Wednesday.'

Claudia was taken aback for a moment. Having been invited, she didn't wish to appear prudish, but she wondered at the frankness of the conversation, until it became obvious that it was a joke. She smiled and said, 'He sounds like a really generous, fabulously hot guy.'

'He is,' Lizzy said, '*my* generous, fabulously hot guy.' She shook her head at Jenny. 'You might have let Claudia weigh you up before you sprang that on her.' She turned to Claudia. 'As you've probably guessed, this is Tony's hotel. They keep this table for us.' She gestured to the three-tiered stand, full of tempting pastries. 'Come on now. We don't allow the calorie police to come to our club. Sensible eating is against the rules for the next hour. Then you've got a week to work it off before the next club meeting.'

Claudia's soul sighed with contentment to be in such good female company. She took a strawberry tart from the cake stand. 'This looks so wicked,' she said with a chuckle, 'fresh strawberries.'

Jenny stared down at her plate and then looked up, with a grim expression on her face. 'It's not the same is it...plain sponge?'

'Not the same?' Claudia queried.

'I normally have chocolate fudge cake, but I can't now, I'm pregnant.'

Claudia smiled, and her eyes shone as she said, 'Congratulations.'

Jenny picked up her pastry fork. 'It's not just any old chocolate fudge cake, it's mine. The pastry chef invented it for me, it's a special recipe.'

'Oh...that really is a big sacrifice then,' Claudia said.

'I've waited all this time to be pregnant, only to go through this gruelling comfort deprivation.' She then chanted as if she was reading a list. 'Can't have chocolate...can't have wine...can't have Brie...can't have coffee...'

'Nor sushi or shark,' Lizzy added.

Jenny grimaced, 'I won't cry over that.'

'It's worth it in the end,' Lizzy assured her, 'and you've only got four months to go.'

Jenny nodded. 'Yes, you're right. At least I don't have to give up sex.'

'There you go then,' Lizzy spoke in a comforting, positive way, 'that compensates. A night of romance and passion makes you feel like a woman, doesn't it?'

'No, it makes me feel like chocolate.' A mischievous glint came into her eyes as she said, 'How about you, Claudia? Does a night of passion make you feel like a woman?'

'I always felt compelled to walk by the sea.'

'That sounds like the past,' Jenny said. 'I'm talking about now.'

'You're fishing,' Lizzy accused, 'trying to find out about Claudia's love life.'

'I lived by the sea for a while.'

'Who with?' Jenny queried. 'What was his name? Are you still together?'

Claudia was trying to think of a way to avoid these questions when something distracted Jenny, and the moment passed.

'Heads up!' Jenny said, 'Talking of sex and chocolate... shedloads of it—coming this way.'

'Who is it?' Lizzy said.

'Don't look!'

'Why should you have all the fun?'

'Because I'm the one who's deprived of chocolate fudge cake. I'm entitled to compensation.' She stared ahead and added, 'I know one of these guys, but I've never seen the other gorgeous, tall, blonde creature before. Wow! He can share my cake any time.'

Lizzy laughed. 'Share your sponge cake, you mean. You wouldn't let him have your chocolate fudge. Behave yourself, you're a respectable, pregnant woman.'

'Well, two out of three isn't bad. Anyway, I'm only looking. I haven't got to give that up too, have I?'

'So what's happening?' Claudia prompted.

'Fraser's making his way towards us and bringing his guest.'

Claudia's heart sighed. Couldn't she just enjoy a little time with friends without having to think about him? She sipped her tea, as if she could hide behind it.

All three of them instinctively stood to greet the two men.

'Sorry to intrude,' Fraser said, and then nodded politely to Claudia, seemingly taken aback to see her there. 'I thought I'd take the opportunity to introduce Yuri Balakirev, originally from Moscow, but now he works in the UK.' He turned to the charismatic Russian. 'This is Lizzy, Tony's wife.'

Lizzy smiled and extended her hand towards the guest. 'Welcome to Merevale.'

He took her hand and performed something between a nod and a bow. 'I am very happy to meet you.'

'So, are you going to be based in London now?'

'Yes, I will be covering for Fraser. He can then concentrate on Wainford, with Tony. But I am staying for a short holiday until after the party.'

Fraser smiled and gestured across the table. 'Jenny's a local treasure, a very talented florist based at the Lakeside Centre. She also does all the floral arrangements in the hotel.'

'Hello Jenny,' Yuri said and reached his arm across the table to take her hand.

Jenny, who had been very bold over her description of him, was now a little timid. 'Hello.'

'The flowers are beautiful. You are indeed very talented.'

'That's very kind of you, thank you.'

'And Claudia,' Fraser said with his eyes fixed on her, 'is here to do some textile restoration, at Larchwood.'

Claudia looked at the sexy Russian and smiled as a rare but irresistible opportunity presented itself. But would it be appropriate? Would it seem pretentious? Dare she act on the impulse that was driving her to talk to this handsome Russian, in his own language? She took his outstretched hand and greeted him. The Russian words flowed from her mouth with ease.

Yuri beamed a smile. *'Vy govorite po-russki?'* he asked. His unmistakable charisma gushed in her direction.

'Tol'ko nemnogo. Ya uchilas' yemu kogda byla rebenkom,' she answered. She wrinkled her nose and gestured with her hand indicating that she was talking of a small child. She then noticed Fraser's frown. Was he annoyed at her for taking the liberty to indulge in a little Russian conversation? Or perhaps he was just confused because he had learned something about her that he never knew before. She enjoyed this secret little pleasure, felt empowered, but decided that it would be impolite to continue.

She turned from Yuri and smiled at the group. Jenny's eyes were wide, and Lizzy was clearly suppressing an amusing thought. 'Excuse us, it's just polite conversation. I can't speak enough Russian to do any more than that.'

'It sounded like a great deal to me,' Fraser said, his tone verging on brusque.

'You would like me to translate?' Yuri offered.

'No, of course not.'

'Congratulations on your new appointment,' Claudia said. 'You have a challenging task ahead of you. Doing Fraser's job won't be easy…good luck, Mr Balakirev.'

'Please, call me Yuri. I will see you at the party on Friday. We can talk again?'

'I don't go to parties anymore,' Claudia stated firmly.

'Excuse us,' Fraser interrupted them. 'We should move on.' He spoke to Yuri, 'We'll get some tea in a private lounge. It's rather cramped in here.'

Claudia sat down again and stared at Fraser as he walked away. She then turned to Lizzy. 'Cramped? Was that a dig at me?'

'No, surely not,' Lizzy said. 'He looked a bit put out, but he's probably just in work mode.'

Jenny stared at Claudia. 'Well I want you to translate, even if Fraser didn't. Yuri was hitting on you. I can read Russian body language.' She wafted her hands impatiently. 'Come on! What did you say to him?'

'I just said I hoped he enjoyed his stay.'

'There was more than that, spit it out,' Jenny demanded.

'He commented that I spoke Russian, and I said that I learned a little as a child.'

'And that's all?'

'Yes, all of it, it's no big deal,' Claudia insisted. 'Just polite chit-chat I learned from my grannie.'

'No fit Russian executive ever chit-chatted to me like that,' Jenny complained. 'He didn't hold on to my hand like he did yours.'

'That's because mine hasn't got a gold ring on it. He won't flirt with a married woman in front of his new boss.'

Jenny laughed. 'It was awesome, so impressive. Did you see Fraser's face? He was gobsmacked.'

'Certainly was,' Lizzy agreed. 'Was your grannie Russian?'

'Her mother was. She was called Zara. She and her younger sister, Alyona, were white *émigré*. They escaped St Petersburg in 1920.'

'Wow!' Jenny gasped, her eyes wide. 'Look at me, having tea with a Russian countess.'

Lizzy was fascinated. 'So Alyona was your great-grandaunt?'

'Yes. They escaped together, just the two of them, too young and indulged to understand what was happening, or why their parents didn't leave with them. Alyona was still only 19 when they left. By some miracle, they managed to get to Paris.'

'Poor girls,' Lizzy said. 'Imagine that, raised in a life of luxury and then suddenly becoming outcasts. Nothing could prepare them for that. And what about the parents? I can't imagine having to do the same for my two. Just putting them in a carriage and making them leave, knowing you might never see them again.'

'How did they survive?' Jenny asked.

'Alyona had dance training. She wasn't a great soloist or anything like that. But she was Russian, and that carried a lot of weight with Ballet Russes, and she already had a Russian name. Zara was a very fine needlewoman, so she joined the company as a seamstress and a dresser.'

'That's so cool.' Jenny's face was alight with wonder.

Claudia felt warmed by their interest and sympathy. 'I have Alyona's diaries, vivid accounts of what happened to her and her new life in England. My grannie left them to me.'

'What an amazing inheritance,' Lizzy said. 'You must treasure them very much.'

'Yes, I do. I've had them translated because my Russian is just conversational and not good enough to do the job. When I get a chance, I'm going to write Alyona's story. I have a score to settle with the family of the man she married.'

Jenny scowled. 'Was he cruel to her?'

'No, he adored her. He sacrificed his inheritance, a big estate, just to be with her. But his family tried to get rid of her. She wasn't one to speak up for herself, so I'm going to do it for her.'

Lizzy looked at Claudia. 'But something bothers you,' she said.

'A bit of a glitch,' Claudia lied. 'I'll sort it out.'

'But it obviously worries you, and we might be able to help.'

Claudia doubted that Lizzy would be able to believe Elsa Hamilton's treachery. Her growing friendship with Lizzy was valuable, and she didn't want to risk damaging it by discussing her mother. 'You've already helped,' she said with a smile. 'You let me join your club. Is there any more tea in that lovely pot?'

Jenny was thrilled. 'When I buy a copy of your book, will you sign it?'

'Love to.'

'In Russian?'

Claudia laughed and said, 'In Russian, with dark, melted chocolate and a gold pen.'

Chapter Five

On her return from the hotel, Claudia was expecting to meet another tall, sexy cousin, with dark hair and a killer smile. But the man that came into the banqueting room was completely different. He was tall and attractive, with fair hair and blue eyes. He had a disarmingly boyish smile, but in all other aspects he was, quite definitely, a grown-up.

'Eliot Gallier,' he called out as he strode across the banqueting room. It sounded more like an announcement. He stopped in front of her and offered his hand. 'And you must be the wonderful Claudia,' he added, with a tilt of his head.

Claudia smiled and clasped his hand, 'Wonderful?' she queried.

'Everybody says so, including Stella, and she can't possibly be wrong.' He glanced around. 'Don't you do this kind of work on a frame?'

'Yes, Fraser passed that to Tony. He's going to get one built.'

'Good idea. That's in Tony's comfort zone, designing functional equipment. This one should be a doddle.' He looked at the tapestry. 'Is Sir Headless ready to dismount now?'

'Yes. If you could lay it out on the floor, adjacent to the window, I can get a look at it in a good light. Then I can run my hand vacuum cleaner over it. This is a very well-maintained house, but I'm sure there must be a cunning spider or two in there.'

'I think you're right.' Eliot looked around. 'Has somebody told you what's happening in here?'

'Yes, Lizzy explained it.'

'Once we get the paintings down, the place might not look so dull.'

'What's going to happen to them?'

'I'm going to store them for the time being. I'm sure to be renovating a fortified house or country hotel somewhere. I'll keep them together until the right opportunity comes along.' He smiled and said, 'If you'll excuse me, I'll go and round up a team to get this tapestry down. Tony's waited a long time for you to come along, so we don't want to hold you up.'

He left the room.

Claudia felt relieved that he was at Larchwood, it was much easier to communicate with him about the work, and he never mentioned the library steps.

She heard a ringtone, looked around to see if somebody had come in and then realised that it was her new phone. This was the first call she'd had on it. Only two people had her number, one of them was Mr Sharpe. He'd caught somebody snooping outside her house, having a look through the windows. The woman told him she was a friend of Elsa Hamilton and commented on the fact that the house seemed deserted.

'A friend, you say?' Claudia said.

'Yes, she informed me that your mother was back in LA, so she had come on her behalf. I told her that she shouldn't be snooping. Then she asked for a forwarding address, but I refused and waited by your door until she left. I'll continue to keep cavey, and let you know if anybody else turns up.'

The time scale had shifted dramatically in Elsa's favour. It was inevitable that she would track Claudia down again, turn up at Heather Brow. But there was no way of knowing when that would be. It was like being stalked by a supernatural being, an invisible presence. Her mother wasn't even in the country, and yet, Claudia could feel the woman breathing down her neck, almost hear the next threat. Her body chilled, but her mind still had no answer.

Claudia's determination to give Alyona a voice had burned brightly ever since she was 14, when she went to live with Grannie and learned more about the diaries and the letters. She knew what it was like to try and make herself understood, to have a say in what was happening. But for a child in an ambitious world, it seemed impossible to be heard. Her only weapon was stubbornness and a sharp wit. She became a difficult child, eventually a stroppy teenager, but her real voice was quickly muted, and she could only push her mother so far before it cost her dearly.

*****

Fraser was frustrated by his meeting, with Yuri, mainly because he seemed to be more willing to talk about Claudia than work. The ease with which he was distracted was worrying. He had a brilliant brain and was very accomplished in matters of education and theory, but clearly, he had found these things very easy and was generally able to get by on his own terms. Not that Fraser blamed Yuri for being seduced by Claudia, what man wouldn't be when a woman greeted him in his own language? But it had been a big surprise.

He returned to Larchwood. As he passed the banqueting room, he called in on Claudia. She was on her hands and knees, wielding a hand vacuum cleaner over the tapestry. She wore a voluminous, old lab coat, and her hair was tied up in a black scarf. She turned off the cleaner and got to her feet. Her face twisted in pain, and she gripped her knee.

'Not the kind of job for a Russian countess,' Fraser commented.

'Riches to rags in no time at all, it happened to a lot of people.' She unplugged the cleaner and started to wind up the flex. 'You're well informed about my heritage.'

'I spoke to Lizzy, at the hotel, she was waiting to see Tony. Your ancestors were obviously very courageous young women.'

'I suppose there must have been a lot of young people forced to grow up very fast.' She spread her arms out wide and asked, 'Do I look like a countess?'

'It's strange to think that had they not escaped, you wouldn't be here.'

'No, I'd be somebody called Saskia, living in St Petersburg, and probably on my hands and knees, cleaning.'

'I'm ashamed to admit that I know so little about you. Lizzy gave me a telling off for that. She's like you, she can tear a strip off a guy without losing her dignity or bruising his.'

Claudia put the cleaner under her worktable. 'You two shouldn't fall out on my account.'

'It's OK. We're good.'

'How was your day?'

Fraser shook his head and said, 'Very frustrating. Yuri never stopped talking about you. It was difficult to get him to concentrate.'

'They're a passionate race. He was probably moved to hear a few words of his own language.'

'I'm meeting him for a working dinner. If he doesn't get his mind on the job soon, it's going to put my schedule out of sync.'

'In that case, for goodness sake, don't take Natalie, or you'll never get his mind on track.'

Fraser scowled, he hadn't come to talk about Natalie. 'She left this morning, gone back to London. She was disappointed, expected us to spend more time together. She'll be back on Friday.'

'Looking amazing, no doubt.' Claudia sighed. 'Oh, to be tall and beautiful.'

'Don't be ridiculous, Claudia, you are...' He looked at her dusty coat, her scarf carelessly tied around her head, cleared his throat and added, 'Of course you're beautiful.'

Claudia laughed. 'You're such a gentleman. You know I look a sight.'

Fraser regarded her affectionately. 'It doesn't matter what you wear, how you tie up your hair, your eyes still shine...you have beautiful eyes.' Then he scowled and tugged at the lapel of her lab coat. 'Where did you find this? It's enormous, did you borrow it from Joe?'

'It's mine,' Claudia protested. 'I bought it online.'

'It's way too big. You should have sent it back.'

'I wasn't going to wear it to the opera, Fraser. I wanted it for this kind of job.' She slipped off the coat, tossed it onto her worktable and then winced and flexed her knee.

'For goodness sake, Claudia, either you're risking your neck on those library steps or crippling yourself by working on your knees.' He put his arm around her shoulders. 'Come and sit down.'

'I'm running late, I need to go now.'

'Just take a minute,' he insisted, half-expecting to be ticked off for being bossy.

They sat on the chaise longue by the window. Neither of them spoke. That didn't matter they had always been able to sit and say nothing.

Claudia broke the silence. 'You seem tense.'

Fraser was surprised to hear this familiar tone in her voice, the invitation to talk about a problem, the kind of response he used to get from her. He turned to look at her face, found her eyes focused on his. He knew this look—understood it. This is what he missed when she'd gone, her ability to embrace him just by listening, being there and understanding his frustrations about his work. Yet, she wasn't always gentle about it. She was quite capable of being blunt. But here she was, his special friend, come home for a visit? He wasn't going to ruin this just because Yuri Balakirev had bluffed his way onto the Gallier payroll with a faultless but ineffective résumé. He dodged her question and asked, 'Did you enjoy your tea with Lizzy and Jenny?'

Claudia smiled. 'Yes, very much, Jenny's a jewel, isn't she? I like her a lot.'

'She certainly is. And is everything OK at your new home?' He almost asked if there was somebody else living with her, but instead he said, 'It's a big change for you.'

Claudia's brow tweaked momentarily. 'Yes, it is, but I like it. I never knew that a postcode could be shared by so few other houses.' She fixed her eyes on his and said softly, 'What's the matter, Fraser?'

'You've got better things to do than listen to my grievances about work.'

Claudia laughed. 'It never stopped you before.'

Her tone and the warm expression in her eyes crashed through his defences. 'It was all my idea to rescue the factory, damn it. I saw it in the local paper when I was visiting Tony and Lizzy. The main source of employment, the lifeline of the whole community, was gone. All that remained was a deserted factory with broken windows. Why is it that when a building stands empty, people want to throw stones at it?'

'Anger perhaps, frustration, kids reacting to their parents' comments about the closure…'

'I looked at that article on the page, the photograph of the manufacturing plant as it stood there, like a lost soul, empty and lifeless. I had this sudden compulsion to put it all back, get it to grow again. I told Tony what I was thinking, and he jumped on-board without a thought. But what am I getting him into?'

'I don't know him that well,' Claudia commented, 'but I doubt you could drag him into something he didn't believe in. He's a Franklyn, it's in his blood to embrace the community.'

'I want to be right up there with him, but this hand-over in London is going to be a damn nuisance, it'll take time I can't afford. Yuri doesn't realise what's expected of him. He wants to do it in his own sweet way. I can't replace him without giving him a chance to stick to the brief, and I don't have time to coach him.'

Claudia's arm linked through his, and she leaned close to him as if they had never been apart, or that there was no conflict between them. His heart quickened. It felt so good.

'Did you really believe that one person would be enough to cover for you?' Claudia said. 'You probably need a whole team. Why not get more people onto it?' She jerked his arm a little. 'You can afford it, can't you? And don't worry about Yuri. He's Russian, he'll see the practical side of it. Besides, he'll still be the chief.'

'It sounds so simple, now you've suggested it.' He gave her a wry smile, 'I'm rather hurt actually. Why couldn't I have made that decision?'

'Because you underestimate what you do. And your mind is dealing with a whole bunch of things. Even I know now that every time you look at that marquee, you feel challenged. Just because you're you, doesn't mean you can't be overwhelmed with life sometimes.'

Fraser knew she was right. Wainford, Yuri, Natalie were all weighing on his mind. And he knew that there was still an issue concerning Claudia. But it seemed that she hadn't changed after all. It was just circumstances that were different. He clenched her hand, and for a wonderful moment, their friendship healed. Then, by some kind of involuntary impulse, he pressed his lips to her knuckles. Claudia withdrew her hand and got to her feet. He had obviously overstepped the boundary, and he kicked himself mentally.

Claudia began to pack her things away. 'Go to your working dinner, draw a new plan on your napkin and tell Yuri to get his act together.' She shrugged her shoulders and added, 'You can tell him I said so if you like.'

'And that's the way forward, is it?'

Claudia slung her bag over her shoulder. 'It's your shout, but it makes sense to me. And tell Natalie that you've got daffodils to plant in Wainford.'

'So you *did* remember,' Fraser said.

'Of course I did. That park holds a lot of memories for me.'

Fraser was disappointed to see her face change, and the light in her eyes fade, the salve of the brief truce drained away. She loved the park, so why did memories of it cloud the mood? 'Good memories?' Fraser queried.

'Some good—some bad. Some very bad.'

'Like what?'

'History,' she said.

'And what about the present? Is there somebody—'

'Goodnight, Fraser.' She had a slight limp as she made for the door. Then she glanced up at the wall above the fireplace and called out, 'Goodnight Silas, you grumpy old toad.'

Fraser couldn't remember ever being at odds with her in the park. Did she meet somebody else there? And was it him who ruined her happy memories? Even worse, was he the one who took her away so abruptly?

His phone rang. It was his PA.

'You wanted me to get back to you if we could remember anything about—'

'And did you?'

'I've asked around and looked at my old notepads. We can remember the paparazzi waiting around the office entrance. We also had a lot of nuisance calls, apparently from the press. You told us to turn them all away. To tell you the truth, eventually, we didn't really know which callers were genuine and which were Press, because they tried harder to get past us.'

'Is that all?'

'One of the girls remembered that we had quite a few calls from the same woman who insisted that she wasn't a journalist, but she wouldn't give her name or tell us why she wanted to speak to you. She came to the office once.'

'What did you do?'

'Asked for ID, but she wouldn't prove who she was. She insisted on seeing you, got angry even, so she was asked to leave. We all assumed that she was after information about you dating Paloma Card—'

'I can remember who I was dating, for goodness sake.'

'It was pretty chaotic back then, so we decided it was better to keep everybody out rather than let one member of the press in. Sorry, we couldn't recall anything else.'

Fraser wondered if that woman in question might have been Claudia. Did that mean she tried to contact him? Yet, the secretary's information raised doubts. He couldn't imagine Claudia being evasive in that way or behaving in such a way as to be asked to leave.

Chapter Six

Thursday morning, Fraser felt more relaxed. Having thrashed out a plan last evening, he had swung into action, and after interviewing several of his executives, on Facetime, he had appointed someone to work with Yuri. Claudia was right, she didn't know a lot about business, but she had a way of nailing the truth that was sometimes quite startling. He smiled to himself as he walked along the parade of shops at the Lakeside Centre. Sometimes, a guy needed advice from a woman, and he should accept that. This morning, he needed the help of another amazing woman.

Jenny was preparing a colourful posy of sweet peas. 'Hi, Fraser, what's up?'

He pressed his palms on the counter, looked at her and said, 'Jenny…I'm in big trouble.'

'Men usually are when they come in here. But your guilt is my gain, and the greater the remorse…'

'Yes, I see how it works.'

'So what have you done?'

Fraser winced and sucked in a breath, as if his teeth hurt.

'That bad hmm?'

'Natalie, my girlfriend, is coming back tomorrow for the party. I want to get some flowers for when she arrives.'

'Ahh!' Jenny said. 'That's nice.'

'We didn't part well on Wednesday.'

'Was it your fault?'

'Not entirely.' He cleared his throat as if it was difficult to mention. 'She thinks we should live together, with a view to—'

'Oh no!' Jenny teased dramatically. 'She said the M word?'

Fraser grimaced. 'Yes, and I said the N word.'

'No wonder you're in trouble. What do the flowers have to say?'

'Say?'

'Are you saying sorry for turning her down?'

'No. It wasn't what we agreed in the beginning. Marriage was never going to happen. Short of signing a document, it was a solid agreement. She was quite clear on what she wanted. But recently, she's changed her mind, and…'

'And…?' Jenny prompted.

'I've handled it badly.'

'Maybe you should go along the parade to the jewellery designer?'

'Don't you think flowers would be more dignified? To give her a diamond bracelet when she really wants a ring would be insulting. Don't you think?'

Jenny shrugged. 'I wouldn't know. I don't get many diamond encrusted insults thrown at me.' She set down the posy and looked around. 'Flowers it is then. So, what will it be?'

'Those pink roses look good.'

'I wouldn't go there if I were you.'

'Why not?'

'Well, as you say, to give her pink roses when she really wants red ones…'

'Then I'll have red ones.'

'If you give her red ones, she'll think you're warming to the proposal.'

Fraser shook his head. 'This is a minefield. I never considered the intricate differences between pink roses, red ones and diamonds.'

The doorbell jingled.

'Claudia!' Jenny called out.

Fraser turned as Claudia approached. She was dressed for rain that threatened to fall at any moment. Her hair was tucked inside a woollen hat. She turned to Fraser. 'Sorry to interrupt. Did the dinner with Yuri go OK?'

'Yes,' Fraser answered, with a smile. 'It went very well. Thanks for your input.' He stood back and said, 'After you, I'm nowhere near done here. Jenny's trying to educate me in the complex language of flowers. It seems you have to have the right ones.'

'Don't expect the flowers to say it all, Fraser, you can't throw your hat though the door and hope for the best, you need the right words too.'

Fraser's brow tweaked into a frown. Claudia had dealt the truth to him in her usual way. He knew the words that Natalie wanted to hear, but he couldn't say them. What was he expecting the flowers to do, work a miracle?

Claudia spoke to Jenny. 'I'm looking for some heather. I've bought a little boiler to try and dye some yarn to match up some of the subtle colour tones in the tapestry. I'd like to include some hand-spun skeins, but I haven't had time to look for a supplier yet. Until then, I'll have to press on with what I've got.'

'You're going to dye it with heather?'

'I'm trying to get to the original colour tones, use what they would have done back then. I found a book on natural dyes. The author had achieved a kind of delicate tone of green from using heather. I'd like to try and get the same. But it can be a bit hit and miss.'

'I have that trouble,' Jenny said. 'It's difficult to match the exact colour tones for the bride's bouquets. I can't boil roses to fit the wedding theme.'

Fraser watched Claudia as she picked up the posy, sighed and gently smelled the flowers, then said, 'These are so pretty. Somebody's going to love them.'

'Sweet peas are great,' Jenny said. 'They come already boiled.'

Claudia chuckled and then looked around. 'So, do you have any heather? I'm going to need a lot.'

'There's plenty up on the brow, where you live,' Jenny said.
'Really?'

'That's kind of where it got its name—Heather Brow.'

Claudia and Jenny laughed.

'Oh, how stupid am I?' Claudia said. 'Is it legal to gather it from the hill?'

Fraser, glad of the light-hearted moment, shook his head sombrely, 'Absolutely not, so don't let anybody catch you.'

Claudia stared at him. 'Or...?'

He narrowed his eyes and said, 'Boiling plants will make people think you're a witch. They'll tie you to a ducking stool and throw you into the lake?'

'Oh dear! Then what would I do?'

'I'm sure Yuri would gallop to your rescue, like a brave knight.' He then regretted his comment. It was just a jealous reaction which was not an emotion he normally suffered, not until Yuri arrived.

'I'm only interested in one knight,' Claudia told him casually. 'He doesn't have a head, and his horse is very lame. A girl can't always rely on her hero turning up at the right time, so she has to learn to take care of herself. But thanks for the warning about the ducking stool.' She made for the door. 'Excuse me, I'll just whistle up my broomstick and get back to work.'

The door clanged, and Claudia was gone.

'You should cut her some slack with the Russian conversation thing,' Jenny said. 'She's not your girlfriend, is she? She can date Yuri if she wants to.'

'We were friends for five years, I'm concerned about her.'

'Well, as she said, a girl learns to take care of herself. It really was only polite chatter. Yuri was flirting, but Claudia wasn't. I don't think he's her type anyway.'

'Who is, do you think?'

'Haven't a clue... How about orchids?'

Chapter Seven

Friday began with a pleasant surprise for Claudia. An arrangement of sweet peas and delicate foliage awaited her when she arrived at Larchwood, it was on her worktable. A little card nestled among the flowers. It was simply signed, Fraser. The coloured petals stood in contrast to the row of metallic tools of her trade, several pairs of scissors, a box of assorted needles, rolls of linen tape and skeins of yarn in a variety of hues. As she leaned and drew in the sweet scent, the thought occurred to her that Fraser wasn't at Jenny's shop to buy her flowers, he must have been ordering a bouquet for Natalie. She was returning today, back into the arms of her lover. The thought induced a faint feeling of nausea in Claudia's stomach, telling her that emotions, she had long since learned to hide, were not so easy to deny anymore. *Work,* she told herself, *get to work.*

'The rain's stopped,' Todd said, as he walked through the banqueting room. 'Going to be hot now...fine for the big bash tonight. Are you going?'

Claudia shook her head. 'Heavens, no, I'm staying right out of the way. I'm going to find an obsolete laundry room or scullery, at the back of the house, where I can dye this wool.'

'And I'm going to be here, doing this job instead of the one I trained for, the one I was born to do.' Todd threw up his hands and added, 'Some people fly straight to the top in no time at all. What's the secret, hmm?'

'It helps if you're a cute baby girl, with attitude and lots of curly hair. If you can speak a few words of Russian...' She shrugged her shoulders.

'You were famous when you were a kid?'

'Until I was 14, then I gave it up.'

'Why?'

'It was my mother's ambition, not mine.'

Todd seemed too exasperated to speak. He walked over to the recess and out of sight.

Claudia felt a sense of guilt in that Todd wanted fame so badly and couldn't even get a foothold on being a jobbing actor. Yet, she hadn't wanted it at all. Elsa Hamilton wouldn't hear of Claudie Hamilton giving up the business. By the time she was 14, Claudia realised that it was no good trying to fight it, she couldn't win. All she could ever do was find petty, annoying things to score points against her mother, along with generally being a difficult child.

Claudia had complained about her hair, one morning, when preparing to go on set. 'It's gross,' she had told her mother. 'It's gotten way too curly in this goddamned heat.'

'Mind your language!'

'If I have to cuss in the script, why shouldn't I say it for real? I wanna have short hair, real short.'

'Cut the American accent, Claudie,' Elsa bit back. 'Speak properly. If they wanted an American girl, with short hair, they would have got one. You're English, you have curly hair, you can ride a horse, swim and deliver dialogue. That's what they pay you for.'

Claudia was astounded. 'Pay *me?* I don't see any of it. Claudie Hamilton, one of the highest paid stars on American TV. Where does it all go...Ma?'

'Don't call me that. Your expenses are astronomical. The profit goes into your trust fund. Stop complaining about your hair. It gets you a lot of work—it always has.'

'That's why I want to get rid of it. I'm not going to be your bread-ticket anymore. I'm going to live with Grannie and go to school like other kids.'

'You've got two more episodes to shoot before you start running off to school with your short, straight hair. You're the *English Girl on the Ranch*, you have an image to maintain. It's in your contract.'

'Other teenage girls—'

'It's staying the way it is.' Elsa quietened her voice. 'And where do you suppose you'd keep your horse if you went to live with Grannie?'

Claudia's body chilled, and she knew that her horse was about to become the next bargaining tool. The pain of that thought hit her insides with a sharp blow. She needed to defy her mother, but it would cost. Independence would come at a high price, and she had to decide if she was brave enough to make a bid for it. At that moment, she decided, fixed her young eyes on her mother, pulled her anger back until it simmered just beneath the surface. 'Two more, just two more episodes, then it's over.'

'Get your things, Claudie, you have to be on location soon.'

'At least Lennie's going to be there today.'

'What's so special about that silly little man?'

'He's my friend. He takes care of me, which is more than I can say about you…Ma.'

Elsa Hamilton had bristled at being called Ma. Claudia had scored a few points in the ongoing battle, but she could never win the war.

*****

By late afternoon, Larchwood House had become quiet and all the activity seemed to be outside in preparation for the party.

Claudia had just enough time to dye the wool and then get away to avoid the guests. She put on her old lab coat and folded up the sleeves. Then she pulled up her hair into a ponytail, wound it around and pinned it close to her head. All the things she needed were in a bag, which she hooked onto her arm. Then she pushed her fingers into the carry handles of the box containing her new boiler. This was not her best look, and she had no desire to be seen, so she paused at the main entrance hall before making a dash past the stairs and towards the back of the house.

'Can I help you, Miss Hamilton?' A woman's voice gave Claudia a fright. The woman was smartly dressed in a business suit, her fair hair was pinned up. 'I am Irena, Mr Franklyn's assistant. I will help you.' She spoke perfect English, but it was clear that it was not her first language. She took the bag from Claudia's arm.

Claudia had seen her from time to time but had never spoken to her. 'I'm going to look for a place to do this job, just a scullery or something with running water.'

'I can see that you are anxious. Is there something wrong?'

'I don't want to bump into anybody. Look at me. Everybody's preparing for a big event, and I'm…well, as you see, dressed for a messy job.'

'Come, I will show you.'

Below stairs, they passed through the butler's hall and then along a narrow corridor that led to a warren of little rooms. Each one had a name, butler's pantry, housekeeper's room, there seemed to be a nook or a cranny for every purpose. 'This might be suitable,' Irena said, as she opened a door. 'I understand that it is called the sugar room.'

Claudia looked around the small workstation of long ago, the old, distressed wall cupboards, a scrubbed pine table and a Belfast sink installed generations ago, long before it became a design feature. She turned on the tap, it screeched and shuddered as it coughed out cold water. She smiled. 'This is perfect.'

Irena handed the bag to Claudia. 'You are easy to please, for sure. There is power in all the rooms, even if they are not used.'

'I'll be very happy here, out of sight, and long gone before the party starts. Don't let me hold you up, you must have quite enough to do. Everything looks amazing out there, you're very efficient.'

'I am efficient because I insist on having the things I need in my workplace, wherever that happens to be at the time.' She looked at the bundle of heather and the bag of salt. 'That is true for you also. But you should open the window. That will not smell like sugar. I will leave you. I am sure you will not be disturbed here.'

Irena was clearly a very supportive person, strong enough to conduct herself in a quiet, orderly manner.

Secure in the knowledge that she wasn't using anybody else's workstation, Claudia wound a scarf around her head, opened the window, pulled on her rubber gloves and set to work.

As the water began to bubble, she thought about Fraser, and how important this evening was for him. He wouldn't give her a thought today. If only she could get to that place, too, become oblivious of him. But she had made a big mistake, allowed herself to become close to him when they sat on the chaise lounge and talked about Wainford. The sudden kiss on her hand, one little touch of his lips, made a mockery of the emotional mountain she had climbed during the past two years. Before that, she had successfully hidden her love in plain sight by being a very valuable friend. She couldn't do that now, too many things had changed since those days. Her throat tightened, and tears spilled from her eyes. She had only learned to live with the pain because she didn't see Fraser anymore, nor hear his voice or know the touch of his fine clothes. Sometimes, when he turned up, it seemed that he had just stepped out of the shower and into her apartment as his face and his neck were lightly scented with a tangy freshness. Other times, he had clearly come straight from a bad day at the office.

She reprimanded herself for getting weepy, ignored her tears and plunged the twigs of heather, along with the salt, into the boiling water, then stirred it with a huge, wooden spoon. After a while, it looked and smelled pretty disgusting—the book didn't mention that. As the concoction gurgled and bubbled, the distant sounds of thudding and banging could be heard. She decided it was maintenance trying to clear up a few more crates. She didn't discount the possibility that there were ancestors in the attic, complaining about their images being taken away to be stored. The thumping sounds seemed to come closer. Doors opened and slammed as if an angry poltergeist was storming through the house.

A voice shouted—Fraser's voice. 'Where are you damn it?'

Then to Claudia's surprise, he called out, 'Claudia!'

'Oh, no!' Claudia sighed. She couldn't believe it. What on earth did he want? He probably wanted her to move her car. She shrugged. They had people for that. It wasn't locked, and Joe could probably pick it up and carry it.

After a few more seconds, the door burst open, and Fraser entered. He was so wound up. 'What are you doing in this…this…?'

Claudia quickly pulled a mask over her moment of weakness and greeted him cheerily. 'Welcome to the sugar room.'

Fraser scowled. 'Is there no end to the absurd situations in which you practise your craft? Nobody uses this place.'

'That's why I chose it. I thought I was out of everybody's way.' Claudia's natural instinct for banter was a handy foil to get through times like this. 'Why are you checking on me? I'm not working on a ladder or kneeling on the hard floor. I bet Todd told you I was here—the snitch.'

Fraser was like a coiled spring. 'I need your help. It's an emergency.'

Claudia was suddenly alarmed, thinking that something serious had happened, maybe Stephanie or Little Eddie was sick or injured. Her insides quaked, as thoughts of accidents, meningitis and other childhood perils ran through her mind. 'What's happened? Are the children OK?'

'Yes, they're fine. I need your help at the party.'

Claudia stared in disbelief. 'Not to wait tables, I hope.'

'Don't be ridiculous, Claudia. I need you as a guest.'

She stared at him. 'Oh, I get it. You want me to sit next to Yuri, so he can speak Russian.'

'Absolutely not,' Fraser said. 'It's Natalie…well… I got a phone call five minutes ago.'

'Is she sick?'

'No, she's just being Natalie. She's not coming, so there's going to be an empty seat. It won't look good.'

Claudia threw up her wet, gloved hands. 'Here was I thinking that one of the children was sick or hurt, and your big emergency is an empty seat?'

'It isn't just a matter of a vacant place at the table, it's the message it sends to everybody.'

'Like having no woman on your arm?'

'We broke up.'

'Oh, I'm sorry,' Claudia said sheepishly.

'Claudia, I don't have time to discuss it. I need you this evening.'

'I don't do evenings.'

'I'm asking you…as my friend.'

'Don't play that card. You've been stroppy with me all week. Now I'm your friend? Surely there must be somebody else listed in your phone?'

'Not at this short notice.'

'So the buck stops at the bottom of the barrel?'

'I didn't mean that…'

Claudia grasped at the lab coat, water dripped from her wet gloves. 'Do I look as if I'm in a party mood?'

'You don't have to be in a party mood, you just have to turn up.' He sighed and then reached his hands towards her. 'Give me a break, Claudia. It's not just me, you know it isn't.'

69

'Don't lay the whole of Wainford on me.' She then thought for a moment. Natalie's behaviour was bitchy. She must have known how important it was to Fraser and Tony. She clearly timed it to jerk Fraser's chain. Although it was tame by comparison, it was akin to her mother's tactics, and Claudia felt a strange compulsion to make Natalie's actions ineffective. She looked at Fraser. His face was expectant, his body language willing her to answer. 'I'll do a deal,' she said.

'Name it. What do you want? A new car, a shopping spree in Paris…? What?'

'Wow! What an opportunity.' She stared into his eyes, 'A car, I can buy. I can even get myself to Paris to shop.'

'Then what—'

'A little humility would be nice.'

Fraser held up his palms towards her in a gesture of peace. 'Yes, you're quite right, I'm sorry.'

'We call a truce for the evening. I don't want to listen to any jibes about Yuri or where I've been for the last two years. I'm not going to spend all those hours with you while you're so—'

'I get it. It's a deal.'

'I haven't finished. I want to talk to you but not in short bursts, as you pop in and out of the banqueting room. We need to thrash out the past properly, so we can find some kind of level ground and move on. It's very important to me.' She noted his look of impatience. 'Sorry to drive such a hard bargain.'

'Don't be cynical.'

'I'll be what I like, I'm doing you a favour. We'll meet up the first morning after your conference.'

'Wednesday will be the last day.'

'Make it Thursday morning, no cancellations or excuses.'

'Agreed,' Fraser said, as if he was closing a business deal.

'Good.' Claudia stirred her potion. 'See you later then. What time?'

'Six thirty.'

'What?' Claudia's composure slipped from her grasp as well as her wooden spoon. 'Six…?'

'The hosts need to be in place before the others arrive.'

'Now I'm a host?' She picked up her spoon. 'I thought I was just filling a seat.'

'Yes, next to me. Is there a problem with that?'

'It's almost five o'clock, how do you expect me to get ready and back here in that time?' Claudia knew her cheeks were bright red and shining from the humid heat. She probably still had tear tracks. The scarf began to droop over her forehead, and she tried to move it with the back of her wrist, but the murky water dripped from her wet glove and rolled down her face.

'Joe will come and pick you up at Heather Brow,' Fraser said, as if it would solve her problem. He peered into the boiler and added, 'Although you don't appear to have left much of it on the hillside.'

Claudia frowned at him. 'I don't know why you're so up-tight. You're at the top of your food chain, you're supposed to be able to manage pressure.'

Fraser stared at her. 'There's going to be lawyers representing Wainford, investors, bankers, people from my business and Tony's. I need this evening to be a success. It has to be relaxed, upbeat and positive. But my best shot at achieving all that is standing here, dripping wet, dressed in a tent and stirring a bloody cauldron.' He glared into her eyes. 'That's pressure.'

Claudia laughed and tried to dry her cheek on her sleeve. She then nudged the scarf up a little. 'Don't worry, I'm going to cast a spell. I'm sure there's a newt or a toad somewhere around. A quick dip of bat, and you'll be a king among men all evening.'

'This isn't funny, Claudia.'

She wrinkled her nose. 'You used to think I was fun in the old days.'

Fraser stopped and sighed and then looked at her for a while. 'Yes, I remember.' A faint smile twitched on his mouth. 'But I never turned up to find you boiling roots.' He shook his head slowly. 'You look ridiculous, you know that?' There was a ring of affection in his voice.

Claudia nodded, painfully aware that she was standing before a man she had secretly loved for five years, her gorgeous, high profile, alpha-male friend. 'I thought I'd make an effort, just in case you dropped by.'

Fraser adjusted her headscarf, took a handkerchief from his pocket and mopped her cheeks. 'One good turn deserves another.'

Claudia allowed herself to feel comfort from the fact that her tear tracks were mingled with the water, and he was wiping them away. If only he could really do that. 'I'd better switch all this off.'

'Yes, go and dig out a posh frock.' Fraser made for the door and then turned back with a startled look on his face. 'You do have one, don't you? Please tell me you've got a prom dress or something.'

'On a scale of one to ten, how posh does it need to be?'

'Twelve,' Fraser answered, quickly, his eyes showing his doubts.

'And all the other women will be dressed up to the twelves?'

'I'm sure they're going to look sensational, but don't worry yourself about them, just get as close as you can.'

'Sure, I'll give it my best shot and see if I can stagger up to a seven. How about that?'

'Claudia!'

'Don't worry, I can scrub up and find a frock.'

'You can?'

She scooped up a skein of wool with her wooden spoon. 'I'll have to, won't I? I don't have time to knit one.'

'Oh hell! This is going to be a train crash. Six thirty...prompt.' He left the room as noisily as he'd approached it. His brisk footfall sounded along the passage, and then his voice echoed across the butler's hall and along the corridor. 'I've missed you, Claudia Hamilton.' It was as if it was safe to say it at a distance.

Chapter Eight

Fraser, Eliot, Tony and Lizzy waited at the entrance to the marquee. Waiters, holding trays of drinks, stood just inside. Fraser looked around at all the stylish trappings of corporate hospitality. It was a family joke that Irena could arrange the weather, and this evening was no exception. Yesterday's rain had quenched the thirsty ground, perked up the blooms in the rose garden, and now the air was still and scented. All Fraser needed now was a partner, but he was regretting his hasty, selfish actions in enlisting Claudia's help. He questioned why he went directly to her instead of examining other options. He wondered if he would always have this knee-jerk reaction of turning to Claudia when life challenged him.

'Fraser, stop pacing about,' Eliot said, 'everything's going to be fine.'

'I shouldn't have done it.' Fraser unfastened his dinner jacket, as if it was stifling him. 'I pushed her into it, expected her to bail me out. She wasn't prepared. I didn't give her enough time.' He looked back at the house. The last couple of hours had been horrendous. Natalie's well-timed phone call had the desired effect, it completely threw him but not enough to give in to her. Her priorities had changed dramatically. She wanted a future, somebody for life, and a gold band to seal the bargain. Maybe she always wanted that and was biding her time until she won him over.

'Fraser,' Lizzy approached him. 'Claudia's made of tougher stuff than that, she's quite capable of turning you down if she didn't want to come.'

'She said she doesn't go out in the evenings. She's going to hate me for this.'

'No, she isn't,' Lizzy insisted, 'she's got more integrity than that. You don't know very much about her, but I'm sure you found that out.'

Fraser smiled at her. 'Yes, I know.'

Grace, Tony's sister, arrived. 'Look at you all,' she called out, with a beaming smile. 'You look fabulous.' She embraced each of them. 'Charlie's really sorry he couldn't make it. I feel awful coming to a party when he's going to be on his feet half the night.'

'Special people, surgeons,' Tony said.

'So are doctors,' Lizzy told Grace, as if to redress the balance. 'You're not on call, are you?'

'Not tonight. I wouldn't miss this for anything. Tony and Fraser...partners.' She smiled and looked around. 'Isn't this great? We haven't all been together for ages. Time we had another wedding in the family.'

Eliot winced and caught Fraser's eye. 'She means us, doesn't she?'

Fraser raised his brow. 'Don't look at me, I've got enough woman trouble.'

Grace hugged Fraser. 'I heard, Tony called me. Is there anything I can do?'

'Thanks, Gracie, I'm fine.'

Eliot looked back at the catwalk. 'Heads up! Here's your partner, Fraser.'

Tony laughed. 'So this is the poor, stressed-out woman who doesn't go out in the evenings?'

'She made it. Good for her,' Lizzy said. 'Wow! She looks amazing.'

Fraser was speechless as he stared at Claudia. Earlier today, he told her that he just wanted her to turn up in some kind of posh frock, but now she looked so fabulous that the wooden walkway across the grass could be a red carpet under her feet.

'She's gorgeous,' Grace said and nudged Fraser's arm playfully. 'You didn't waste any time.'

'Oh, she's just a friend,' Eliot said with a laugh. 'The kind of good chum you turn to when you need somebody to bail you out.' He slapped Fraser's shoulder. 'Don't stand there choking on humble pie, go and meet her.'

Fraser's feet remained on the spot as he continued to stare. Claudia, confident and at ease, approached as if she did this all the time. She wore a black dress, with thin shoulder straps. The skirt was slightly above her knee and had a dressing of beaded chiffon that swung and danced about her thighs with every step she took. A far cry from her Peter Pan hair, a glossy cascade of waves bounced as she walked. Fraser had never met a woman who could go through a metamorphosis like this in such a short time. She had joked that she was brewing a spell to make him a king among men, but she was the one who had been magically transformed. Tension drained away as he walked towards her with his hands outstretched. He felt a huge surge of admiration for her, or was it just plain lust? To his surprise, restraint was needed to keep his greeting to a polite, chaste kiss on the cheek. Nevertheless, he ventured to kiss both sides of her face. The touch of her skin made his lips tingle, as he savoured the delicate, sweet scent of her. He felt vulnerable, like a teenager on his first date, afraid to flirt, scared that he couldn't control the powerful physical reaction below his bespoke belt. He called on his age and experience to help him out of this gripping reaction. 'You look…' His throat dried and made it twitch. He swallowed and said, 'You look sensational.'

Claudia smiled, it lit up her beautiful, brown eyes. 'Did I get close to a seven?' she teased.

Fraser shook his head slowly. 'Please don't give me a difficult time over it.' He nodded towards the family. 'They already did that on your behalf.'

She brushed his cheek with a kiss. Her mouth lingered by his ear as she whispered, 'I'm not promising.'

The illusive touch of her breath on his face was intoxicating, and she wasn't even flirting with him. If she did, he was going to be in big trouble.

They joined the family group.

Lizzy embraced her. 'I love your hair, how on earth did you do it in such a short time?'

'I don't have to do it, I was born with it,' Claudia said. 'I didn't have time to straighten it properly.'

'Nor me,' Grace laughed, as she ran her fingers down her straight, glossy, dark hair that was cut in a neat bob. 'Hi, Claudia,

I'm Grace, Tony's sister. We'll get to know each other better during the evening, yes?'

'Yes, we'll do that.'

Eliot took Claudia's hands and smiled. 'You look a million dollars,' he told her, 'but I'm so disappointed.'

'What?' Claudia looked startled.

'I hoped you'd come in your shabby chic. That lab coat is really something.'

'I almost did,' Claudia said, 'I don't recall packing my posh frocks.'

Eliot spoke to Grace, 'Let's get a drink, Gracie, and make ourselves scarce. The hosts can do the meeting and greeting bit.'

Claudia turned to follow, but Fraser seized her hand. 'Will you stay?' he said. 'Greet the guests with me?'

Claudia smiled. 'Sure. No problem.'

Fraser felt ten feet tall. The pressure he experienced just a few minutes ago was history. Claudia had, as usual, come to his rescue. There was never a time when she wasn't there for him. Her apartment was a haven, a place to go where he closed the door on the fast lane outside. An evening with Claudia was a shot in the arm, a tonic that wiped away the frustrations of business and set him back on his feet. Now he realised that he knew no more about her than that. It never occurred to him to dig into her life, to ask about her past, school, college, boyfriends... Those were things that you asked when you dated somebody. Every day, since she arrived at Larchwood, he had learned something new. But the most significant discovery was that he had befriended just a small corner of an amazing woman.

'Fraser, Yuri's here,' Lizzy called out to him.

For a moment, he was still lost in his thoughts. Then he looked towards the walkway.

'Is that his girlfriend?' Claudia asked. 'That dress is fabulous, but she still looks very business-like, cool and confident.'

'No, that's Paige Morgan, joined the company a few weeks ago, keen to work in the UK. She's a very shrewd, ambitious woman, hungry for success. I've asked her to work with Yuri.'

Yuri approached, with his Russian charm in full flow. 'Ah, what a wonderful surprise, my beautiful countess is here after all.' He took Claudia's hand. 'I did not expect to see you this evening.'

Fraser deemed Yuri's flirting to be bad form, but he could see how skilful Claudia was at finding a balance between dignity and self-preservation. Even so, he was glad that this overbearing flirt wouldn't be sitting next to her. He'd already seen to that.

Claudia stepped back a little, seemingly putting more space between them. 'I hope you enjoy the evening, Yuri.' She gestured to the waiter. 'A glass of Champagne would be a good start, don't you think?'

Yuri nodded and smiled, then moved on.

Fraser shook Paige's hand. 'Welcome to Larchwood,' he said. 'And thanks for making such a quick decision.'

'No brainer,' Paige said. 'I can't wait to join Yuri's team in London.'

'Keep him focused, will you?'

Paige nodded. 'I'm on it,' she said with a crisp, positive tone.

'This is my good friend, Claudia Hamilton.' Fraser chose his words carefully, making sure not to take liberties with Claudia's status for the evening.

Paige smiled and shook Claudia's hand. Then she suddenly stared at her, and after a long, potentially embarrassing pause, she said, 'Claudia Hamilton?'

'Yes,' Claudia's brow puckered a little at Paige's stare.

Paige then slowly shook her head and a look of wonder came into her face. 'It *is* you, isn't it? I was thinking that you reminded me of somebody but…you're not a lookalike, it really is you.'

'I'm so sorry?' Claudia said politely, 'I don't think we've met before.'

Paige smiled. 'You haven't met me, but I've met you, Claudie Hamilton…Bobbie.'

A good-humoured wince came into Claudia's face. 'Oh dear, are you going to blast my past at me?'

Paige clasped Claudia's hand in both of hers. 'But you're very much part of my past too.' Her words were warm and genuine.

'I'm surprised you recognised me,' Claudia said.

'You look exactly as you did in the Christmas special is why. *English Girl on the Ranch*,' she chanted and softly sang a couple of lines from the credit song. 'I was such a big fan. I watched you every Saturday. A feisty little tearaway, that's what they called you.'

'Both sides of the camera I'm afraid.'

'Back then, I had a lot of surgery. I couldn't get about or go outside for a long time. But every Saturday afternoon, I could be a little tearaway, with Bobbie. I went with her on all those adventures. Fearlessly riding that horse, hanging from trees, falling into rivers…God, how that used to scare me. I'd hug a cushion while I watched you hanging onto floating logs, grasping at overhanging branches…'

'Bobbie was always falling into the water.'

'Next time you see that feisty little tearaway, you tell her that she changed the life of a wimpy, sick kid, pulled her through a real hard time, taught her how to fight back. I wasn't expected to amount to much, but look at me. I just landed my dream job in a tough business.' She smiled. 'Who knew? Catch up with you later.' She moved on and, once more, became an executive.

Tony, Lizzy and Fraser turned and stared at Claudia.

She frowned at them. 'What?'

'English girl on the ranch?' Lizzy queried.

'I was in an American TV series when I was a kid. They needed an English girl with a lot of unruly, curly hair. Some feisty kid, who could ride, swim, climb trees and not freak out when she had to fall into a freezing cold creek. It didn't come over here.' She shrugged. 'My mother's a casting agent. I worked all the time until I was 14.'

'What kind of work?' Fraser said.

'Kid's work…films, TV, commercials for baby soap, school kit, toys, cough medicine… Whatever my mother could persuade me to do.'

Fraser shook his head in disbelief. Two hours ago, he invited a woman who was boiling bits of heather. Now she stood by his side, charming, dignified, gracious and not the least bit phased by the flow of guests arriving at the marquee. He always had a fabulous woman with him at times like this, world-class stunners that could be seen on magazine covers, but tonight, he wouldn't change his partner for any other woman on the planet. She was, through and through, beautiful.

The sunlight filtered through the marquee and cast a warm light around it. The tables, each one laid for eight people, were placed around a wooden dance area. Cutlery shone and glasses sparkled. The centrepieces of fresh flowers and candles added a vibrant splash of colour. There was a carpeted dais for the musicians.

When they were seated, Fraser poured Cristal into Claudia's glass, he knew it to be her favourite but never questioned how she came to like this particular vintage. But then he thought how ridiculous it was to know that and not the fact that she was a child star or that she could speak Russian. He waited for her to pick up the glass and perform the subtle little ritual that had always fascinated him. She would smile and watch the bubbles before taking a sip. Then she would pass her tongue over her lips, as if to make sure she tasted it all. But he'd never asked her what it was all about, in case she stopped doing it. It was her secret, her special memory—like the pinecones. It was something he'd always loved about her and kept it locked away in his memory, as if it was a jewel in a safe.

Fraser felt disappointed when she didn't do it. Instead, a smile lit her face as she raised her glass and said, 'To people who plant daffodils.'

When dinner was over, they danced, held each other close and he felt comfort in the regenerated friendship. His friend had returned to him, but his reactions toward her were not the same. This became clearer when the Tango was announced, and Yuri swiftly moved into action and led his countess, who had clearly accepted rather than cause a scene, to the dancefloor. Her Russian blood, albeit diluted, had obviously attracted him. Jenny was right, Fraser had no claim on her, he had to acknowledge that. Yet, his precious friendship had become entangled in this physical attraction, and it made him nervous as he watched them dance. Claudia's hair shimmered, her feet moved professionally, her skirt waved and rippled as her hips turned about and revealed brief glimpses of the lower part of her thigh. Her skin was golden in the soft lighting. He sat and devoured the sight, consumed with fascination and the sudden hot sizzle of erotic energy throbbing through him. Yuri began to show off, but Claudia didn't let him steal the thunder and rose to it effortlessly, with so much style. She was a delicious blend of grit, intrigue and tantalising sex appeal. He wanted to fence with the grit, flirt with the intrigue and take the sex appeal to bed. Oh god! How he wanted to take her to bed. The thought shocked him, and he gulped down some water.

Yuri ended the dance with flair, spinning Claudia, snatching her close again, spreading the palm of his hand across her beautiful naked back, between the narrow straps of her dress and her defined shoulder blades. A snap of jealousy hit his gut and, once more, shocked him.

'Wow!' Grace said, when Claudia returned to the table. 'You tango like an Argentinian gypsy. You obviously had lessons.'

Claudia was very casual about it. 'My mother dragged me off to lessons for everything, dancing, swimming, riding, tennis, fencing…yada, yada, yada.'

'What's your tennis like?' Eliot asked. 'We could have a game.'

'Pathetic,' she said. Then she laughed. 'But I had a great coach who taught me how to serve really stylish double faults. I'm rubbish at fencing too.' She smiled, cunningly, as she added, 'But I can ride a horse, like a Texas Ranger.'

'You sure can,' Paige said, 'and so could Mathew Jay. The way he drove the cattle was amazing. Do you ever see him?'

The question seemed to take Claudia by surprise, the light suddenly faded from her eyes. Fraser almost felt the change in her as he committed the name, Mathew Jay, to his memory.

'I don't see him anymore,' Claudia said.

'He was gorgeous in that Christmas special,' Paige continued enthusiastically. 'Was he as nice as he seemed?'

Claudia smiled but a look of sadness lingered in her eyes. 'Yes…a beautiful man.'

Fraser could see that Claudia hadn't relished this topic of conversation. He took her by the hand. 'Let's go and get some air,' he whispered.

Chapter Nine

They walked to the lake. Claudia took off her shoes. When they got to the water's edge, Fraser scooped her up into his arms and carried her to a fallen tree that had, for some years, been a seat. She gasped with surprise and then laughed. The garden was lit, and a faint glow spilled onto the lakeside. The music and the voices faded, and all seemed still. There was barely a ripple on the water, as all the wildfowl were settled.

Claudia's voice broke the silence. 'This night air's going to make my hair curl up even more.'

'I can't wait to see it happen.'

'I hate it,' she said. It wasn't a casual comment. 'That's why I used to keep it so short.' She looked towards the lake. 'You must have had such fun here when you were boys.'

'Yes, Grandpa Franklyn invited us every summer. It was expected that we agreed to come. He was a big influence in our lives—old-fashioned but an amazing man. I suppose that's why we're close. Between school and Larchwood, we lived as brothers. We once tried to make a boat out of sawn-off bike wheels and a sheet of polythene. We paddled it quite a way out, and then it capsized and we had to swim for it. We arrived in the kitchen, soaking wet, looking forward to Stella's offer of hot chocolate and brownies, but Grandpa Franklyn sent us back to recover the wreck. We didn't know how, but he said we had to work it out. Tony designed a raft, with a winch, which was far more stable. We managed to drag it back, then we got the hot chocolate and brownies.'

Claudia laughed. 'Well the Wright Brothers didn't fly on day one. They kept trying.'

'Maybe if they had a sheet of polythene and a couple of sawn-off bike wheels, they might have achieved it sooner.' Fraser felt the urge to ask about Mathew Jay. Of all the things he'd found out about Claudia, this was the most intriguing. He resisted the temptation for a while, but curiosity got the better of him. 'Tell me…this beautiful man…I get the impression that he was special?'

'Mathew? Yes, he was. Why do you want to know about him?'

'You never talked about him.'

'No, I didn't.'

'Maybe I'm jealous.'

Claudia nudged him like she used to when he said something ridiculous or made a bad joke. 'Idiot!' She seemed to think out her next move very carefully. Then she said, 'An English actor.'

'And…?'

'Don't you think we've talked enough about me this evening?'

'Not nearly enough. I'm way behind on your history.'

'He played my uncle when I was that feisty little tearaway kid that Paige talked about.'

'But you weren't a kid in the Christmas special.'

Claudia shook her head slowly. 'No. When I finished college, I was in debt, like any other graduate. So when I was offered a one off mini-series, including a Christmas Special, I took it. When I met Mathew again, I was all grown up. He didn't ruffle my hair anymore or raise his hand for a high-five when we finished a scene. As soon as the filming and the promotions were finished, we came back home together. We went to live by the sea for a while. Then we moved back to London because he wanted to do some theatre. We were together until five years ago.'

'About the time we first met in the park.'

'Yes but…' She shrugged as if to shake off a sad memory. 'It was all over by then.'

She clearly wanted to move off the subject, and Fraser had to quash his burning curiosity about it. 'Did you do any more acting?'

'No, I'd made enough to pay my debts and buy a few posh frocks for the promos and interviews.' She pinched some of the fabric that rested on her thighs and said, 'This one included. Didn't you notice how so last season it was?'

'Absolutely not, you look fabulous. Besides, you of all people must know how to care for textiles, keep them looking new.' He thought for a moment, not wanting to stir the calm atmosphere. 'You were very successful. Why were you so short of money?'

'That's just a detail in a long, tedious story. Not for tonight. I've had such a fabulous time. I don't want to talk about those days.'

Fraser had no idea of the time they sat there. Claudia wanted to know more about Larchwood, and the childhood experiences he had with his cousins. They were easy to talk about.

Eventually, the music stopped. He and Tony had agreed that the party wouldn't go on too long because the sound carried across the lake. He glanced at his watch, the evening, he had worried so much about, had flown by.

'I must go home,' Claudia said.

Fraser frowned. 'Home, what, now? I'm disappointed. I hoped you'd stay over.' He noted Claudia's shocked expression. 'Not that kind of stay over. Stella prepared rooms, just in case.'

'I'd like to go home,' she said, 'I wasn't expecting to come, remember?'

She put on her shoes and insisted on walking.

They arrived back at the marquee. Tony and Lizzy were sitting at the table with Paige. Yuri had already left; Eliot and Grace had gone back to the house to make a cup of tea.

Paige got to her feet and thanked Tony and Fraser. She looked at Claudia. 'It's been such a pleasure to meet you.' She hugged her, and then she beamed a smile and added, 'But why didn't you tell me about the box set?'

Claudia frowned. 'Box set?'

Fraser could see the change in Claudia's face and he asked, 'What about it?'

'Re-released! Every episode,' Paige said. 'I'll be able to binge on them after a tough day. But I guess I'd better get myself a bigger cushion.' She left with a big smile on her face.

'I have to go.' Claudia hugged Lizzy and then thanked Tony, who kissed her cheek. She turned to Fraser. 'Thank you, Fraser, it was a lovely party.' She started to walk away.

Fraser caught her up. 'Hey! Hold on! What is it? What's wrong?'

Claudia didn't stop, she was clearly suppressing anger. 'Nothing, I'll deal with it.'

'Deal with what? What's this all about?'

She stopped walking and looked at Fraser. 'My mother sold me out. Nobody asked me about the box set.'

'Perhaps it was a buy-out in the first place. They wouldn't need your permission.'

'Elsa Hamilton would never agree to that. Otherwise, she would have to relinquish control, and that's something she never does. This must have been arranged months ago. And she's got the cheek to turn up to my house and make demands on my inheritance?' She moved on.

'Claudia, wait!' Fraser caught her up and walked by her side. 'What demands?'

'Did Lizzy tell you that my grandmother left me some precious, family diaries written by my great-grandaunt?'

'No, I don't think she'd deem it appropriate to do that.'

'Well…my mother wants them, and she's trying to take them from me. I can't let her do that. They're too precious. She'll abuse them just to make some quick money. I promised my grannie I wouldn't let her have them.'

'Will she contest the will—take it to court?'

Claudia scoffed. 'I wish! At least that would give me a chance. She doesn't get a lawyer, she finds much more effective ways to beat people into the ground.'

'Such as…?

'She finds a weakness, makes threats, and she won't stop until she wins.'

Fraser was perplexed. Claudia was smarter than this. Why did she think it was so difficult? 'Come back to the house, and we'll sort something out.'

Claudia became exasperated. She stopped and faced him. 'Why do you presume I'm being naïve? You don't seem to understand that she takes what she wants. That's why I moved from London, to give me some thinking time. Do you think I would have gone to all that trouble if it was straightforward? She's looking for me as we speak. When she finds me, she'll make a move to force me to hand over the diaries. When I deny her, she'll increase the pressure. She'll continue to do that until I give in. She's very good at what she does. I won't have a clue where she's going to come from. Your conference is more important than my lifelong quarrel with my mother, so don't get tangled up with her.'

'This is too fantastic for words. I can't believe she'd deliberately—'

Claudia glared at him. 'Then stay out of it.'

Fraser put his arms around her, 'Claudia, darling,' he pleaded softly. 'This isn't us. We don't do this.' He pressed a light kiss on her face then embraced her, held her tightly, and she relaxed into his arms. 'Come back to the house, and we'll talk.'

Claudia broke free. 'We'll talk on Thursday, like we agreed. I have to leave.' Her eyes watered, and for a moment, she seemed to wilt. 'You don't need my problems on your mind as well as your own. Goodnight.'

Fraser watched her walk away. He wanted to understand her problem. What could be so bad that would induce her to pack up and move? Why would it be so difficult to deal with her own mother?

*****

Claudia walked towards the main entrance of the house. Even though the box set wasn't part of the battle, she felt the sharp pain of her mother's distant prod. Time was running out. It had all been used up on this unexpected twist of meeting Fraser again. Her eyes watered. 'Don't blub, Claudia,' she whispered as she walked. 'Don't let her win. You'll find a way to stop her before she can get any closer.' She squared her shoulders and continued to walk. 'Just don't blub.'

Irena met her by the house. 'Mr Gallier called and said you are going home.'

'Yes, is there a taxi company I can call?'

'Friends and guests of the Franklyns do not need to call a taxi. You look upset, I will take you myself.'

As they drove from the Larchwood gates, Claudia expelled a quivering sigh. 'I'm afraid I caused a bit of a scene.'

'Please tell me that you poured your drink over Yuri Balakirev's head?'

'No, I didn't do that.'

'That is a disappointment.'

'I was unfair to Fraser. He wants to help me, but he can't.'

'Do not be concerned about him. He is a powerful man, accustomed to dealing with difficult situations.'

'He can't believe I have a malicious mother. This family is so close, he doesn't understand that a relative could scheme against you, cause you great pain.'

'Then he is very fortunate. My ex-husband placed me in a dangerous position, my children also. That is why I left my home in Ukraine and came to the UK.'

'I thought *I'd* made a brave move.'

'It was no more than you have done, I think. If it was to get away from your mother, then indeed she must be a very dangerous person?'

'Yes, and it doesn't help that Fraser thinks I'm being paranoid. He thinks it can be settled with a good lawyer, but he has no idea what I'm up against.'

'It is easy for a man to believe a woman is worrying about nothing, when he does not fully understand her problems. He also has many people to help him. You are a woman alone in a difficult situation. So do not hesitate to let me know if there is anything I can do to help you.'

'That's very kind, Irena.'

'A woman does not forget her own troubled past.'

'But I'm not your responsibility, am I?'

'I consider all women, at some time, to be my responsibility. We go through challenging times, and so we should help each other…yes?'

Chapter Ten

On Wednesday, even though the conference was still in session, Lizzy insisted that they keep the tea-and-cake date. As usual, the table by the window was reserved.

Jenny prodded her lemon tart with a pastry fork. 'Well, there's one thing about being off chocolate, you get to explore other experiences.'

Claudia watched her as she sampled some of the crumbling pastry, laced with yellow filling. 'How is it?'

Jenny's left eye screwed up, and she spoke out of the corner of her mouth. 'Tangy!'

'That's good, isn't it?'

'My palate doesn't do tangy.' She sipped her tea and then looked at Lizzy. 'When are you going to Italy?'

'Third week in August,' Lizzy said. 'It's going to be fabulous, just enough summer left. Tony's looking forward to it. He was really concerned that we hadn't seen much of the family this summer. We'll have time to catch up.'

'Is Fraser going?' Jenny asked.

'Yes, he's meeting up with his parents. They can take a few days before the grape harvest. I presume Natalie won't be there now though, unless they make up.'

Jenny's eyes sparkled as she told Claudia all about Villa Firenze, Tony's facility in Tuscany, for corporate entertaining. It was run more like a hotel, with lots of rooms, huge lounges. Dining is mostly al fresco under the pergola. 'It's fabulous,' Jenny said. 'The pool is kidney-shaped, and the steps are like a fan in the recessed part. You just want to plunge into it. And there are tables and chairs and loungers, and it's all lit at night.'

'You've been?'

Jenny shook her head. 'No, but Grace and Charlie had their wedding there. I've seen the videos...fabulous.' She became distracted and looked across the restaurant. 'Incoming!'

'Who?' Lizzy asked.

'Fraser.'

'Oh no!' Claudia sighed. 'I thought he'd be busy.'

Lizzy frowned. 'What's wrong? I thought you two were OK.'

'We still have...issues.'

'Friends aren't supposed to have issues,' Lizzy commented.

'I'm not even sure we're very good friends anymore.'

'Well, he's making his way over to us, and he looks very serious,' Jenny said.

'Sorry to interrupt,' Fraser said, 'mind if I join you for a minute?' He was carrying a magazine.

'Course not,' Jenny said, 'you look a bit tense.'

Fraser sat by Claudia. 'I'm good. I just...' He paused and laid the magazine on the table. 'One of the receptionists showed me this, Claudia. I thought you should see it.'

Claudia frowned. 'What is it?'

Fraser flipped through the magazine and stopped at a double page feature. 'Pictures...of you.'

Claudia expelled a gentle laugh. 'I don't think so. Nobody's asked me for any pictures since I was 14, and why would they?'

'You should look.'

Claudia peered at it as if it was going to sting her, and she drew a sharp breath as if it had.

Lizzy leaned over, and Jenny moved from her seat to get a clearer view.

'What's it all about?' Lizzy said.

'It's my mother,' Claudia said, her voice was flat and unemotional. The headline read, *Successful LA casting agent Elsa Hamilton, tells of heartbreak over estranged daughter.* It was a huge spread, several pages, pictures of Claudia when she was a small child, and one as a 12-year-old sitting up in a tree. In the largest picture, she was a little older and on horseback, her wild, curly hair flying, her face beaming as she raised her Stetson hat in the air. The horse was rearing. The large print below it said, *Claudie Hamilton—English Girl on the Ranch.*

Lizzy pointed to a small picture. 'Oh! And look at that little princess. Is that you? Your eyes look so sad.'

'I told you, my mother had a casting agency. Somebody was looking for a bright four year old who could deliver a few simple lines of Russian dialogue, and if she had lots of curly hair, it would be an advantage. It was a no-brainer. Little Claudie Hamilton was a busy girl after that. I wasn't very co-operative, but my mother always managed to persuade me—one way or another. Some kids are brilliant, and they're really up for it, but I didn't want to do it.'

'You looked happy enough on that horse,' Fraser commented.

'He was a real pro, he was trained, but my mother wouldn't allow me to do any stunts on horseback. On that occasion, we were shooting stills to promote the last series. The photographer said, "Make it look interesting, Claudie." I reared the horse up, the photographer was delighted, but Mother was furious. That's what made me laugh.'

It seemed that Elsa Hamilton had managed to fast track the process of getting her story in the magazine, but that wasn't surprising. She would have found a way.

'There's more,' Fraser said as he turned the page.

'Who are these two guys?' Jenny said.

'The small man, sitting on the ranch fence by me, is Lennie. He played a stableman. We were good friends.'

'And the tall, lean cowboy standing by you?' Fraser prompted.

Claudia became silent. She could sense her mother closing in on her, creeping nearer with all the power she needed to threaten that, which was so precious. She felt sick. She had made no progress in her plan to win this battle, and her nemesis was way ahead of her. 'Please,' Claudia said, 'this isn't easy for me. All this is part of my mother's plan.'

Fraser's brow puckered a moment. 'Plan, what do you mean?'

'She has no idea where I am, but she's looking for me. This is designed to encourage people to give her information about where to find me. Somebody's going to tell her or post it on social network.'

'Why don't you just call her?' Fraser said. 'Perhaps she's suffering some kind of remorse after you took such drastic measure to—'

'Lose contact?' Claudia's voice challenged him. It silenced him for a moment. 'I've already explained to you, Fraser, not only is she still exploiting me, she wants everything else I have.'

'But she can't just take it,' Fraser insisted.

Claudia's heart was racing, and anger was rising inside her. She tried to keep it under control, but she couldn't hide the tremble that crept into her voice. 'She can, and she will.' Claudia knew that Fraser wasn't convinced and was maybe even thinking she was paranoid, and all she had to do was talk to her mother or get a lawyer—something straightforward and practical. 'Why am I sitting here trying to convince you?'

'Families go through these times, Claudia.'

'Including yours?' Claudia challenged. 'Does your mother do stuff like this to you? Would she take something that was yours, just because she wanted it?'

'It's natural for her to feel bitter at being left out of the will.'

'There's nothing natural about all this.' She flipped the page back to the centrefold. 'She's been the bane of my life since I was that old.' She pointed to the image of the little Russian princess. 'And she isn't finished yet, so I don't want to hear you sympathising with her.'

'I'm not sympathising,' Fraser insisted, 'I want to understand. She says she just wants to make it up with you. I mean, look at this spread, it's—'

'Heart-breaking?' Claudia interjected. 'Is that what it says to you?'

'No, of course not. But you've jerked her chain, maybe you can meet up with her and make it clear to her that you're entitled to the legacy.'

'There's no way of getting to her. See how innocent she looks, grieving for her...what did she call me?' She glanced down at the text on the glossy pages and read out, 'Claudie, my darling girl.'

'None of what you say is making sense. Claudia, you've had a lot on your plate lately, maybe you need to take a break and think this—'

'Don't you dare!' Claudia snapped. Her voice was quiet but forceful. 'Don't you dare lay this on me. You know nothing about me or my mother or my life.' She fixed her eyes on Fraser's face. 'I don't need your help. I can manage my own nemesis. I always have done, because even my father couldn't help me.' She leaned closer to him and said quietly but firmly, 'Yes, Fraser, I've even lost touch with him. But don't worry, Mother tells me he's happy. He's gone to Cornwall to be a painter. What a pity he couldn't have given me his change of address. I guess I've inherited that from him.' She was angry, but the restaurant was very busy, so she kept her voice down as she stabbed her forefinger onto the magazine. 'This isn't a doting mother making a plea to her daughter, it's Elsa Hamilton letting me know that she's going to trample me into the ground to get what my grandmother bequeathed to me—Alyona's diaries. She plans to build on the scandal, turn them into a novel and then make a trashy movie. She doesn't care that Alyona got all the blame and was accused of stealing Richard from his fiancée. But she never got to speak up for herself. Her voice has been muted since 1921, and it's time she was heard. I'm going to make that happen for her. I'm going to write the novel properly, with her point of view, the way it really was. And nobody, including you with your misguided reasoning, is going to stop me.'

Lizzy reached out for Claudia's hand. 'I'm so sorry. This must be really horrible for you. Please let us know if there's anything we can do to help? We're here for you, aren't we, Jen?'

'Too right!' Jenny said. 'If she finds you at Larchwood, you can come and stay with me.'

Claudia's eyes burned and her throat tightened as she whispered, 'Thanks, girls, that means a lot, it really does.' She was comforted by their unconditional support.

She looked at Fraser, he was being polite, but it seemed to frustrate him that he hadn't convinced her of his views either. 'I've already warned you, Frazer, don't let her get into your life. Your conference is more important than her.'

He closed the magazine and said, 'I appreciate that this is a very difficult situation for you, Claudia, but it wouldn't hurt to run it by a lawyer, get some kind of support for goodness sake.'

'Now you can understand how good she is? You, my special friend, believe her...and not me.' She stood up and grabbed her handbag. 'You can look at it from any angle you like, but I won't sit here while you make her look like a bereft parent. If you want to play happy families, go ahead, tell her. Be the first. But I promise you if you do, you'll be able to hate me for losing touch a second time.' She spoke to Lizzy and Jenny, 'I'm sorry, girls, I have to go.'

'Claudia! Stay,' Fraser pleaded. 'Don't leave like this.'

Claudia glared at him. Her disappointment sent a gripping pain through her heart. 'Stay until I see it your way, is that what you mean? I don't need two people trying to make me do that. Along with all those lessons my mother dragged me to, I had classes in voice projection, but the strange thing is that I can't make myself heard.' She left very quickly and weaved her way through the tables with as much dignity as she could scrape up. She was about to reach her car, when she heard Fraser's voice calling. She ignored it. He arrived just in time to push his hand against the door and prevent her from opening it.

'I just want to say one thing. Just one thing, Claudia, and then I'll leave you alone.'

Claudia's shoulders sank, as if she was fresh out of energy.

Fraser grasped her hands. 'It doesn't matter what goes on between you and your mother, I'm on your side. However it turns out, do you understand? I'll be there for you—not her.'

Claudia looked up, and as she did so, he pressed a brief, firm kiss on her mouth and then walked away.

Chapter Eleven

Claudia arrived at Larchwood on Thursday morning. Stress gripped her whole body, but she was determined to be strong, frank and honest with Fraser. Something in her life had to be settled, she couldn't juggle it all like this forever. Fraser had no idea what it had cost her when she walked away from him and their chummy relationship. It broke her heart, she was so much in love with him, and he never knew it. But he'd know it today, she would hold nothing back.

Reluctant to get out of the car, she waited a while. The view of the lake was uninterrupted now that the marquee had been taken away, and with it, the happy memories of the party. The music, the heady scent of the sumptuous flowers, the ever-changing montage of fabulous dresses as the guests moved about, dances with Fraser when the sensuous entwined with the sensual and reached every nerve-end of her being, a reminder of how she used to feel. She glanced at the lake where Fraser had carried her across the rough ground, an old-fashioned gesture, but she had to admit it was fun. In one of Richard's letters to Alyona—Claudia's favourite that she kept apart from the others—he wrote, 'It is all as a dream of sweet reality.' That's how it felt last Friday evening, until Elsa Hamilton's long, bitter reach plunged her back into a reality that was not so sweet.

Fraser had suggested they meet on the terrace. It could be approached in two ways: either by the French windows, in the drawing room, or she could walk around the outside of the building until she found the semi-circular structure, with an hour-glass balustrade and steps leading down to the grass. She found it deserted, so she waited.

It wasn't long before Fraser came out, via the French windows. To her relief, he was casually dressed in jeans and sweatshirt, so he wasn't likely to look at his watch and then dash off for a business meeting. It seemed that he was keeping to the bargain. He rested his hands gently on her shoulders, bent his head and kissed her cheek, the way he always did in the old days. He smelled fresh and slightly scented, as if he'd just taken a shower. She was distracted by it, imagined how the water would roll over his shoulders and down his body. Even through her tension, the image lingered, and she had to remind herself that these thoughts had no place in her head.

'Did the conference go well?' she asked, to distract herself.

'Yes, brilliantly thanks.' Fraser answered. 'We're back on familiar ground now.' He seemed relaxed, and a beaming smile lit his face. That was worse than the virtual water rolling down his body.

'So it's going ahead?'

'Yes, but I promised this morning to you, so work is off the agenda.' He frowned at her. 'You're very pale.'

'I didn't sleep well.'

'Not worried about this, surely?'

Claudia was envious of his calm, unruffled mood. 'Why wouldn't I be?'

'I know I was the one asking all the questions at first, but don't you think we're dragging it on a bit? Do we really need to have a post-mortem now? We got along really well at the party so—'

'We called a truce for the evening, that's why. I don't want to patch this up. I want it all on the table, then we can...' she stopped and a gulped down the tension in her throat. 'All your questions, "Where did you go? Why didn't you contact me? What the hell happened to you?" They're still in your head and still unanswered. They're going to come out again one day. I don't want that, I'd rather answer them now.'

Fraser nodded and gestured towards the rose garden. 'There's a seat over there.'

They went down the terrace steps, strolled to the garden seat and sat down. Claudia wasn't sure she could get him to listen to everything she needed to say, he was so strong and decisive at the moment. When they sat down, Fraser remained silent as if to give her the time to speak.

'You asked what happened to me,' Claudia began. 'I moved in with my grannie. Then my phone was hacked, so I changed my number. But I couldn't reach you on yours.'

'I switched it off and left it in my office. I was seeing...' He paused for a second and then added, 'I was seeing somebody, and we had problems with the press. I used a temporary one for a while.'

'She wasn't just somebody, the whole world knew her. Before long, everybody knew your face too, and you were surrounded by paparazzi, whether you were with her or not. It made it impossible to reach you.'

Fraser scowled. 'They were photographers not bodyguards, you could have got past them.'

'And make them wonder who it was knocking on your door? Who knows what they would have made of it. Imagine the headlines, Fraser Gallier, in love-rat triangle.'

Fraser sighed and nodded. 'Yes, I can see how difficult that would have been. But was that your last option?'

'Do you remember that evening we watched a film about two people who made a bargain. They agreed on a venue and a particular day of the year when they should meet up if they ever lost touch.'

Fraser smiled. 'Yes, I remember. They chose Paris.'

'Ours wasn't Paris, was it?'

Fraser expelled a brief laugh. 'The park, any Wednesday lunchtime as long as the daffodils were still in bloom.'

'You make it sound like a joke.'

'It was, wasn't it? We joked about films all the time.'

'But it was worth a try, don't you think?'

Fraser became serious. He stared at her and said, 'You went to the park to look for me?'

'Yes, two Wednesday's, I walked and waited, but you didn't show. I went on the third week, and there you were...'

Fraser's brow twitched, and his eyes closed tightly as if a bad feeling rushed through him.

Tears lingered on Claudia's lower lids, the shards of pain she felt on that day hit her heart, and she spoke the angry words that she failed to speak back then. 'You had six other days in the week to take your Latino lover for a stroll among the daffodils.

Wednesday was my day…my daffodils…my friend. And you gave them all to Paloma Cardini.'

Fraser leapt to his own defence. 'It wasn't a stroll, there was a photographer along the path. It was just a stupid photo shoot to get an upbeat, spring time picture.'

'I know we weren't in a relationship. I knew I couldn't have you, but it broke my heart anyway…I was so in love with you.'

'Love?' Fraser stared in disbelief. 'Claudia, I didn't—'

'Of course you didn't know. You weren't meant to.' She could see how shocked Fraser was as she continued. 'I always bluffed my way through it. Successfully it seems.' She expelled a nervous laugh. 'I'm an actress, aren't I? You have no idea how much pain that final breakup caused me, so I didn't want to hear how upset you were that first day I arrived here.'

'I wasn't just upset, I was cut up about it…genuinely. I was never too busy to be there for you, Claudia. I thought you knew that. You could have approached me anywhere, anytime…'

'That would have taken more courage than I had.'

'Courage?' Fraser queried. 'To talk to me?'

Claudia intended to be honest, leave nothing unsaid, but she felt for him, and she was in danger of aborting her plan and suggesting another truce, postponing the things she had come to talk about. Her thoughts re-grouped, and she spoke again. 'I was feeling very vulnerable. My grandmother was becoming frail, my life was changing dramatically, and I was about to experience the learning curve of my life. I was so scared about what was happening to me. I wanted you to hug me, and tell me everything was going to be fine.'

Fraser moved closer to her as if to comfort her, but she backed away. Fraser sighed. 'So you walked away.'

'I decided that the best thing to do was to go home and get the hell over you, learn to move on without you, forget the ridiculous fantasy that my stupid mistake would somehow become a blessing.'

'Mistake?'

Claudia told herself not to weep, but her eyes defied her. She ran her fingers over them and brushed the tears away. 'I said goodbye, to the memories, the daffodils and the guy who planted them, and then…and then I left the father of my child walking in the park with his lover.'

Fraser's face drained, and his eyes stared in disbelief. 'Jesus Christ!' he whispered on a heavy sigh. 'This isn't a joke, is it?'

'Oh, Fraser,' Claudia sighed. 'You didn't just forget our arrangement, you forgot the one time we broke the rules. In your defence I realise that you were in a bad way, grieving for your business friend. It was a terrible accident, it hit you hard. I can understand you needing some kind of comfort. My part in it wasn't a comforting gesture. I loved you. I wanted you. And there you were, in my arms, wanting me all of a sudden.'

Fraser got to his feet and stared around him as if an answer was hiding among the roses. He suddenly turned back, his eyes narrowed as he said, 'Ever since you arrived here you gave nothing away. You really are an actress, aren't you?'

'All my life,' Claudia answered. Her task was almost done, she had told him, now she braced herself for the backlash. 'What was I supposed to say? Did you expect me to tell you on the doorstep within earshot of Natalie? I thought you two were getting married for goodness sake. I came here to work out how to solve a very serious problem with my mother, and suddenly there you were, presenting me with another one.'

'I wasn't expecting…Dear God! This is really serious.'

'I know. Having a baby is a very serious business, Fraser.'

Fraser walked a few paces. His shoulders lifted and fell as he breathed. He turned about on the spot. His hand clamped to the back of his neck. Then he glared at her. 'You waited all this time to tell me?'

Claudia could see he was shocked, but she had no intention of continuing to take all the blame. 'We pushed the boundaries of our relationship, then early the next morning you were gone. What was I supposed to think about that?'

'I wrote a note.'

'A note, great, every girl likes a note the morning after. Especially one that said it shouldn't have happened and wouldn't happen again because you valued my friendship far too much.'

Fraser was not taking it well. He glowered at her. 'That's the truth,' he snapped. 'How many more times have I to tell you how important you were…you are to me?'

Claudia composed herself, but anger was very close to the surface. She went to him, took him by the arm and said, 'I think you should sit down again. After all, I already knew all this. I was just nervous about telling you. Obviously, I was right about that.'

They returned to the bench. Fraser said, 'My note…I tried to be tactful.'

'Tactful?' Claudia shook her head. 'Pregnancy isn't tactful, Fraser. That little testing stick has got a very loud voice. It yells out, "Welcome to the silly girl's one-night-stand club."'

'How can you joke about it?' Fraser retorted.

Claudia looked at him, with a sudden air of weariness, and shook her head slowly. 'I've done all the weeping, the heartache, and the backache, along with all the other aches you develop along the way. I've hung around clinics, trying to convince myself that being pregnant was perfectly normal and natural. But daily retching and piercing pains down your sciatic nerve do not feel perfectly normal…or natural. I wasn't one of the chosen ones, the lucky girls who breeze through it all with no debilitating symptoms.' Fraser kept his eyes fixed on hers, but he didn't speak. It was as if he felt in honour bound to let her say her piece. 'I've done all that. Did it on my own. I had nobody to hold my hand for hours and hours—36 actually.' Fraser winced but said nothing. 'I had nobody to swear at. No fingers to squeeze. No loving man to look at me with tears in his eyes and whisper, "Thank you for your pain, thank you for our beautiful baby."' She paused a moment, gulped at the lump in her throat and added, 'Why the hell shouldn't I joke about it?'

Fraser took a breath as if to speak, but then he failed to say anything. Claudia observed the disturbed expression on his face, and she could almost hear the workings of his mind. Was she joking? Being sarcastic? Jerking his chain? What the hell was happening here? She pierced a stern look into his eyes. 'And please don't insult me by questioning whether the child is really yours.'

'Then don't insult me by suggesting I would.'

'Don't you see, I couldn't allow the news to leak out just anywhere? We needed to talk about it together, quietly and privately, like now. There was no way I was going to have my child plastered all over the papers.'

'Do you have to be so brutally blunt? Just give me a minute to get hold of this. I don't even know what kind of questions to ask.'

'Was it a boy or a girl? Did it thrive? Did I keep it? Put it up for adoption?'

'Dear God, you didn't—?'

'No, I didn't.' Claudia composed herself. She felt for Fraser and didn't want to hurt or upset him, but she had to fight her corner just the same. This wasn't easy. He was a wealthy and powerful man, and she had to keep up with him. 'Fraser, this isn't why I wanted to talk to you about it. I got over you and moved on. Now the past is just baggage. I'm concerned with the present. Our child's name is Justin—your middle name—and he has your surname. Justin Gallier is almost a year old.'

Fraser's control slipped, and his voice lashed out as if he could suddenly see a child in his mind. 'There was never a time in a whole year that you could have told me this? The paparazzi have long-since stopped chasing me about.'

'I'm not here to be hot-seated, so let's just stick to the facts. I'm a single parent, I'm doing great, but since we met again, the rules have changed. You've got a second chance. If you want to join me in raising Justin, then we'll arrange something. If you don't, you can continue your childless existence, which is what you always wanted, and I won't tell a soul. We've been fine without you, and we can carry on the same way.' Claudia, having said her piece, became calmer and much stronger.

Fraser was still restless. He got to his feet again, 'You can't do that,' he argued, and suddenly they were on opposite sides. 'We have other decisions to make.'

'Like what?'

'Where he should live, am I not supposed to provide a home for him?'

'No.' Claudia was irked by his suggestion. 'He has a home.'

'Which you fund on your own.'

'It's a perfectly nice cardboard box,' Claudia said, peeved at his attitude. 'I even cut a hole in it so we'd have a window.'

'Stop it, Claudia!'

'Well for goodness sake, Fraser, women can actually do bread-winning now. We have a nice home, two in fact. I buy him the best clothes, the best equipment, the best food—he's thriving.'

'But don't you realise that he's heir to everything I own?'

Claudia gasped. 'You sound as if I borrowed him from you, but now it's time to give him back.' Her voice grew louder as exasperation set in. 'You expect me to start doing things your way just because my son might have expectations?'

Fraser lashed back swiftly. 'If only you'd let me know from the beginning, we would be in agreement by now. It's obvious that your stubborn streak kicked in back there in the park. You decided that you'd, get the hell over me, as you put it, and keep my child from me.'

'As I recall you never wanted children.'

'And did you at that time?'

'Justin wasn't planned, but he's here now, and he lives with me, and if anybody wants to bequeath him an estate, they can come and knock on my cardboard box and tell me. And don't start putting his name down for schools, either.'

Fraser was suddenly forceful. 'Who needs a father when he has you? You can be both I suppose?'

'No, Fraser, I can't,' Claudia almost yelled at him. It shocked them both and quietened them. They both took a moment to recover, and then Claudia said, 'I can only be a mother and a breadwinner. That's the whole point of this discussion. Please, Fraser, I hate fighting. This isn't about finances. If it was, I could have made a fortune out of you long ago. I told you, he wants for nothing, except—'

'Except what?' Fraser scoffed. 'What the hell am I supposed to give him?'

Claudia found it hard to make him listen to her. He was so wound up. 'Your money would give him many advantages but there are other far more important things he needs, and you can make them possible.'

'What are these illusive things that you, the super-parent, can't provide?'

'A father, grandparents, uncles, aunts and little cousins,' Claudia answered. Her voice was now calm but she remained strong. 'You have a wonderful extended family, and there's so much love and respect between you. Since my grandmother died, there's none in mine, so I can't provide that. But you can. A little boy needs affection from his father too. Seeing Tony with his children has taught me that. And that's why I decided to tell you instead of saying nothing and moving on again.'

Fraser stood silently, then he ran his fingers over his forehead as if to make his brain work better. After a while, he said, 'You realise that you can't deny him the financial security I can give him?'

'You can give him as much money as you like, load his little piggy bank with cash, and get your PA to remind you when it's his birthday. But if you can't give him emotional security, then leave him alone. I won't allow him to grow up hankering pointlessly for your affection.'

Fraser nodded, 'I understand what you're saying.' The effects of shock still reflected in his face as they stood in the silent aftermath of emotional conflict. 'Justin will be welcomed into the family,' he said at last, 'and most certainly loved by us all. You know us well enough to believe that. Can I see him?'

'Yes you can. But you should take a little time. Talk it over with your folks. Come to Heather Brow tomorrow, about three. Justin has a nap after lunch, he'll be in a good mood after that. You really don't want to meet him, for the first time, when he's being a little monster.' Claudia respected his feelings and spoke softly. 'I'll be taking tomorrow off as well as the rest of today. Larchwood needs me gone for a while.'

'Can I...bring him a gift?'

'Of course you can. He's your son, you don't need my permission to do that.' Claudia turned from him, but really wanted that hug denied her back in the park. She wanted to comfort Fraser, she knew she'd shocked him, hurt him even. But maybe he was too angry for her to embrace him, this was not a good day for a rebuff. The contact, the discussion about the child, the heat of their words had brought back feelings long since dismissed, and she now questioned her claim that she was ever over him. The love and the need for him were right there where they used to be. She needed to regain her ability to bluff. She looked at him and said quietly, 'Are you all right, Fraser?'

'Sure, I'll work it out.'

'See you tomorrow.' She turned from him.

'Claudia!' Fraser called out. When she turned back, he said, 'Who takes care of him when you're here?'

'Molly, my landlady, she's a nurse and a childminder. Justin loves her, and he can stay in his own home where he's secure.

It's the best arrangement we've ever had. He likes the farm, loves flowers, and he can say "Cat" in a high squeaky voice.'

*****

Fraser was stunned, and a strange mixture of emotions tugged at his insides. He wasn't afraid of responsibility, but this was unlike anything he had ever faced. The reality of learning that he and Claudia had made this baby was shocking. The guilt of not supporting his own child and his mother began to grip his conscience, even though he resented Claudia's secrecy. His status as a father seemed so flimsy. He thought of that night, the only time they broke the rules. The memory was vague because he hardly knew where he was at the time. He never did remember how he got to Claudia's apartment. The news of his business friend had poleaxed him in the way a healthy, active man in his prime feels, when one of his peers is suddenly stuck down. It seemed like a lottery, and he was close to the man who lost. All he could think about was being with Claudia. She didn't hassle him or question him about it. She allowed him to get through it in his own time. She circled his chest with her arms and rested her head on his shoulder as she whispered, 'I'm so sorry.' Then she gave him a glass of wine and sat quietly by his side on the sofa. She listened to the concoction of random thoughts spilling from his mouth, things he needed to say. She was privy to his burning tears. The warmth of her company wrapped around him, like a blanket, shrouded him, absorbed him until he was aware of nothing but her and his lost friend. He hardly drank the wine, but he felt drunk all the same, the intense grief and the consuming comfort brewed a potent drug, and he fell asleep. His dreams were haunting until he became aware of Claudia, as she tried to move him.

'You can't go home like this,' she told him and persuaded him to go to her spare room. His body felt weak but hot, and he couldn't clear his head, but with Claudia's help, he managed to get into bed. She brought him some water, but his hand shook, so she closed her fingers around his while he drank it down. He reached for her, but she made him lie down. He couldn't let her go, his comforter, his rock. She lay by his side. 'Sleep now,' she told him.

Sometime during that night, still half-sleeping, half-waking, they entwined together, languidly. No great passion or fires burning to urge them into a union, it was like a gentle, compelling journey, and he lost himself in her. It was almost supernatural, dream-like. A sensual experience without the frenzied striving, but the engulfing height was reached all the same. He left early in the morning under a cloud of remorse for what had happened. He wrote a note. Claudia deserved better, but he couldn't bring his head together long enough to think rationally. It had haunted him. But when Paloma Cardini came into his life, like a fireball, she distracted him completely. She was the antidote—a hot, sexy movie star—erotic by night but chaotic by day. He had since questioned his actions. Was it a ploy to get back into his old ways, a panic reaction to the night he'd spent with Claudia, because it had drawn emotions from him that he never allowed himself to feel?

Tony and Eliot sat at the table on the terrace. Fraser wanted to tell them straight away, while they were together.

'I know what you're feeling.' Tony spoke calmly and steadily. 'I've been there, remember? Maybe Louisa meant to tell me that Stephanie had been born but left it too late. It was a dreadful thought that my little girl could have been adopted as a foundling, and I would never have known about it…about her. I understand that anger, that tearing inside you. I'd still feel it now if Lizzy hadn't taught me to forgive. We'll help you do that, but you'll have to hold it down until you can deal with it properly. Claudia's very independent, she might just as well have moved on from here, but she had the courage to stay and face you. You need to find a way to embrace it all rather than constantly asking why.'

'Is that all she asked you for,' Eliot said, 'a father, grandparents…us?'

'Yes, she can care for him and meet his needs, but she's come to realise the importance of a loving family.' Fraser paused a moment and then continued, his voice low and a little unsteady. 'Aside from her grandmother, she had no experience of that. I guess that's why she didn't think it was important, until now. I know I'm as much to blame, but he's almost a year old. I feel so cheated, betrayed somehow.'

Eliot looked at Fraser. 'I suppose it hurts all the more because it's Claudia. But she's admitted that she was wrong about the child needing a father and family, given you a choice whether you want to be involved or not.'

Fraser knew they were trying to help him through this. Their comments made sense, but he couldn't shake off the bitter feeling. He never wanted children, but once he knew that Justin existed, he felt an overwhelming need to protect him and couldn't accept that he'd missed the opportunity to do that until now.

Chapter Twelve

Fraser strolled through the garden. It wasn't quite time to leave for Heather Brow. His insides were churning, and his head still ached from a lack of sleep. A brief visit to Wainford did nothing to ease his frustration. Claudia seemed to be well and truly in control of the situation whilst he was still trying to believe what was happening. He stood by the small tree that had been planted in memory of Louisa, Stephanie's birth mother. He'd seen the tree many times and respected it for what it was, but at that moment he realised just how much strength and backbone Tony needed to forgive her. But how could he follow Tony's example and forgive Claudia? Where would all that understanding and forgiveness come from? There was certainly none in his angry soul at this moment. He strolled on to his car that was parked at the front entrance.

Lizzy came out to see him. She was calm, but he knew her well enough to know that she was very concerned. Her voice was soft, but the message was clear. 'Don't judge her, Fraser. Whatever you think, it hasn't been easy for her.'

'But it was the way she wanted it.'

'No woman wants to go through pregnancy on her own, then take a new born baby back to an empty house. Do you think she enjoyed standing there, trying to make the right decisions? You've been concerned about the responsibility you took on at Wainford, how worried you were about letting the people down. But to be responsible for a new life is a lot more frightening than that. I had it all, a husband, private care, family, and still I found it challenging. I can't imagine doing all that alone.'

Fraser desperately needed a deep breath, but his lungs stopped short. 'I need to buy a gift for Justin. He likes cats. Shall I get a soft one? Would that be OK?'

'Yes, just a little one that he can hold easily and put in his bag when he goes out.'

'Bag?'

Lizzy smiled. 'All children come with a bag. They need one for when they go out—nappies, change of clothes, drink, little book, comfort item…'

Fraser nodded. 'I can see that I'm starting a long way behind. Cat it is then…small cat.'

When he reached Heather Brow Cottage, Fraser had to admit that it was a lovely spot, and the cottage was picturesque. Claudia was indeed coping very well. He got out of the car and looked around at the hillside. He imagined Claudia gathering heather to dye her yarn and then recalled the way she stirred it in her noxious potion, her scarf slipping down her forehead…and that ridiculous lab coat. He had no idea that the person in the sugar room would turn up looking like a star, tango like an Argentinian gypsy. He had learned more about her in the past two weeks than he knew before they lost touch. But he never suspected for a moment that she was the mother of a child—his child.

The door of the cottage was open wide, and he assumed it was an invitation to enter. He could hear Claudia's voice talking cheerfully. Then he heard baby laughter, it stopped him in his tracks. The infectious chuckle and babbling sounds continued and caused a shiver to ripple down his back. He fully intended to approach this moment with dignity and control, so he followed the voices that were now accompanied by a loud knocking sound.

Claudia greeted him with a nervous smile. He had never seen that kind of uncertainty in her face. She then raised her chin, as if to call on an extra margin of courage. 'Hi, come and join us.'

Justin was sitting in his high chair up against the table, a wooden spoon was clenched in his little hand, and he was banging it on the neighbouring chair. He stopped, his round, blue eyes stared at Fraser, the fingers of his other hand grasped at his soft, fair hair that fell into small loose curls. Fraser thought the child might cry, so he stood still and spoke quietly, 'You two seem to be having fun.'

'Stella gave me a recipe for chocolate brownies,' Claudia said. Then she smiled at Justin, 'We made some for tea, didn't we?'

Justin smiled back at his mother and revealed four perfect little white teeth.

'Then they'll be very special,' Fraser said.

Claudia looked at Fraser, and the hint of insecurity returned to her eyes. 'Would you like to sit down?'

Fraser felt like a stranger meeting her for the first time. 'Thank you.' He sat at the end of the table, conscious of the look of uncertainty on Justin's face. 'I don't want to upset him,' he whispered.

'He's OK. He'll work it out. Don't scowl or grimace and you'll be fine.'

'Hello Justin,' Fraser said. He was most certainly out of his comfort zone.

Justin pointed to the windowsill. 'Fowa,' he said with a little squeak in his voice.

Fraser responded with a smile. 'Yes, flowers.' He was impressed with the child's gesture of friendship by pointing out a vase of flowers. It seemed a mature thing for such a small child to do.

Justin continued to babble about nothing in particular, but it seemed to mean something to him.

'He has your eyes,' Claudia said, which Fraser saw as some kind of laurel branch. Yet, there was no sign of her usual soothing, evenly paced voice. She then continued, as if she was reading a product description. 'We've been very lucky. He's a beautiful, healthy boy developing as he should be. There are no known family illnesses that might come to visit him. Erm...' Her voice began to quiver, her eyes grew pink. She cleared her throat and continued. 'He's... he's had his injections... Oh, is that a problem? Do you believe in immunisation?'

Fraser looked at her. 'I haven't come to challenge you about his welfare, Claudia. Anybody can see that he's very healthy and happy.'

Claudia stood up, turned from him and leaned against the work top, her shoulders rose and fell as if she was trying to take a deep breath. He never thought that such a difficult moment would ever exist between them. He went to her and rested his hand on her shoulder. 'Come on now,' he said gently, 'I told you I'd be there for you whatever happened. It might take me some time to catch up with you, but I'm here. What about these brownies? Stella used to make them in the holidays,' he said, lifting the mood up a notch, 'they're great with a glass of cold milk.'

'I thought you had them with hot chocolate.'

'Only when it was snowing and we'd been out tobogganing.'

'And when you capsized in the lake,' Claudia added, with a faint smile.

They returned to the table. Justin was still unsure, but didn't make a fuss. Claudia spoke to him. 'This is Daddy. Are you going to say hello?' She encouraged him to raise his hand and wiggle his fingers by way of a greeting. She turned to Fraser and added, 'That's all right, isn't it? You'd like him to call you Daddy?'

Fraser wasn't a man to be easily knocked off his guard, but Claudia's words bounced around his head, like a pinball game, as a very startling reality leapt into his mind. He'd only ever considered the remote chance of eventually being a father. He would provide for his children, the usual cliché things, roof over the head, food on the table, clothes on their backs, the best education. He would protect them, advise them and be there to support them on sports days, school productions, graduation...Yet, he never considered, until that moment, that he would be a little boy's daddy. That seemed to be a different role altogether. Like his father, and like Tony's father, a full-time, hands-on, proactive daddy.

'I wasn't deciding for you,' Claudia explained a little anxiously. 'I just...'

'Of course,' he said softly, 'that's fine...I like it.' Fraser felt that he was travelling around this learning curve at a terrifying speed. He'd played with Stephanie, carried her, swung her around, but he hadn't, thus far, ventured into much interaction with little Eddy, save to pick him up and look through the kitchen window at the lake.

They ate brownies and drank milk. Justin seemed to be playing with his fingers, and Fraser feared that it was anxiety, but Claudia explained that it was a sign, he was asking for more milk. He also had one for when he was hungry.

Fraser was, once again, impressed with the child's ability to communicate. 'That must be very useful for you,' he said.

Claudia smiled and added, 'It seems that babies can learn to understand signs before actual words. I like to give him as much self-empowerment as I can. That way he'll survive better in a crisis. If I'm not there.'

'Crisis? Not there?'

'Things happen.' She smiled. 'He has verbal ones for when he's angry.'

'We all have those,' Fraser replied, with a faint chuckle.

'He's learning words though. He knows how to say "sore" when he's hurt, and he knows what sleep means. Which is more than I do these days,' she added, with a frown, 'he's got some more teeth coming.'

After brownies and milk, Justin relaxed and offered his last handful of cake to Fraser, who took it graciously.

'Don't eat it,' Claudia whispered, 'he's squashed it.'

Fraser deemed it to be a kind gesture, indicating that he was making progress, so he ate it and hummed his appreciation. 'I have something for him,' he said, 'is now a good time?'

'Sure, I'll clean him up, and we can go into the other room.'

To Fraser's relief, Justin smiled and grasped the fluffy toy, testing it with his mouth and then pressing his little forefinger onto it to examine it further. He then cried out with a sudden jolt of his body, 'Cat!'

*****

Fraser stayed much longer than Claudia anticipated. He was more interested in Justin than she expected. The child sat on the carpet, rooting in his treasure box. He produced a variety of possessions and thrust them at Fraser, as he performed a running commentary of babble, intended to be conversation. Fraser talked back to him as if he understood. Then Justin tossed a small, homemade, laminated book onto his lap. Claudia had made it for the child, pictures of Fraser, some in business clothes, some in casuals and some lounging on Claudia's sofa, back in London.

Fraser looked up from the book and frowned. 'Why are all these shots of me?'

'He might not have had you in the flesh, but he could know what you looked like.'

'Like some dead hero?' Fraser's eyes hardened, 'Is that what you were going to tell him? That I was dead?'

'If all I wanted was a model, I would have made him a book out of Mathew's pictures. He would have been a great absent father, he looked pretty impressive on a horse.'

Fraser cut Claudia with a chilling, piercing stare. 'I just don't understand. How could you do it?' he challenged, yet his voice was soft. 'How could you keep this miracle from me?'

'I told you why, Fraser,' she defended, her voice controlled and steady. 'This visit is just for you two to meet, then we can work out how we're going to raise him. If you're going to pick a fight, will you please not do it when he's in the room with us?'

'Yes, of course, I'm sorry. I didn't expect to feel so emotional about it. I came to meet a stereotypical baby, not a real person who would communicate with me, show me the flowers, share his cake... These unexpected feelings have changed my perspective. It scares me...shocks me...' Justin made his way back around the furniture until he reached Fraser's knees. Fraser picked him up and sat him on his lap. 'A son,' he whispered, 'I have a son, and if you hadn't arrived here unexpectedly, I would never have known about him.'

Claudia said nothing, but she was hurt. Bringing Justin to this stage had been so hard, and she was proud of it, but Fraser's attitude just seemed to cancel all that out.

*****

It took no time at all for Fraser to become totally besotted with his little boy. All Claudia's efforts to juggle time, energy, dedication, career, sacrifice as well as a powerful love for her son, couldn't measure up to the fun things daddies can do so much better than mummies. Daddies can throw you up into the air and catch you again, run you around the garden on their shoulders, fly you round and round, like an aeroplane. Justin very quickly learned to recognise the new parent in his life. The child would shriek, jig about with excitement or crawl across the floor towards Fraser when he arrived. It seemed, to Claudia, that everything mummies did was expected, but daddies only needed to turn up, to be a hero.

Another high chair was installed in the kitchen, at Larchwood, so the boys could have meals together and babble to each other. Stephanie, being altogether a more grown-up child, sat on a proper chair with a cushion. She included Justin in her life as if he'd always been there, like another little brother. Justin Gallier had his tiny feet well and truly under the Larchwood table.

Claudia was desperate to get some ground rules in place, but it was clear that Fraser was enjoying his new role and wasn't ready to move on to more down-to-earth things, like custody. He seemed to revel in his new life as a daddy, and it defied all previous beliefs that children were not for him.

Chapter Thirteen

'But if Alyona and Zara lived and worked in Paris,' Jenny said, 'how come you're English and not French?'

'Diaghilev brought his company to London, so the girls came too. Alyona met Richard, and she wouldn't go back, so Zara had to stay with her. I suppose it wasn't as simple as that at the time.'

Lizzy smiled. 'Did Richard wait for Alyona at the stage door?'

'No, it was much more dramatic than that. One night, after the performance, Zara was still dealing with the costumes, so Alyona waited for her outside the theatre. She took off her shoes, her feet were hurting so much because of the gruelling performances. She was still very homesick, pined for her family and the old life in Russia, but didn't understand why it all happened. Then suddenly, it all overwhelmed her, and she felt the urge to run. She kept on running through the streets until she arrived at Westminster Bridge, exhausted, gasping for breath, sobbing and calling out for her father.'

'Why her father and not her mother?' Jenny asked.

'He promised to follow on and find them, but...'

'They were both so young, I suppose that was probably the only way to make them leave without their parents,' Lizzy suggested.

'What then?' Jenny asked. Her eyes were wide, like a child listening to a bedtime story.

'A handsome cab stopped, a gentleman leapt out and ran towards her.'

Lizzy laughed. 'You're kidding. That really happened?'

'Alyona said so in her diary. She even describes his white silk evening scarf fluttering as he ran, his top hat falling from his head and rolling along the pavement. It's so vivid.'

'Standing there, clutching her shoes and crying, he must have thought she was going to jump,' Jenny said.

Claudia nodded. 'He threw his arms around her and never let her go again for the rest of his life.'

'Ah,' Jenny sighed.

'Her affair with Richard was considered outrageous in 1921. He broke his engagement to a very suitable young lady, which annoyed his family intensely. The family and friends all had a go at poor Alyona, blamed her entirely and called her all kinds of dreadful names, tried to make her give him up. In desperation, they threatened to disown him. So Richard walked away from his rightful inheritance to a huge estate. Had he been single, then maybe Alyona would have enjoyed a life of luxury again. But it wasn't to be.'

'What if he did inherit?' Jenny said. 'Would you have got it?'

'No, I'm descended from Zara. Alyona and Richard didn't have children.'

The tea and cake arrived.

'Oh, brilliant!' Claudia sighed. 'A nice cup of tea to wake me up a bit.'

Lizzy looked sympathetic as she said, 'Is Justin not sleeping?'

'No, poor baby, he's still snotty, grumpy and teething, so you can add dribbly to those symptoms. He feels very sorry for himself.' She sighed. 'So do I. Molly offered to take him for a night, but they don't want anybody else when they're not well, do they?'

'Do boy babies get worse colds than girl babies?' Jenny asked.

'I don't know, but it's so hard because you can't explain that it isn't forever. I'm sure he's missing Fraser too. But he's very tied up with handing over to Yuri and Paige.'

'Justin's got time to get better before we go to Firenze,' Lizzy said. 'Then you'll have loads of babysitters and get plenty of rest.'

Jenny looked at Claudia in surprise. 'I didn't know you were going.'

'It never occurred to me to go, but I couldn't deny Justin a chance to meet his grandparents. Fraser needs this holiday, and being in sole charge of Justin wouldn't leave him much time to enjoy his family.' She paused to sip her tea, and then she said, 'I won't get involved, I'll just be there if I'm needed. We'll be like a divorced couple being very polite and civil for the child's sake.'

'I'm sorry, Claudia,' Lizzy said, her voice was laced with concern. 'It must really hurt.'

Claudia nodded and expelled a long sigh. 'All around the ranch and back.'

Jenny stared at her. 'Around the ranch?'

'When I was a kid, I was often in scenes with a retired jockey called Lennie,' Claudia smiled affectionately, 'the little guy in those pictures in the magazine. He was my rock. We had to hang around an awful lot. One day, we made up a new saying, something to explain how we felt. How much Lennie missed his wife and kids, how far I'd go for a hot dog when I was hungry. That's what we came up with, all around the ranch and back.'

'So if anybody wants to know how much I miss my chocolate fudge cake, I say, all around the ranch and back.' Jenny laughed. 'I shouldn't complain, I'm fit and well.' She suddenly widened her eyes and beamed a smile. 'Just think,' she said, 'we'll all be mums.'

'Yes, we will,' Lizzy smiled, 'all three of us.'

'We can bring our babies to tea-and-cake day,' Jenny continued.

Claudia frowned. 'What?'

Lizzy looked horrified. 'Babies…at tea-and-cake day?'

'It'd be such fun…wouldn't it?' Jenny reasoned.

Lizzy and Claudia answered together with a positive 'NO!'

*****

It was late afternoon when Fraser left his office. He decided to take a walk in the park before going home to his apartment. It was the first time he'd been in London since Justin came into his life, and he was surprised how hard it was to be separated from him. His London life pleased him once, but now it seemed empty. The Wainford project was distracting, and his main business was losing favour. He hardly recognised himself at all.

The weather was warm, something drew him to the park. The summer flower displays were magnificent. He thought about

Claudia, and what might have happened had he remembered to come and look for her.

He recalled how simple it all used to be back then. Each time he tapped his knuckles on her door—it was always the same rhythmic knock—she would open it, smile and step back to let him in, all in one movement.

One evening he had walked in, kissed her cheek as usual and then declared, 'I brought dinner.'

She had peered into the bag, 'You brought groceries,' she contradicted. 'You even left the till-receipt in.'

'I thought we could cook.'

'I can't prepare it, my fingers hurt.'

He held her hands and inspected them, 'What did you do?'

'Work, fine textiles need small needles. They push into your fingers.'

He hugged her. 'Poor thing!'

'Thing?'

'Just an expression…would you prefer, darling, sweetheart honey?'

'Claudia would have been fine.'

'Sorry about your fingers. Can you hold a wooden spoon and a wok?

'Sure.'

'I'll do the labouring. You can do the magic, conjure up something fabulous.'

They chatted, laughed and talked as they cooked and drank wine. Later they sat on the rug, leaned against the sofa while they watched the movie about the people who made a pact to meet up, in Paris, if they lost touch. After that she looked at him, tilted her head, smiled and said, 'Are you OK now?'

'Yes, I'm good.'

'Was it a really bad day?'

'Frustrating, annoying, stifling…'

'You often say that. Why don't you get out?'

'Out? What do you mean, out?'

'Move on, do something else? You're just going through the motions of enjoying your career. Just because you're successful doesn't mean you can't give it up.'

She always seemed to know, despite his efforts to hide it, that he had arrived with a burden on his shoulders. But she helped him bear the weight and during the evening it lifted. It's what she did. As he re-lived moments from that evening, he recalled that he had hugged her simply because her fingers hurt, but she had no such comfort from him after her hours of travail to bring his beautiful son into the world…36 hours…Jesus Christ!

He phoned Claudia, she gave him an update on Justin. His cold was upsetting him, and he had some teeth coming through, but it was all perfectly normal and would pass in a few days.

Chapter Fourteen

It was way past midnight when Fraser arrived at Merevale. He hadn't planned to drive back tonight and he was tired but presumed that Claudia would be more so. He went straight to Heather Brow. The downstairs lights were on. Claudia was obviously still up and about. He rang the doorbell, then knocked and called out, 'Claudia, it's Fraser.'

Claudia opened the door. Justin was in her arms, whimpering and sniffling, tears rolled down his cheeks. The strange thing was that he didn't react to Fraser, he clearly only wanted Claudia.

'You're a welcome sight,' Claudia said, 'but this is a grumpy household at the moment. He's just had the paddy from hell.' Fraser followed her to the kitchen. She was dressed in short pyjamas and walked about barefoot on the tiled floor. He felt impotent as he watched the way she functioned so efficiently, one arm holding the baby and the other preparing a drink.

'I came to help,' Fraser said, 'but you don't look as though you need it.'

'Don't be fooled by my ability to function in my sleep.'

Fraser reached his arms toward Justin. 'Come on now, it's Mummy's turn to sit down.' He sat at the table and put Justin, who was still gulping and whimpering, on his lap.

'What are you doing here, Fraser, it's almost one in the morning?' Claudia seemed to be in a daze.

'Did I scare you?'

'Course not, I'm too tired.' She looked at her little boy. 'Poor baby, I just gave him something to help ease the pain. It should kick in soon. Then he'll feel better.' She looked at Fraser as if she'd remembered something. 'I'm sorry I never asked you how you felt about managing baby pain.'

'I trust you completely, Claudia, you don't have to check that kind of thing with me.' He looked at her and shook his head. 'You need some rest.'

'I'll be fine if I can get five hours.'

'You call that a night's sleep?'

'No,' she said, 'three hours is a night's sleep, five hours is hibernating. You've caught me at a bad time. I suppose it looks as though I can't cope.'

'Nonsense!' Fraser looked at her face and at her eyes that fought to stay open, her beautiful hair scrunched and tousled over her shoulders. It was seductive seeing her that way. It gave him ideas and certainly memories, though they were hazy and dream-like. He had once held her in the night, and the treasured proof of that union was now beginning to fall asleep against his chest. 'Do you want me to take him up now?'

'No, leave him until he's really sound asleep, otherwise he'll spring up again when you lie him down.' She looked at him, and a faint smile twitched on her lips. 'I'm glad you're here. I have something for you. I should have given it to you sooner, but it wasn't unpacked.'

'That sounds intriguing.'

Claudia went into the hall. Justin's lungs shuddered. It was the first time he'd seen his son like this, and it wasn't going to be cured by a shoulder ride or an aeroplane swing. He uttered a few soothing words and then gently kissed the top of Justin's head.

Claudia returned, she carried a small attaché case which she placed on the table. 'Here you go. This is for you.' She sat down, her whole being seemed to sigh as she did so.

'What is it?'

'When you don't have a family or a very wide support network to help you take care of a baby, it's perhaps more worrying than normal. If I met with an accident, what would happen to him?'

The reality of her words struck Fraser sharply, but he said nothing.

'Somebody would meet his needs while he was a child, but then he'd be alone as he approached his late teens. It wouldn't turn out good for him. I know I should have done more to contact you, but that wasn't his fault, and I decided that he'd be better off with a financially secure father who would do right by him. I knew that much. I knew you'd set up some kind of safe situation for him. So I always carried instructions to contact you at your London office. I'll still carry your details, so you'll be the first point of contact in the event of…'

Fraser felt chilled at the thought of Claudia not being there. 'That must have been very hard for you to deal with.'

'It's hard for anybody.' She fixed her eyes on his face and added, 'You've made provisions for him, this isn't so different. His documents, medical history and such are kept here if you want to see them any time. But everything in the case is yours. There's an album of photographs. He's well-documented at each stage of his development.' She pushed the case towards him. 'It might fill a few gaps. And maybe you'd want to scan some of them to send to your parents.'

'Thank you. I have to go back to London fairly soon. I'll be alone, so maybe that would be a good time to look through it.' He hesitated a moment and then said, 'I saw my lawyers in London. I'll bring you up-to-date on that when you're feeling better.'

'You're a wealthy businessman, but…' her voice faded, and she paused.

'What's on your mind?'

'I know your brilliant lawyers could run rings around me, but please don't ever use that power to fight me for custody.'

'Get that notion out of your head. I won't do it.'

'But what will happen when the love of your life eventually comes along, and you set up home together, have a family. You'll want Justin with you?' A sob snatched at her lungs. 'You'd have to prove that I'm an unfit mother, but you can dig all you like, you won't find any mud to rake up from my past, no drugs, no scandal, and I'm not going to go home and leave my child crying in the playground, no matter how tired I get.'

'For God's sake…' Fraser whispered, reached his hand across the table and grasped her fingers. 'I wouldn't dream of doing that. Why would I fight you? What would be the point in you giving him a chance to be part of my family if I was going to take him from his mother? We might still have issues, Claudia, but we're moving past them now. This is tired talk. My legal advisers are there for things I'm not qualified to deal with. I made a new will and set up a trust fund for Justin. That's what it was about… Understand?'

Claudia nodded.

Fraser smiled, 'I should buy two houses, and we can be neighbours. Justin can stomp between us when he can't get his own way.'

Claudia smiled. 'I did that.'

'You did?'

'I left home when I was 14, went to live with Granny.'

'Teenage rebellion?'

'I would have done it when I was five if I knew how.'

'You were close to your granny?'

'Yes, I miss her so much. But Justin was very small, so I didn't have time to dwell on her passing for long.' She looked at Justin. 'He's sound asleep now.'

'I'll take him up,' Fraser whispered.

When he returned Claudia was sitting down, her elbows rested on the table, and her hands covered her face. He sat by her and put his arm around her. 'He's fine,' he said. 'He's much cooler. I'm sorry you've had such a rough time.'

'It makes you feel so hopeless,' she said. 'When I first got him home, I tried so hard not to feel like the worst mother on earth, but sometimes it's overwhelming, as if you're drowning.'

'I'll stay and listen out for him. You go and hibernate.' He leaned back and looked at her. 'Are you going to object?'

'No chance,' she said, wearily. 'I have a spare room. It doubles as a study. The bed's already made up, and you'll find towels in the cupboard on the landing. I'll show you.'

The room clearly doubled as a study. There was a desk that was neatly organised, but it was mostly taken up by notebooks, journals and a box of letters. Fraser stared for a while and thought how ordinary they looked for something so important. He wondered if they were worth all Claudia's efforts to save them. None of it made sense, and he couldn't believe that a good lawyer wouldn't sort it out. He looked at Claudia and smiled. 'Go and get some rest. I just need to get my bag from the car.'

Claudia slid her arms around him and leaned her face against his shoulder. 'I'll be fine tomorrow, so you must get back.'

'We'll see. Are you going to bed or are you going to sleep right there against my chest?'

She looked up at him, 'Better not, last time I did that, I ended up in big trouble.'

Fraser smiled. 'All the same, it's a pleasant thought.'

'Yes it is,' she agreed wearily and then left the room. 'Goodnight!'

Chapter Fifteen

After a long day at the office, followed by an evening conference, Fraser arrived at his London apartment, pulled off his tie and unfastened several buttons of his shirt. It was far too quiet, and he wasn't enjoying the solitude, it made him restless. Claudia had often told him that he was in the wrong game, that he was bound to it because his father had started it years ago. She was right, he was disenchanted with it, but it was successful and afforded him a good life with many advantages. He considered that to be a good balance, and the advantages would always be there for Justin. Yuri and Paige were up to speed now, it was a relief. The Wainford project would take him away from London for the time being, but it didn't concern him, his life wasn't here anymore. It seemed he'd left it behind on a heather-coated hillside where his little boy lived. His trip back, to help Claudia, had been brief, both mother and child were very quickly recovered, but the experience of their little family closing ranks had been somehow fulfilling. His thoughts prompted him to take a look at Justin's papers.

He moved the occasional table up to the sofa and spread the contents of the small attaché case on it, files, papers, albums, notebooks describing special times or anecdotes about Justin's everyday life. He poured through the pages, smiled, laughed and even felt his eyes heating up.

Something fell from between some paperwork. A data stick landed by his foot. It wasn't marked in any way. He was curious and inserted the stick into his laptop.

There were four files. The first was simply marked Justin. It contained video recordings, moving images of a baby in all his stages of development, sitting up, crawling, plunging his tiny fingers into his food, all the vital landmarks in a child's early life.

He wanted to open the other files, but his eyes refused to focus, even though he blinked and rubbed them with his fingers. It was getting late, he was exhausted. He leaned back and closed his eyes for a moment.

He awoke with a start, thinking he'd heard his door slam, but nobody had a key, so he assumed he'd dreamt it.

'Fraser, darling!' A familiar voice called. It wasn't a dream.

'What the…?' He quickly got to his feet as Natalie burst in.

'I've been to a party. You don't mind if I crash here for the night, do you, hon? It's nearer than my place, and I can't go back, because I've had a row with Damien.' The words tumbled from her lips, and it was clear that she wasn't expecting her request to be refused.

'Another Damien?'

'No, he's the same one. I went back to him when we broke up.'

'From what you told me about him, you'll have an even bigger row if he finds you here. For God's sake, Natalie, I might have been with somebody. How on earth did you get in?'

'I borrowed a key, weeks ago.'

Fraser felt invaded by her arrival and her assumption that she could just drop by. 'Then you should have given it back.'

'Oh Fraser, don't be so boring.' She wrapped her arms around his neck. 'I'm glad you're here. I've missed you so much.'

'And after letting me down at an important time, you expect to kiss and make up?'

'It was mean, I admit it. It must have caused you a lot of hassle, and I'm—'

'Don't tell me you're sorry because you're not,' Fraser bit back. 'That was the intention, wasn't it, to tell me when it was far too late to make other arrangements?' He peeled her arms from around his neck. 'And you'd do that to a man you wanted to marry? How do you treat your enemies?'

'Come on, Fraser, don't be like that. You survived didn't you?'

'I did more than survive.'

'So, there you are, you managed to find somebody. What was she like?'

'Beautiful! She can dance a tango like an Argentinian gypsy, and she even speaks Russian. Not only that, but she got ready and arrived on time…imagine that.'

'If she's so fabulous, why isn't she here?'

'You know I don't date on a work day.'

'Then you'll be seeing her again?'

'Oh yes, that's for sure,' Fraser said casually, deliberately keeping details from her.

'She's not here now, though, is she?' Natalie said and wrapped her arms around his neck again, pressed her body against him.

'Natalie, stop playing games.' He felt the familiar moves of her body, it was what she did if she turned up unexpectedly, and he was distracted by work. There had been times when his body language shouted down his work ethic, but that was before they broke up. He put his hands on Natalie's shoulders and stepped back. 'You should go now. I'll get a chauffeur to take you home.'

'Don't be so dull, Fraser. Why can't I stay here?'

'We're not together anymore. You can't just let yourself in whenever you've had a row with your jealous boyfriend.'

Natalie snatched up her bag, found the key and slapped it in his hand. 'Don't bother about the car, I'll get a cab. Have a nice life with your quick-change Russian dancer.' She slammed the front door as she left.

Fraser, completely surprised by his restraint, returned to the sofa and the laptop, to check out the other files. The first one pre-dated Justin's life, so he was curious as to what it could be. What he didn't expect was to see Claudia smiling back at him.

'Hello Fraser!' Although she smiled, he could see uncertainty in her eyes. Her Peter Pan hair had grown into a wavy bob. She looked cute. 'I decided to make a video diary to explain a few things. Truth is I'm pregnant.' She stood up and rested her hand on her rounded abdomen. 'See?'

Fraser quickly pressed the pause button, so he could take in the image. He was transfixed. A wave of emotion flowed through every part of him—mind and body alike—to see where his son, yet foetal, was seemingly being comforted by his mother's hand on his head. When he released the pause button, Claudia's voice continued.

'This potential little bundle is yours...well ours,' she said, and she sat down again. 'I'm not blaming you,' she hastened to add, 'it's my own fault. I should have resisted you that night. I guess we both fell off the platonic waggon, so to speak.' Her approach was very practical, whereas he was still in the grip of emotion.

'But things go wrong in life,' Claudia continued, 'and what would the little thing do if something happened to me? So I keep your details in here.' She pinched the chain of her ID necklace. 'It's what people look for in emergencies, isn't it? It has your office number and my lawyer's number. I wouldn't be able to protect your reputation, but the child's wellbeing and safety are more important than that, don't you think? Well that's all I needed to say so...so...maybe I'll record an update sometime. At least I've taken precautions for the baby's safety. Bye for now.'

Fraser quickly opened the next file, anxious to see more. Claudia explained that she was well into her second trimester and held up a small print of her scan that she forgot to show him the first time.

'It seems that this little black and white smudge is probably a boy. I can't call him little smudge, so he's got his father's name already, well, your middle name actually. This is Justin Gallier.'

Fraser pressed the pause button again, rooted through Justin's little case and retrieved the scan. He looked at it for several seconds, and then put it at the end of the table, away from the other things, before watching more of Claudia's message.

She told him about her day job in a textile store, so she didn't have to travel to commissions, that often involved working quite high off the floor, and she didn't want to take risks. She went on to explain that she wouldn't normally have stayed so long because of the heavy rolls of fabric. But everybody was so kind, they were helping her work the extra weeks, so she could have longer maternity leave.

'Of course, Justin isn't a little smudge anymore,' Claudia said, 'he's lively, kicks about a lot. He gets fidgety at times.' She laughed. 'Like his father,' she added. 'He's probably drumming his little fingers too.'

Fraser laughed at her reference to it.

'Anyway, Fraser, it's good to talk to you. I've got nobody else to nag and shout at, and you can't answer back, can you? Hope all this wasn't too mumsy for you. I'm really tired, so I'm off to bed.' She chuckled. 'I sound like Samuel Pepys—supper, diary, bed.' She stopped, looked straight at the camera and seemed to draw a nervous breath. 'Everything's so different now. I miss my work, and I miss my life. I miss you too…so much.' A sob caught in her throat. 'These wretched hormones,' she complained, 'they make you want to blub at the slightest thing.' She cleared her throat and smiled. 'Goodnight Fraser.'

Fraser sat for a moment, still feeling shaken and incredibly guilty to see this beautiful, courageous woman dealing with the changes in her life. There was one more entry. He hesitated, unable to bring himself to look at it, he felt emotions unlike any other he'd known. But curiosity overcame him, and he opened the last file.

'Hi Daddy!' Claudia called to him from the screen.

Fraser snatched his breath and stared, his pounding heart resounded through his body, his head, his ears…

'Look what we made,' Claudia said with a beaming smile and shining eyes, even though her face was pale. Her hair was now, almost to her shoulders. 'The only thing we ever made together before was dinner. These little beings are a lot more complicated than preparing vegetables. He's got all the important things, toes, fingers and the little parts that you fathers deem to be important.' She lifted up the tiny body so he could be seen, the feet of his onesie hung empty beyond his toes.

Fraser stared, mesmerised and hardly able to believe it.

'I just got out of hospital,' Claudia continued as she put the child in the crook of her arm. 'I'm thrilled of course, but for goodness sake, I don't know how to look after a baby. I mean, you don't even have to qualify to take one home. You can't adopt a cat without being checked out. If your body knows how to grow him and get him born, why can't your brain download all the other stuff you need at the same time?' A look of uncertainty filled her eyes, and she was silent for a moment. 'To tell you the truth, Fraser, I shouldn't say this to you at this stage, but I'm so scared. I'm supposed to nurture him, teach him things and keep him safe. I have to make decisions about jabs and inoculations and scary stuff like that. Look at him, he's so little and vulnerable, and I don't know if I can do all those things. I wish…' She reached out her free hand. 'I wish you could hold my hand right now, wish I could feel your fingers closing around mine. I'm being ridiculous I know, but I've never needed anybody so much as I need you now.'

'Claudia, dear God, don't tell me that,' Fraser whispered.

Claudia went quiet for a moment, and then she suddenly snapped out of her doleful moment and smiled. 'But isn't he fabulous, Fraser? Aren't you proud of him?'

'Oh, God, yes,' Fraser said, as if she was actually standing there, talking to him. 'At least now you know I am.'

She held the child close. 'I don't regret this for one second. I wouldn't have missed that night with you. I thought that, just once, I could be close to you and then go back to hiding how I really felt.' She thought a moment and then said, 'Was it so bad to let my guard down just once? Did you have to be so remorseful about it? Leave me that note?' She frowned and shook her head. 'I'm really sorry but…' She drew a long breath and composed herself. 'I really do need to get over you. Even if I contacted you, I could never have you. And I can't live with a broken heart forever. I'll let you know about him, as soon as I feel tough enough to run the gauntlet again. I'll try, I really will try. But first, I have to let you go.' Her throat seemed to tighten, and she uttered, 'Goodnight my long, lost lover…goodnight.'

The screen went dark. Fraser searched for another file, another message, but there was nothing. He had never felt so much emotional conflict. He was boiling with frustration, his chest felt as though it would burst. All he could think of was that hand reaching out to him, but it was beyond his reach, locked in technology and time. His chance to be there was gone, frittered away while he indulged in a reckless affair with Paloma Cardini. He could have had it all, a wonderful woman who needed him, even loved him. All he had to do was turn up at the park, one Wednesday lunch time, when the daffodils were in bloom.

He packed Justin's papers and albums back in the case, hastily threw a few things into a go-bag and left his apartment.

Chapter Sixteen

Claudia was about to leave the house when her landline rang, it was Eliot.

'Todd hasn't turned up this morning,' he said. 'If we don't get the place emptied, before we go to Italy, the decorators can't move in while we're away. The whole schedule's going to hell. We've only got a couple of weeks... Did he say anything to you yesterday?'

'No, but don't worry, Eliot, I think he's got an audition. I know he's been rehearsing a new piece, I've heard it so often I've learnt it myself.'

Eliot sighed in exasperation. 'I hope he's better at acting than he is at this job. Sorry to bother you, Claudia. I'll get somebody else in.'

Claudia was anxious to leave, she had a very busy day planned. Justin was already with Molly, so she was good to go. As she left the house, Fraser was just pulling up on her drive. He seemed in a hurry as he got out of the car and approached her.

'Hold on, Claudia, I need to talk to you.'

'What's the matter? I wasn't expecting you back for another couple of days. There was no need to rush, Justin's fine now.'

'I came back late last night. I had to see you.' He seized her and pulled her into a tight embrace, his arms were clamped so tightly around her, she could hardly breathe. 'I needed to hold you,' he uttered against her ear. Then he released her.

'What's wrong?' Claudia peered at his pale, tense face, his tired eyes and said, 'You don't look so good.'

'Can we talk?'

'Now? I need to leave. I have a very tight schedule today.' She took a small notebook from her bag, flipped the pages and then peered at it. 'I'm going to a craft supplier in Bowbury, but if they don't have what I need, I'll have to go further afield. Then

I'm off to meet somebody about some hand-spun yarn. It's a place called…Roughingmount.'

'You can't find anywhere nearer than that?'

'I don't know this region, and there's no time to keep searching. I found this place so I'm going. I haven't a clue where it is. It could be in Middle Earth for all I know.'

Fraser looked at the notebook. His tension eased as he took control. 'It's pronounced Rowmont, and it could well be Middle Earth, quite a long drive from here. You can't possibly go in your own car, and don't even think of protesting.' He wouldn't hear of Claudia attempting the gradients and the rugged terrain, of Roughingmount, in her small vehicle. 'You should take this one.'

'I can't take your car.'

'It's not mine, it's one of Tony's pool cars. And if he were here, he would insist too. You can drop me off at Larchwood.' Claudia began to protest, but he pressed the ignition key into her hand and added, 'I'll be here for Justin. Don't start rushing from place to place, take your time. Just concentrate on what you have to do.'

'Fraser, I know how to—'

'You've never been there, don't underestimate the conditions.' He fixed his eyes on hers as if to thrust home his advice. 'Maybe I should drive—'

'For goodness sake!' A cold wind induced Claudia to hug her short jacket across her chest. Grey and purple clouds loomed above, warning of heavy rain. It wasn't going to be a very pleasant trip. 'Anything else,' Claudia said, 'or can I go now?'

Fraser's tension returned, and it unnerved Claudia. She still half-expected him to challenge her about custody, and moments like this made her suspicious. Considering he had something pressing on his mind, he was taking his time, and the wind was already undoing her efforts to groom her hair.

At last Fraser spoke. 'Justin's case…'

'What about it?'

'I found your video diary among some papers. It fell out when I was going through them.'

'Fell out?' Claudia frowned. 'But I put it in an envelope and taped it to the album, it's marked very clearly.'

'It was loose, it fell out,' Fraser insisted.

Claudia groaned as she realised what had happened. 'You weren't supposed to have that one, it wasn't edited, it was a mess. Please tell me you didn't watch it all,' she said ruefully.

'Of course I did—every second of it.'

'I went to a lot of trouble to cut out all those ridiculous...hormonal tears.'

'They're not ridiculous,' Fraser snapped, and then held up his hands in a silent apology. He looked grave and showed no signs of relaxing. 'That's why I need to talk it over with you.'

'Why? We need to move forward not backwards. That's all in the past now.'

'In your past, maybe, but not in mine.' Fraser looked into her eyes. 'That frightened woman in the diary needed me.'

'She got over it...moved on.'

'She hasn't moved on, she's still there reaching her hand out to me, trapped in some kind of computerised time warp where I can't reach her.'

Claudia could see how the video had upset him, and she felt guilty for her carelessness, and that she should help him get past it. 'I didn't feel all that doubt just because you weren't there, all mothers go through it. I still need you now, Fraser, we have to make proper arrangements for Justin. My life's in limbo and I have to get hold of it.' She glanced at her watch. 'Fraser, I really do have to go.'

'Just a couple more minutes—please. I have a proposition to put to you.' Suddenly words came out of Fraser's mouth that shocked Claudia into silence, and all she could do was stare as he continued. 'What could be better than both of us under one roof?' He reasoned. 'No passing backwards and forwards to different homes. No daddy days and mummy days, just one family together. Our son will be raised by married parents,' he concluded decisively.

Claudia could see that he didn't expect to be turned down. She stared in disbelief. 'That's not a proposition, Fraser, it's a proposal.' The picture he presented was a dream that Claudia never believed possible, but it wasn't a proposal from a man full of love for a woman, it was a practical solution from a man who wanted to be a good father and take hold of that needy hand that reached out to him on the video. She wished that he would just pick two or three weekdays to spend with Justin, work out an amicable agreement for Christmas and holidays, like everybody else. Then they could all learn to live with that. She felt a pang of irony in her heart. There was a time when this would have been an exciting idea. But it wasn't welcome today. 'We don't need to be married,' she told him firmly. 'Children cope with this situation all the time.'

'Yes, when it's the only solution. But Justin doesn't have to cope, he can have us both.'

'You respect and admire me, you could probably enjoy spending nights with me, and you're even in love with your son.' She looked straight into his eyes and said, 'But you're not in love with me...are you? You never have been.' The words almost choked her. 'The main thing is that we remain friends and not become competitive or bitter. Surely this is what we're supposed to be discussing not hypothetical ideas of marriage.'

Fraser put his hands on her shoulders. 'It's not hypothetical,' he protested, 'I'm very serious.'

She remained strong, but her heart still felt the pain of knowing that even if they were married, she couldn't truly have him, not all of him—nobody could. 'My life isn't a defunct factory to be salvaged, Fraser. You're basing your proposal on your need to be there, for Justin, and to help you come to terms with the fact that you can't change the past. I'm not Paloma Cardini or Natalie. I'm five foot seven, I wear a tatty, old lab coat for work, and deep down I'm still a feisty little tearaway who has more kick-off buttons than most women. How can you possibly see yourself tied to me in marriage?'

'I don't see it as being tied. We can do this,' Fraser insisted, 'we can build on what we have.' He clasped her hand. 'At least think about it.'

Fraser's eyes seemed to plead with her, they were soft and suddenly full of warmth, and she was tempted to agree as the love she once felt threatened to flood back into her soul. Her heart was telling her that it could work, he might even fall in-love with her, but her head said that they would probably break up eventually. Then Justin would be the one to pay. She dragged herself from the grip of temptation. After all this was presented as an agreement, not a proposal for a happy marriage. That's all it was, a deal.

'I'll think about it,' she told him so that she could get away. 'But you must remember that I have issues to settle with my mother. And I just don't seem to be able to find the time to work it out. And please don't start talking about lawyers again, I have to find another way.'

'But why won't you accept that you've got the law on your side, she can't just—'

'She can!' Claudia's patience snapped, 'Don't you dare underestimate what I'm up against.'

'It's not like you to be so...' He stopped suddenly.

'Go on, Fraser, say it... Obsessed? Paranoid?' Claudia was becoming angry at his patronising attitude towards something that was potentially very damaging. 'Is that what you were going to say?'

'Let me help you?' Fraser pleaded.

Claudia turned from him and stared at the hillside. The wind whipped at the heather, and the clouds were tinted with purple.

'Claudia?' Fraser prompted and stood close to her.

'You really must try and understand what kind of person my mother is. People like her are very clever at what they do. You can't nail them down. When I was four, not much older than Stephanie, I made a film. I played a little Russian princess. You saw the picture in the magazine. A dialogue coach taught me the Russian lines. She was nice—kind. It was fun, just a game. But when it came to filming it in the studio, it was a different game, and I didn't want to do it anymore. I suppose it was the activity, lights, people rushing around. My mother swung into action and said she'd arranged to have my new kitten taken away. She would get him back when I'd done the filming—like a good girl.'

'But that was just a bluff, surely.'

'No, you see, that's what the kitten was for—why she got it in the first place. It was to give me a weakness that she could tap, something she could use to make me co-operate. As soon as I finished my last series of the ranch, as it came to be called, I threatened to leave and live with my grannie so I could give up working and go to school. Mother said that if I did, she'd sell my horse. I called her bluff.'

'And did she?'

'Of course she did. Losing my horse was the price of my freedom.' She turned to him and could see the confusion and disbelief in his eyes.

'But you broke away,' Fraser reasoned, 'you were brave enough to face the consequences. What can she do now? You don't have a kitten or a pony anymore.'

'No, but I do have a baby. He's my new weakness now, don't you see that?'

'You can't be serious, she wouldn't use him.'

'She would, and she will if I don't sort it all out first. Somebody will have contacted her after seeing the spread in the magazine. Goodness knows what they might have told her. By now she could have her greedy hands full of ammunition to weaken me. If she finds out about Justin…'

'She won't hurt him, I promise you.'

Claudia shook her head wearily. 'By the time you know where she's coming from, it'll be too late. You won't be able to do a thing about it. All your lawyers and advisers put together won't scare her one jot. She'll think of something. Probably try and discredit me. Report me to the social services. Suggest that I'm unstable, and all those years as a child star have taken their toll.' She shrugged her shoulders. 'I wouldn't be the first, would I? I'd be a risk, an unfit mother.'

'She can't prove that.'

'No, but they'll check it out, and during that time, I wouldn't be allowed to take care of Justin or even be with him alone. Social services don't rush these things. I called her bluff over my horse, but can you see me doing the same with Justin? She'll win, get the diaries and walk off as squeaky clean as a new pin. Then she'll make her trashy movie out of Alyona's life. My promise, to my granny, will be on my conscience for the rest of mine.' She gulped down the tension in her throat. 'Of course, she might go straight for you, first. In that case, I'll still lose because I won't let her hurt you either.' Her heart sank when she saw that Fraser was still struggling to understand the gravity of her situation.

'Then, are the diaries worth it?'

'Excuse me?' Claudia bit back. 'Fifteen years ago, you joined your father's company out of sheer loyalty. You didn't want it. You slogged to keep it alive and then turned it into an empire, far removed from what he started. Now he's living his dream, making wine in Tuscany. Look what Tony did for Larchwood, saved it from crumbling into the ground.'

'Where's all this leading, Claudia?'

'When the Galliers and Franklyns in the world go to great lengths to be loyal and protect family and property, it's looked on as noble and admirable. But when I do it, I'm paranoid, overreacting and misguided. I'm supposed to hand over my family treasure, whatever the cost, then marry you to make things simple.' They both stood in silence, having reached some kind of stalemate. Claudia then said softly, 'I hate to fight, and I certainly can't fight two of you. I have to go.' She walked towards the car. 'By the way, it's Justin's birthday the day after tomorrow.'

'Yes, I noticed from the papers.'

'Could you ask Tony and Lizzy if he could celebrate it here with Stephanie and Eddy? His only nursery friends are in London.'

'Sure, let's have a great party. I'll get Stella to do a cake.'

'Brilliant. Are you going to drive to Larchwood, or shall I?'

Chapter Seventeen

As Fraser had returned unexpectedly, he and Tony decided to take a day to reflect on the situation, at Wainford, talk over one or two issues. They had coffee at the hotel, but work wasn't the first item on the agenda.

Tony was hard-pressed to gulp down his sip of coffee before the surprise caused him to gasp, 'You proposed?'

'Yes, this morning, before she left. If we were married, it would be so much better than raising Justin in two separate homes.'

Tony leaned his arms on the table and stared at his cousin. 'Is that how you proposed, with a domestic arrangement? You say she's special, important, valued, all those things, but I don't hear the word love mentioned.'

'Of course I... She's always been very special.' He paused for want of the right words to explain himself. 'It's a confused kind of feeling.'

'That's because the rules used to be simple—no marriage, no kids, no long-term commitment... The best they could hope for was monogamy while the relationship lasted. Why don't you just admit that you're in love with her and ask her properly?'

'What?'

'You're afraid of her, because you're just as crazy in love with her as I am with Lizzy. So you keep your real feelings hidden behind this friendship, that's so bloody important to you.'

Fraser frowned, his fingers fidgeted on the table. 'I wouldn't describe my feelings like that.'

'I never had trouble with women either, until I fell in love with Lizzy. It's frightening at first.' He stared at Fraser, 'You've got some soul-searching to do. This isn't fair to Claudia. You hardly know a thing about her. Get to know the woman you're so afraid to love, and stop treating her like a pal who might make a good house-share buddy.'

Tony's words hit Fraser hard, but then his cousin was so secure in his marriage. 'Don't forget you're a Franklyn, you're genetically designed to be locked in passionate, powerful feelings for your wife.'

Tony sipped his coffee, and then he stared at Fraser. 'That isn't an exclusive emotion just for the Franklyn family. Besides, you've only got to take one look at Silas to know that it's a recent trend. It can happen to anybody.' He then spoke as if he wasn't sure whether to say any more on the subject. 'I think she's in love with you.'

'No, she isn't, she used to be, but she got over me.'

'Sure she did. Claudia's strong and independent. She doesn't need you, but she sure as hell loves you, anybody can see that.'

'I can't.'

'That's because she's hiding it from you. And you try and win her over with an outmoded offer to make an honest woman of her? If you're not careful, she really will get over you and move on. Then Justin will have someone else to take him for a walk, a swim, a romp on the lawn and shop for a Christmas tree. The little chap will be calling two men daddy.'

Fraser was shocked. Another man in the equation didn't sit well at all, Mathew Jay was bad enough. She might even go back to him. She hadn't really forgotten him, that was obvious. The idea raced around his head like a spiky little spit venom. Some other father in Justin's life? Some other guy in Claudia's bed?

'That hit home,' Tony said with a chuckle.

Irena approached them and spoke discreetly. 'Mr Franklyn, you are wanted in the private lounge. It is a matter of some urgency.'

'Something wrong, Irena?'

'I do not wish to speak of it in public, if you would come now please. Mr Gallier should come also.'

Fraser exchanged a puzzled look with Tony and then followed Irena. He wondered if somebody from the factory had a problem. It was a pity, as he had planned to spend a quiet day at Larchwood, pick up Justin early and spend some time with him. This plan became more pressing after Tony's tough love speech.

What actually met them in the lounge was the last thing he expected. His eyes fixed on the tall, sophisticated woman, dressed in immaculate and very expensive clothes.

She approached Tony and held out her hand. 'Mr Franklyn?'

'Yes, good morning.'

'Thank you so much for seeing me.' Her voice was low and authoritative.

Tony introduced Fraser. 'My cousin and business partner, Fraser Gallier.'

'Yes,' she said smoothly, as if she already knew who he was. It made him feel uneasy. She offered her hand in greeting, but, to Fraser, it looked more like an invitation to kiss her fingers. He clasped them very briefly and gave her a polite nod. Neither he nor Tony knew this woman, but she seemed to know them. Could be she was a sleeping investor, in Wainford, come to check on them.

She looked around the room. Fraser wondered why. It was like any other in a well-run, high-calibre hotel, easy chairs, sofas, coffee tables... She asked about the architecture, the history of the place, if it was originally a mansion house. Tony responded politely and informed her of several interesting facts about its origins.

Fraser had met enough powerful people in his career to be able to recognise that she meant to be in control, and this pause to discuss her surroundings was to give her time to weigh them up, make them wait for her to speak, a classic controlling technique. But he knew that Tony wasn't likely to play that game with a stranger, and his cousin addressed her politely.

'What can I do for you, Mrs...?'

She responded swiftly as if to steal Tony's advantage. 'Hamilton, Elsa Hamilton.'

The name gave Fraser a jolt. He was glad Claudia was out for the day. He had no intention of referring to her. He kept quiet.

'I'm here on a flying visit,' Elsa Hamilton continued, still owning the room. 'I came by train from London to Bowbury and took a taxi the rest of the way. Consequently, I arrived very late last night. It was a relief to find a good hotel. I wasn't sure what would be here to greet me.'

'I hope you had a comfortable night, Mrs Hamilton,' Tony said. The two of them were like opponents in a poker game, neither showing their hand.

'Unfortunately, I've woken up with a dreadful headache,' Elsa Hamilton said. 'I'm prone to migraines, so I'll try and be brief.'

'I'm sorry about that,' Tony said, 'how can we help you?'

Her brow creased, she shook her head slowly, and a wounded look came into her face. It was in contrast to the arrogance she had first displayed. 'My Claudie,' she said with a weary sigh.

Fraser's insides jerked again but more violently. Claudia had anticipated this. She tried to tell him that this woman would turn up, and how she would use anybody for her own betterment. It sounded incredible, but this visit was beginning to make him doubt his original opinion. He felt the need to see where this was heading, to find out how hard Claudia's mother was going to push today.

'Claudie?' Tony was still playing it carefully.

'My lovely daughter, I believe she's working for you. Can you tell me where she lives?'

Tony didn't hesitate to answer. 'I'm afraid not, Mrs Hamilton. As her employer, I can't give such details to anybody.'

Fraser was surprised at Tony's approach, he seemed to mistrust this woman immediately.

'I must know where she is. She has some valuable property of mine, things that my late mother was saving for me. She hasn't forwarded them, and I'm growing concerned.'

Fraser was shocked. The woman's claims were disturbingly innocent, and not at all like Claudia's version of the story. Yet, he knew that Claudia loved her grandmother and wouldn't lie about being a benefactor. He felt for her, she had taken such drastic steps to keep this woman out of her life, and here she was. Somebody had obviously seen the magazine and had made contact. They must have told her that Claudia worked for Tony, he was well documented, so finding out about the hotel wasn't difficult. But it seemed she hadn't found out about Larchwood or Heather Brow. He was anxious to know if she had learned any more.

'I can tell you this much, Mrs Hamilton,' Tony said. 'Claudia is a very reliable person. I'm sure the property is safe with her.'

'The thing is,' Elsa Hamilton said with a sudden switch of mood from the wounded mother to friendly associate. 'There are a number of diaries, a valuable family history, you see. They contain personal details of my great-aunt Alyona's life with an English gentleman. As you can imagine, I feel responsible for the safekeeping of her personal account of it. I can't keep flying over to England, to find Claudia. If I could take possession of the property, I shan't need to bother her again. I'm not sure she realises the true value of them.' She strolled around a while and then said. 'I'm flying back to LA, this evening. I don't have much time.' She frowned and shook her head, as if Claudia was a naughty child who'd played the wag from school. 'My girl makes such rash moves. You see there's some jewellery, handed down from my Russian grandmother. It needs to be in a safe place.'

'Why do you think Claudia hasn't secured a place of safety for it?' Tony said politely, but not losing his air of authority.

'Well, she gets over-tired and forgets her medication.'

'Medication?' Fraser swiftly re-joined the discussion. He wished he hadn't and knew he'd just fed Elsa Hamilton a glimmer of weakness. After all, this was a person who could coldly take a child's kitten away. He knew that was how this woman operated, and Claudia was right, she was good at it.

Elsa Hamilton raised her brow. 'She's not going to admit she needs it, is she?' Then having just dropped the bombshell, she dismissed it as if the damage was now done, and she could move on. 'But you must ask her about that yourself. I have to insure the jewellery before I can travel back with it.' She fixed her cold, grey eyes on Tony, 'Perhaps it's in your hotel safe?'

'I haven't heard of any valuables like that,' Tony said. 'We don't know anything about Claudia, other than what you published in the magazine. She just does her work and then goes home—simple as that.'

'I don't know what to do.'

By now, Fraser knew that this woman was going to keep on playing her cards, one at a time, until she felt she'd played the right hand. He watched her stealthily, coldly, place the next one.

'I could get the police on to it I suppose, after all, it should be with me. And then there are the diaries.'

'She's never discussed this with me,' Tony told her.

'She's very well-practised in being a disruption to my life.'

Fraser was angry to hear of Claudia being discussed in this way. 'Disruption?' he queried but remained cool.

'She's spent her whole childhood working on it. If you saw the magazine, you'd know that she was a child actor.'

'I glanced at it,' Fraser lied, 'one of the staff had it here.'

Elsa Hamilton shook her head ruefully. 'You should have seen her. She was a little star…amazing. There was nothing you could throw at her that she couldn't do. When she was four years old, she made her debut. Delivered a considerable amount of dialogue, in Russian…so convincing. It took a little persuasion, she's very stubborn, my girl. But I bought her a kitten for doing it so nicely. She was so fond of that little cat.'

Elsa Hamilton then fixed her attention on Fraser. It seemed deliberate. 'I could have turned her into a bigger star than that sultry, Cardini woman that was all the rage a couple of years ago.'

Fraser wanted to say, out loud, she already is, but he kept it in his head, he needed all his concentration to keep up with her and find out where this was going.

'I mean, people are already saying, "Paloma who?"'

The way she fixed her cold, grey eyes on him when she mentioned the name, gave Fraser chilling confirmation that she knew what she was saying. It was aimed at him.

'She threw it away,' Elsa Hamilton continued. 'She could have made the transition and had a fabulous adult career. Her genius…wasted, and for what?' She scoffed. 'To go and live with a man 15 years older. He seduced her, took her away from the world.'

It irked Fraser to know how much Claudia treasured the memories of her relationship with Mathew, but she had known him from childhood, they had worked together. Elsa Hamilton couldn't possibly blame him.

'So you see,' Elsa Hamilton continued, 'this latest little escapade is just another chapter in Claudia's reckless life.' She cast her eyes up to the ceiling. 'She's so chaotic. It probably goes with the talent.'

'I haven't seen that in her,' Tony was swift to contradict her. 'Her approach to her work and her organisation is immaculate.'

'She's a calm sort of person, I grant you that, but she always is—at first. She gets ideas and then backs out. She wanted *English Girl on the Ranch* to be available in a box set. I thought it was a ridiculous idea, but she would have it her way. So what could I do? I agreed.' She raised her palms towards the ceiling. 'But is she grateful?'

That moment hit Fraser like bolt of lightning. He was with Claudia when she found out about the box set. She was livid and very hurt. It even caused a row between them when they'd been so happy during the party. If Elsa Hamilton had caused him to doubt Claudia, he most certainly didn't doubt her now. This woman was a total fraud, lying, manipulating and scheming to cheat Claudia. Now she'd come to try and con Tony into helping her get her hands on the diaries. Fraser knew he must keep this woman at bay until her flight time. Arrange to head Claudia off and warn her. But then Elsa Hamilton still hadn't got what she came for, and she could clearly operate at a distance and wouldn't stop until she succeeded. This move, of trying to involve Tony, was a bold one, arrogant and callous. She seemed to have played Plan A, and she hovered as if to regroup, ready to strike again with Plan B.

Tony and Fraser had an extra sensory instinct to stand close together as she prowled about. She then looked at them and smiled, 'Your project sounds very exciting.'

Fraser thought he'd got the measure of her, but this comment shocked him. It was as if she had a repertoire, some order of delivery, like a stand-up comic, but she wasn't funny. Each level of attack was more probing and severe than the one before.

'What a fine thing to do,' Elsa Hamilton said smoothly. 'You must be looked on as a couple of knights in shining armour in…Wainford, isn't it?'

'We're not do-gooders,' Tony contradicted, 'it's just business.'

'Situations like that are so fragile, aren't they? You have to keep the confidence of your workforce and the investors.' She suddenly widened her eyes as if she's had a fresh thought. 'You're not looking for investors, are you?'

'No,' Tony and Fraser answered swiftly.

Fraser knew that was to shock them, and was most definitely in the script. 'We've had a lot of experience between us, so we're going to make it work.'

Her mouth smiled, but there was no light in her face, it was merely a patronising smirk. 'Yes, I'm sure you are.'

Fraser suddenly felt as though he'd been hit in the gut. She clearly knew, all along, who he was, so what else would she aim at next—Justin? He totally understood Claudia's fear for their child, and now he felt it too. This was the most devious and dangerous person he'd ever met. The reference to Paloma was aimed at him to let him know that she had something on him. His relationship was in the public domain at that time. That's what worried Claudia about being seen with him. This cold, scheming woman could start an ugly rumour and have it in papers and magazines in no time, she'd already done it to Claudia. By the time he'd proven his innocence, the Wainford project could be well and truly scuppered. All Claudia's efforts to keep him out of this were based on the certain knowledge that Elsa Hamilton would use him, and here was the proof staring right at him. How was this to be handled? This woman had virtual talons, poisonous claws that could strike anywhere. She could say anything, lies, rumours, accusations... All she wanted was that dogeared, battered pile of notebooks on Claudia's desk. It seemed so simple.

'Tell you what, Mrs Hamilton,' he said, as if he'd come to a decision. 'I can call Claudia and tell her you're here. But it'll take some time, she's away. Gone to the Welsh border, up in the hills, to buy some hand-spun yarn.' He knew that Elsa Hamilton wouldn't be able to even imagine where Claudia had gone, let alone attempt to follow her. 'Claudia's very gifted and particular about her work you see. She's trying to match textures and colour tones perfectly to blend in with the original work. I'll call her as soon as there's a signal.'

'That's very civil of you, Mr Gallier.'

Fraser chalked up a point for himself for gaining control for the moment. He had to be sure Claudia stayed away from the hotel. He swung into action and called on his gentlemanly charm to play his hand. 'The way I see it, Mrs Hamilton,' he said with a polite smile, 'the sooner this misunderstanding is dealt with the better. I totally understand how frustrated you must feel. The situation has obviously gone on quite long enough.'

'It's such a relief to find somebody who understands my predicament. Claudie is under the illusion than she's going to write Alyona's story, but she's just not capable. I can get it written.' She frowned and shielded her eyes from the daylight streaming through the window. 'Do you suppose it's possible to have them sent on after I leave this evening?'

'They're not our property, Mrs Hamilton,' Tony said, steadily. 'We can't answer that.'

'I have to admit I need to do something about this headache, it's getting worse as we speak.'

'Why don't you wait in your room,' Fraser said, 'and I'll get back to you when I have news? We'll do what we can to help.'

'I'm glad you see it that way, Mr Gallier. I'll do that.' Fraser escorted her across the lounge and opened the door for her.

She stopped, still scowling with pain, but she managed to look him in the eye and say, 'Congratulations, by the way. I understand you've made a granny out of me. That was careless, wasn't it?'

Fraser's heart jerked, and he could barely bluff his way out of the shock. She knew about Justin, and that comment, disguised as a joke, was perfectly timed and indicated that she would go to the lengths Claudia feared. He closed the door and leaned against it. When would this woman stop? There were other children at Larchwood, would Stephanie and Eddie be at risk? There was no end to it, except to give her what she wanted.

Irena emerged from an adjoining room that she used as an office.

'Did you hear any of that? Tony asked.

'Yes, I did. I took detailed notes.'

'Now we know for sure what this woman is capable of,' Fraser said. 'You weren't fooled even at the beginning, were you?' he said to Tony.

'Claudia talks to Lizzy. She convinced me some time ago.'

'And she knows about Justin,' Fraser said. 'Now I see why Claudia moved so quickly.' He was very shaken and breathed steadily to regain his composure.

There was a knock on the door. The receptionist came in. 'Sorry to interrupt, Mr Franklyn, but Mrs Hamilton has asked for a doctor. Said to tell you personally that she's anxious to get rid of her migraine in time for her flight tonight.'

'I will arrange it,' Irena said.

The receptionist thanked her and left the room.

Fraser tried to call Claudia to warn her to stay away. He needed time to work something out. She was unavailable, so he assumed that she was driving. They hadn't parted well today, and he felt the need to make his peace with her.

'The migraine will be very debilitating,' Irena said. 'Mrs Hamilton has done a lot of travelling over a short time, and now she faces all the inconveniences of another long journey.'

'My heart bleeds for her,' Fraser scoffed.

'It is unfortunate for her,' Irena agreed, 'but good news for Claudia.'

'You're up to something, Irena,' Tony said. 'I can tell by the way you're delivering clues instead of information. What's on your mind?'

'I realise that it is against your policy to use the plane for only one passenger, but this is an emergency, is it not? If Mrs Hamilton could make the return trip in the comfort and privacy of a private plane, then she could be persuaded to leave immediately. We could get her airborne while she is still feeling unwell and more likely to be persuaded. When Claudia returns from her trip, her mother will be somewhere over the ocean.'

'A tempting idea,' Tony said. 'She thinks we're co-operating, so she might agree to it.'

Fraser thought of Claudia, and all the years she had lived with this woman. How was a child to deal with such a parent? What could she do to protect herself from the web of control around her where her mother was intent on draining every last drop from her, like a venomous spider would drain a fly? He was angry, not just with her but with himself for failing to understand Claudia's fears. But it was futile to think that there was a way to stop Elsa Hamilton. It was inevitable that the diaries would be hers eventually. He was sickened by the thought. He looked at Irena and said, 'Get that despotic bitch the hell out of here.'

Despite the cloudy sky, Elsa Hamilton wore dark glasses and a wide brimmed hat, but it was clear to see that she was unwell.

They arrived at the small, local airfield where the plane waited. Irena escorted her up the steps while Tony and Fraser looked on.

'I feel as though I've just been sucked into a spy game,' Tony said. 'We have all the elements, a Ukrainian agent, a dangerous woman in a big hat and a giant chauffeur waiting for us in a black limo.'

They laughed, as much from relief as good humour.

'I wish it really was funny,' Fraser said. 'I feel like hell. I can't stand to think of what Claudia's been through. I just didn't grasp the degree of danger she was in.'

'You've got time to put that right. Talk to her when she gets back.'

Irena returned, Fraser thanked her.

'That is a very dangerous woman. I will do all I can to help Claudia.'

'If you get a chance to help her, whatever it is, don't wait for permission, just go ahead and do it.'

They watched as the plane taxied along the runway, picked up speed and then rose into the sky. It was soon out of sight.

Chapter Eighteen

Claudia found herself driving along miles of hill roads, thankful for the loan of Tony's vehicle, as it was definitely more robust than her own. As a child, she was accustomed to travelling in style, chauffeur-driven cars, first-class flights, five-star hotels… But that was the business, the public image created by Elsa Hamilton, and totally wasted on a feisty little tearaway. If Claudia accepted Fraser's proposal, these things would be part of her life again. There would be no need to consider every commission on offer, she could just choose the best ones, spend more time with Justin, write Alyona's story without having to think of bills and expenses. Then she reasoned that she didn't need to be Fraser's wife to enjoy more security, she could probably have all that anyway simply by being Justin's mother.

'Stop it, Claudia,' she said aloud. 'You need to focus. You're miles away from Rowmont. Then you've got to find Ridge Farm. That sounds a lot more remote than Heather Brow and certainly a lot higher up.'

She pulled over and parked by a farm gateway. The journey was taking much longer than she expected, and she needed to call Fraser. There was no signal. In her frustration, she tossed the phone onto the passenger seat and moved on again.

The wind whipped at the trees, and the rain beat down onto the car roof. Claudia pressed on, took wrong turns, backtracked to find the right ones. Small, white signposts, impossible to read until she'd gone past them, pointed to other places, but none directed her to Rowmont, whichever way it was spelt.

There was an oncoming car, so she made for the pull-in, just ahead, to allow it to pass.

The driver lowered her window and called out, 'Keep your eyes open, there's a lot of debris from the trees.'

'Thank you. Am I going the right way for Rowmont?'

'Oh yes, but it's a bit rugged. You should be fine in that vehicle, but don't hang about. Storms up here don't take any prisoners.' The car moved on.

Claudia felt nervous in this isolated place where the trees thrashed about, and the wind dashed against the side of the car. Even though it was early evening, the sky was dark, and it looked more like night time. A flash of lightening took her by surprise. She gasped and gripped the steering wheel tightly as a clap of thunder followed.

'Give me a break!' she called out loud. 'I just want to find this farm. Is that too much to ask?' Then, as if her cry had been answered, she spotted a sign, marked Ridge Farm. Visibility was bad, but she could just see the turn. Once committed, there was no chance of turning between the dry-stone walls that flanked the track.

Rain began to pelt so fast that it made one constant roaring sound. The wipers were on the fastest setting, even then she could only see for a second at a time, as the rhythmic beats of the blades afforded her precious glimpses of what seemed like a dark tunnel ahead. Small, yellow lights glimmered in the distance. Claudia sighed with relief. 'Please be a house,' she appealed. Another flash of lightening lit up the hillside, and she had a split-second snapshot of a property. 'Please let this be Ridge Farm.' She braced herself for the next clap of thunder. Then she followed the lights that guided her towards the house. It stood stout, square, grey and fearless against the aggressive elements. It seemed to look down with its yellow, window eyes and arched gable brows.

As she parked, Claudia could see a silhouette of a person in the porch. It was such a welcome sight. She turned off the ignition and grabbed her bag. As she opened the car door, the wind seized it from her hand and jerked it violently back onto her shoulder. She cried out with both pain and frustration, but there was no time to dwell on it, so she grasped it with both hands and lunged at it stubbornly until it closed. There seemed no point in locking it for who would take it from this remote place?

As Claudia made a dash to the sanctuary of the porch, the figure called out to her, 'Come on in.' Once inside, the woman turned her back on the heavy, latched door and forced it closed, shutting out the roar of the storm. She laughed and said, 'I think

Mother Nature always intended me to live up here, that's why she gave me a big backside to shut this door. Let's get you dried off a bit. I'll get you a towel.'

'Thank you. I'm Claudia. I'm sorry I'm so late.'

'Don't worry yourself about that.' She handed a towel to Claudia and smiled. 'I'm Sandy.' She was tall, with long, thick, wavy hair, tied back with a coloured chain of wool. 'You chose a fine day to come. We're very exposed. Storms hit hard here.'

Claudia rubbed her hair and then shook her head; her curls began to spring up. 'Do you have a land line?' she said anxiously. 'I can't get a signal, and I need to make a call. I'm really late getting back.'

'No problem. I've put it down somewhere…' Just as she located the phone, it rang. 'It's my husband. I won't be long.' Sandy talked for a short while and then told him to stay in his studio until after the storm. She handed the phone to Claudia and said, 'You got here just in time, this is a mean one and it's not finished yet.'

'Well, I'm safe now, but I'd feel better if I could call my…call home.' No sooner had she spoken, there was a loud bang as the next thunderbolt hit the house, took out the lights and plunged the place into darkness.

'It's all right, just stand still,' Sandy said. 'The emergency power will come on in a second.' Just as predicted, the lights came back on, dim at first and then brightened up. 'We're well prepared for this kind of weather.'

Claudia was glad of the emergency lighting, but the phone was dead.

*****

Fraser was at Heather Brow cottage, with Justin, who was fretful, and didn't understand this break in routine. He was accustomed to being with other people during the daytime, but this was evening, and he seemed to expect Mummy to be there. What's more he seemed to think it was his daddy's fault and demonstrated his frustration by throwing things on the floor. This was the first time Fraser had been in sole charge of his son at this time of the evening, it seemed to have a greater concentration of rules. Supper was a battle, but a tactical choosing of Justin's favourite things helped get over the problem. At least the child was fed. Bath-time was easier, warm water, bubbles and squeaky dolphins had a soothing effect, and Justin's mood improved. Bedtime meant favourite books—no problem—but the goodnight song was not so straightforward. Fraser knew it was a Russian translation of Brother Jack, but neither the English nor the French version would do. Nor would incy wincy spider, winding bobbins or wheels on the bus.

'Din, din, din,' the child whined, it was what he called the song. Until that moment, Fraser had fooled himself that he'd learned how to care for his son. However, it was clear that there were other aspects he had yet to conquer. He also knew the cry was not just for the little song but for his mother to be there to sing it. Fraser gave up on bedtime, took Justin back downstairs and sat him on his lap to watch kid's TV. It was against the rules, but the normal routine wasn't working.

Once Justin was asleep, Fraser took him upstairs to his cot. Downstairs, the house felt so empty. It made Fraser restless and anxious for word of Claudia, she was running late, but he felt sure she hadn't intended to be this long, probably hadn't realised how much those narrow, hill roads can slow you down. The weather was still windy and dark, but the track up to the cottage was visible through the sitting room window, it was deserted. His male logic told him that he was worrying unnecessarily, that Claudia's journey would take a long time, and she was bound to be late. Signal bars could be fickle, so phone calls couldn't always be made. Yet, his doubts told him that she wouldn't let these hours go by without calling. It just didn't fit, and he pivoted on that perilous edge between logic and suspicion.

A phone call to Larchwood yielded nothing except Tony's reassurance. 'Claudia's not accustomed to those hill roads,' he said. 'And if she's driving, she won't use the phone. She knows you're here for Justin. Elsa Hamilton has put us all on edge today. Try and relax.'

Fraser noted that Tony's male logic mechanism was still in place, so he made an attempt to take his cousin's advice. He sat in an easy chair with the baby alarm clutched in his hands and tried to make sense of this strange, eventful day. He would have to tell Claudia about it. But perhaps they'd have a glass of wine and talk it over quietly. He smiled at the thought, leaned his head back and closed his eyes.

*****

Claudia looked at the brightly coloured, chunky, woollen jacket, one of Sandy's products. 'Can I buy this too? I have to work in some draughty places sometimes, so I'd be glad of it.' She put it on and hugged it around her.

'That's what it's for…you won't feel the cold in that.'

'And I'm looking forward to trying this black wool. It's already the right shade and texture. I won't have to dye it.'

She looked at her watch and sighed. 'I don't know what I was thinking, trying to pack so much in one day. I should have been home long ago.'

'Try not to worry, I'll make some tea.'

The kitchen was vast, and a large, round, oak table stood on the slate floor. Two fireside chairs, dressed in patchwork throws, were placed by an old, well-used, solid fuel cooking range set in an inglenook fireplace. Sandy approached it, ducked under the skeins of wool that hung from the low ceiling, and set the kettle on the hot plate. It clunked and the water that ran down the sides spat and sizzled beneath it. A golden Labrador slept against the oven door, alongside a lop-eared rabbit and a cat. Sandy didn't seem to notice them but moved her moccasin-shod feet around them without looking down, as if she had some kind of domestic radar.

Claudia sat down and smiled at the diversity of the bedfellows curled up together. The cat and rabbit were oblivious of the storm, but the dog wasn't too sure. He looked up now and then but settled to Sandy's calming voice. Claudia had never been in a kitchen like this. It served as a workplace as well as a living space. A range of pots was displayed on a shelf, bunches of aromatic herbs and dried flowers hung from the iron hooks in the beams. This was the home of people who knew what they wanted from life.

The kettle began to sing and very soon made a rumbling sound. Then it coughed and gurgled as the boiling water was poured into the pot. Before long, Sandy handed Claudia her tea in a chunky, hand-thrown mug, along with a wedge of fruitcake. She took a bite, it was wonderful.

Claudia's granny used to say that there were some people with such good souls that you couldn't help but tell them your whole life story on the first meeting. Claudia now knew that her grandmother was right. She didn't tell Sandy much, just the part that concerned Justin and Fraser.

Sandy listened attentively and then said, 'So are you going to marry him?'

'No.'

'What's the problem, you're good friends, he respects you, and you've got a child to raise?' She regarded Claudia, sympathetically, 'You're afraid he'll break your heart, is that it?'

'He already did that before Justin was born. I've spent all that time trying to get over him. I thought I could do it.' She drew a long, tense breath. 'I should be over the moon, shouldn't I? It's just that he's being a gentleman, doing the right thing. I don't need that. I can take care of my son, earn my own keep, so why would I accept a proposal that's just an honourable gesture?'

'Life's a bit of a bitch up here on the ridge. We've got our bit of land, the pottery studio and the grazing rights on the hills.' She shook her head. 'Not much time for moonlight and roses. But we know we're in it for the whole journey, and that's romance enough for us.' She listened for a moment and then said, 'The storm's moving on. It's about time too.'

'Thank goodness, I can get going soon. It's getting so late.'

'The weather's still bad, but at least the thunder will stop.'

Chapter Nineteen

Fraser woke up, he was still in the armchair. He checked the monitor and then realised that it was his phone that woke him.

Tony's voice was low but brisk. 'Fraser, you need to come, right away.'

Fraser's heart pounded, and his fingers clamped tightly around the phone. 'What is it?'

'We don't know. The police won't say over the phone.'

'Police?'

'Just come, Fraser…now.'

Fraser had never known such fear and dread, his whole body felt weak, and he could hardly control his voice when he phoned Molly. She came straight away. It was clear she was distressed. But she said nothing other than to reassure him she would stay with Justin.

At Larchwood, Fraser found Tony and Lizzy in the small lounge. Lizzy stood by the window, she was pale and extremely tense. Two detectives had just arrived. One was a fairly short man in late middle age, he wore a tweed jacket. With him was a tall, attractive woman, wearing jeans and a black jacket over her shirt.

A loud, pulsating sound beat in Fraser's ears, as if his blood was rushing to his brain and had nowhere else to go. He became aware of Eliot, who stood close to him. The fact that they were all together was grave.

The man introduced himself. 'DCI Brent…and this is DS Grant. We're already known to Tony and Lizzy, but we haven't met before, Mr Gallier.'

'Fraser,' he corrected automatically. 'What…what's happened?' His voice jerked from his throat.

'A vehicle, registered to Tony, has been found in Rowmont,' DCI Brent explained.

'Found?' Fraser queried, his taut throat almost blocked out the sound.

'The car was loaned to Claudia,' Tony continued. 'Claudia Hamilton, she's working here, but she's also—'

'My fiancée,' Fraser interjected instinctively as a moment of clarity helped him stake a claim to the role as Claudia's next of kin. He pulled his thoughts into shape. 'We have a baby boy,' he added. Even in his state of shock, he thought it might add weight to his claim. 'So where was it found?'

'In the valley below Rowmont Ridge.'

Then Fraser's mind struggled to comprehend what the detective was saying. It was like a fog filling his head. He fought his way through it. Whatever this was all about, he needed to hold it together. 'Are you saying it went over the ridge?'

'But it doesn't appear to have rolled,' DS Grant was quick to reassure him.

DCI Brent continued to explain. 'A farmer and his son were walking the valley to check on their sheep after the storm. By then, visibility wasn't good, but they saw the lights from the vehicle. Said the engine was still warm, but they couldn't find a driver. The local police are searching the area, and I believe they have a team of volunteer hill-walkers out there. But you can appreciate that Rowmont is moorland, it stretches for miles in every direction. They haven't been able to find her yet.'

Fraser then felt numb, stunned as if he'd received a heavy physical blow, and he couldn't regain his breath. 'Dear God!' he gasped and stepped back to steady his balance. Eliot gripped his upper arm to support him.

DS Grant spoke up again. 'It seems that the car door was open, but there was no evidence of injury inside the vehicle. The windscreen is intact, the steering wheel undamaged, and there's no blood. Also, Claudia's personal things seemed to be untouched. Items from a craft shop, skeins of natural wool, handbag containing a small notebook and a wallet with cards and cash in it. The phone was loose in the car.'

'If these things had been taken, we could consider that it was a robbery,' DCI Brent said. 'But that doesn't appear to be the case.'

'Then what?' Tony said. 'What the hell could it be?'

'That's still under investigation.' His phone rang, and Fraser stood rigid with fear. DCI Brent looked at him. 'I'm afraid they had to call off the search for the night.'

'No!' Fraser protested loudly as fear and anger surged through every part of his body. 'We have to keep looking. I'll go…I'll find her.'

'Fraser,' DS Grant said. 'You're needed here.'

Fraser's chest felt as though it would burst as he gasped in short, ineffective breaths, and his vision blurred into a red fog. 'I can't leave her out there. I have to go.'

DCI Brent put his hand firmly on Fraser's shoulder. 'Try and calm down a bit, so we can explain.'

Fraser responded and fixed his eyes on the detective. 'Explain what?'

'She might not be there, Fraser. She could be anywhere. And you need to be here in case somebody calls.' He kept his eyes fixed on Fraser and added, 'Unless, of course you've already had a call? And maybe that's why you want to get away.'

'What are you talking about?'

'Have you had a demand for cash?'

Fraser was stunned by his question. 'What? Why would I?'

'You think she's been kidnapped?' Lizzy suddenly called out in fear and moved from the window.

Tony put his arms around her. 'We don't know yet, sweetheart. Just hang on until we can work out what we should do.'

DCI Brent continued, 'If your fiancée has indeed been kidnapped, it's important you tell us whether anybody has contacted you.'

Fraser shook his head. 'No, I've had no calls, not even from Claudia. I was expecting her to walk in any…' His voice faded, and then he braced himself and continued. 'Nobody's called.'

'Does she normally call in?' DCI Brent asked.

'She never leaves loose ends about our son's care,' Fraser told him.

DCI Brent took his phone from his pocket. 'The local police found some photographs on her phone and sent them through to us. It looks as though an old pickup van was blocking her way, and she took these.' He found the pictures on his phone. 'Does this vehicle look familiar?'

They looked, but nobody recognised it. Nor did they recognise the man in the pictures, but tension increased even more, knowing that they were taken by Claudia. Fraser's fear turned him cold, and he became quiet.

'You must wait here, Fraser, if a call comes, we assume it'll be for you. The search will resume at daylight, but, for the moment, we're treating this as a kidnap.'

Fraser sat on the edge of the sofa, his elbows were braced on his thighs, and his head rested on his hands as he prepared to wait for the phone to ring. He even found himself hoping that Claudia had been kidnapped because it was the lesser of the unthinkable evils that were possible.

The family sat and waited hour after hour.

Daylight began to creep across the lake. Suddenly DCI Brent's phone rang, giving everybody a severe jolt. 'Yes…. In the valley?' He listened a moment and then added, 'Halfway down. We'll leave straight away.' He looked at Fraser. 'They've found her.'

It sounded as though it was a body and not a living person. Fraser could hardly breathe. 'Are they sure it's Claudia?'

'Identification is confirmed because she's wearing an ornamental ID tag round her neck, with your contact details. Air ambulance is taking her to casualty at Bowbury.'

'Casualty?' Fraser said, grasping at the hope that she was alive.

'She's unconscious and hypothermic.' He looked at DS Grant. 'We should get over there.'

Chapter Twenty

Fraser ran, from the hospital car park, to the emergency entrance and saw the two detectives.

DS Grant approached him, she spoke quietly. 'All we know is that Claudia was found halfway down the ridge and some distance from the vehicle. She's in the trauma unit, they won't allow us in yet. She's still being processed.'

'Processed?'

'She's still unconscious. We'll get back and run checks on the photographs.' DS Grant handed Fraser a card and lowered her voice even more. 'For Claudia, just in case this turns out to be…what I mean is…'

'I know what you mean,' Fraser said quietly, but it was a horrific fact that he hadn't yet considered. 'I'm sure the doctors will detect the signs and let me know.'

'She can call me any time. For now, we need to find out who this guy is in the photographs. I'm so sorry about all this, Fraser. If there's anything I can do, just call me.'

Eliot caught Fraser up, but he didn't ask any questions, he just stood quietly.

Fraser continued to claim that he was Claudia's fiancé and mentioned once again that they had a child. Someone showed them to a relative's room. There were times when the invitation to take a seat was not a welcome courtesy. Sitting was definitely not going to happen. Eliot's silent, strong and compassionate presence continued, as it had all the long hours of waiting through the night.

Fraser gulped down the tension in his throat and looked at Eliot's face. 'Times like this,' he said, 'you think of all the things you should have said to somebody when they were fit and well.'

'It's usual to feel like that.'

'I love her…so much. What's wrong with me for God's sake? I couldn't even tell her that.'

'You've got the rest of your life to tell her.'

'But what if this is already the rest of her life? What if it's all going to end in there?'

'You can't speculate, Fraser. Concentrate on keeping yourself together. Claudia's alive, she's strong, and, by all accounts, she's stubborn. The qualities a person needs to beat things like this. You should be the same.'

Fraser gripped Eliot's shoulder and said, 'You're right. I shouldn't leave it all up to her.'

After a while, they allowed Fraser to see Claudia, but they were still assessing her condition. His gut clenched like a vice as he approached the bay where she lay on a bed that seemed to be covered with tubes and wires. Her head was braced, and a mask covered her mouth and nose. There was a swelling on one side of her forehead. The rest of her body was covered in a blanket.

'Just a couple of minutes, Mr…?'

'Fraser Gallier. Can you tell me anything?'

'We're trying to find out the extent of her injuries. She can't tell us where the pain is. She's had a blow to the head, and she's hypothermic. We have to take her for a scan now to check for internal injuries.'

Fraser watched as they wheeled Claudia's bed away.

He re-joined Eliot in the relative's room. 'I should arrange for a private room for her.'

'Clearly, the care and attention she gets won't be any different, but it might make you feel better.'

'It would if I have to arrange ongoing care for her.'

'What do you mean?'

'She's still unconscious. What if she's going to be in a coma for weeks, months…?' He gasped in a shuddering breath. 'Who knows how long? I must make plans for that…take care of her. But what about Justin?' His eyes closed tightly as he winced at the thought of trying to make Justin understand.

Eliot gripped his shoulders and stopped him pacing about. 'For goodness sake, stop rambling. Wait until you know more before you commit her to a permanent sick bed.'

Two hours later, the registrar brought an update. 'The good news is that her temperature's rising slowly, and she has no spinal injury but has bruising to her legs and her left shoulder. She has a head injury and that appears to be the main cause for concern. All the procedures requested by the police have been completed.'

'And...?'

'I can't tell you anything about that, I'm sorry. I'm sure the police will let you know. You can see her now, but I'm afraid she still isn't conscious.'

Eliot accompanied Fraser when they were shown to the side ward. Fraser approached the pale, still body that lay on a bed with rails on each side of it. She was covered with blankets. He had never seen Claudia so lifeless. In his mind, he scooped her up from that clinical bed, held her close to his chest, kissed her face, whispered against her beautiful curled hair. But in fact, he didn't know if he could even touch her hand. Her eyes were closed, her breath was shallow. He gently rested the back of his fingers on her cheek and wondered just how cold she would have been before the improvement. A monitor, by the bed, made beeping sounds, and he began to fear that they might stop.

Claudia's eyes flickered and slowly opened. Fraser harnessed the urge to react. He quietly leaned towards her and said, 'Hello, my love.' Claudia stared at him blankly, but he smiled at her. 'You're doing really well, sweetheart, really well.' But the beautiful, brown, shining eyes, that he knew and loved, were now vague and dull. They could be staring at any other man in the world, a total stranger. His throat jerked, and his chest tightened as he stood upright again. 'She doesn't know me,' he whispered. 'There's no recognition on her face, she doesn't know me,' he repeated.

'It's far too soon to expect it, Mr Gallier. Give her time,' the registrar said. 'You must be exhausted yourself, waiting all this time for news. Why don't you go and get some rest? Come back later. We'll call if there's any change.'

Chapter Twenty-One

Molly told Fraser that she would give Justin his supper and get him to bed. So, Fraser returned to the hospital, sat by Claudia's bedside and watched as she drifted in and out of consciousness. Time passed, measured by the metronomic bleeps of the monitor. He pressed a faint kiss on Claudia's face and rested his hand gently on her fingers where they laid on the bed. 'Come back, Claudia,' he whispered. 'I love you, please come back.'

Justin was confused, the next afternoon, when Fraser picked him up from Molly's, because they didn't go straight to the cottage. His hand reached back towards it as he cried out for his mummy.

'Mummy's at work,' Fraser lied.

'Mummy work,' Justin echoed tearfully. He knew what it meant, and it comforted him for a while. Fraser was amazed how Claudia had prepared their child with as much self-empowerment as his age allowed, taught him little things that helped him through confusing times. He knew that the word "sore" meant pain or unwell. He knew a couple of signs for when he was thirsty or hungry. Claudia lay in a hospital bed, injured and shocked, but even in that situation, she shielded him. She had always made sure Justin would be protected, still wore her ID necklace.

Lizzy had arranged to put a cot by Fraser's bed, at Larchwood, so Justin could be close to his daddy.

When the child's bedtime arrived, it was clear that even well thought-out plans could go very wrong. The cries for Mummy and the bedtime song returned, and there was no way he would be fobbed off with the expression, Mummy work, any longer. Every tear that spilled down the child's face stung Fraser's heart as he stood by the cot, trying to comfort his fretful son. He came to realise that a baby can be exhausted and still fight sleep, so he made a decision.

He picked up Justin, gathered up the comfort items, along with the many things that fitted into a baby's bag, and went down to the kitchen. Once he had a mission, things looked better.

It was Stella's evening off, so Tony and Lizzy had eaten early with the children. Tony was making coffee, a sign that his children were already settled in bed. 'Can I help?'

'No, I'm fine, thanks.' Fraser put Justin in his high chair and got him a chocolate chip biscuit, he would stop breaking the rules at a more convenient time. 'How's Lizzy?'

'Distraught, stressed, but putting on a cheerful face for the children.'

'Give her my love, I'll let her know as soon as there's any change.' He located the first-aid kit, took out some plasters and a small bandage and placed them on the table, along with a small Teddy. Justin didn't understand enough words for a full explanation, but with the help of his little repertoire, he would understand a simple one. Teddy was going to be the patient. He was sore, he needed a plaster on his head. Together they applied the plasters and then a bandage.

'Sore,' Justin said, and his little brow puckered.

Fraser sighed with relief that Justin understood. He smiled. 'Yes. Teddy's sore.'

'He seems much calmer,' Tony said. 'That was a good move. He might settle now.'

'No, he's going to see his mummy.'

'Are you serious?'

'Yes, positive. She has no visible injuries other than the bump on her head and some bruises. She hasn't recognised me yet, so that might be a problem. But it's worth a try. She looks peaceful, he'll cope with it a lot better than not seeing her at all. He can get a glimpse of her to see that she's sleeping before the nurses kick us out again.'

'It's getting late now. We can take care of him.'

'It's OK, we'll make it. She's in a private room now, so we won't be disturbing anybody else.'

'Fraser—'

Fraser flashed a determined look at his cousin. 'He wants his mummy! Who am I to tell him he can't see her?'

'What will you do if he kicks off? He's exhausted.'

'We have to try. Come on, Tony, put Lizzy in that hospital bed and little Eddy in this chair. What would you do? This might not be a good idea, but he wants Claudia, and he's going to see her. I have to stop his little heart breaking somehow?'

'And how's your own heart?'

'Battered,' Fraser said with a weary smile. 'But I'm getting hold of the priorities now.'

The teddy was wrapped up in a little blanket and put in Justin's bag, along with his cat, two books and a drink. He glanced around to check if he had everything and noticed the birthday cake on the worktop. He shut his eyes and sighed, 'For Christ's sake it's Justin's birthday.'

Tony embraced him and said, 'It'll keep. We'll get it together tomorrow. Lizzy and I will make sure he gets his party. You're right, you've got to do something. Take care, and keep your mind on the road.'

When Fraser arrived at the hospital, the nurse questioned his decision to bring Justin.

'If he doesn't get a glimpse of his mummy, I'll have a sick child on my hands. We just want to sit with her for a couple of minutes, and then we'll go. If it doesn't work, I'll take him straight out.'

'OK, give it a try.'

In the room, Claudia seemed unchanged. Justin's body jerked up and down when he saw her. Fraser held a finger to his lips. 'Shh! Mummy's sore.'

Justin's chin crumpled, but he remained quiet. Fraser carefully put down the bag, sat on the chair by the bed and put Justin on his lap. 'So far so good,' Fraser whispered to himself, but he knew that confusion about the strange surroundings was contributing to Justin's quiet behaviour.

'Mummy sleep,' Justin said.

Fraser smiled at his little hero son. 'Yes, Mummy's asleep.' He fumbled in the bag and took out a book. Justin was drawn to it, and they talked about the animals in the story. The child almost fell asleep but deliberately jolted himself awake.

Fraser reached into the bag and found the cat in the belief that it was the missing detail. Justin was delighted to see it and let out a loud cry of 'Cat!' His voice pierced the clinical silence.

Fraser winced and feared that their visit would be over. He looked at Claudia. Her eyelids flickered, and her head turned towards them. For several seconds, she looked at them, her eyes still blank. Fraser watched and waited. Claudia blinked and stared, and then her mouth tweaked into a faint smile. Fraser hardly dared think that the smile was for them. Claudia would smile at any child, and Justin was very softly calling to her. Then her arm stretched out towards him.

'Hello Justin,' she whispered, her voice was croaky and tight. 'Hello, my lovely boy.'

Fraser almost passed out with relief, but he drew a long breath and said, 'He's been so brave. He was desperate to see you.'

She looked at Justin and smiled. 'I need a cuddle,' she said softly.

Fraser protested. 'I don't think the nurse would agree to that.'

'I wasn't going to cuddle the nurse,' she said, 'I was going cuddle my little boy.'

Fraser's heart pounded as he hardly dare believe this was happening. Her eyes were still not so clear, but her brain was very much intact. She was shaken and unwell, but even in that state she could make a sharp comment. He stifled a shuddering sound that rippled through his vocal chords. 'Are you sure?'

'Yes.'

'He might hurt you. Do you have any pain?'

'Only because I can't reach him.'

Fraser gently put Justin on the bed. The exhausted child nestled against Claudia, as she put a bruised arm around him and held him.

'Din, din, din,' Justin uttered.

Claudia's husky voice, muffled against his head, whispered the song, and within seconds, Justin was asleep.

Fraser sat back in the chair. Relief swam over his body and threatened to make him sob like a child. He held back this urge, yet large tears spilled over his lower eye lids and down his face to his jaw.

Claudia raised her arm from Justin's back and reached out to Fraser. 'Hold my hand.' It was like the video, when she reached out to him, but this time he was there. He stood by the bed, grasped her fingers and bent to press his lips on them. Then he placed her hand back on Justin's body. He knew he had taken a big risk, but it turned out to be a moment of healing for all three of them.

*****

The next day the police were allowed to interview Claudia. She felt Fraser's hand clasp hers, his voice made her feel secure as she sat, propped up in the hospital bed and wondered why it took two detectives to ask the questions.

'Take your time, Claudia. Just tell us what you can remember,' DCI Brent said.

'I'm really sorry about the car,' Claudia said to Fraser. 'I know it was irresponsible to take the Ridge road, but I just wanted… It was so late, and the weather wasn't improving. I needed to get home.'

Fraser frowned at her comment. 'Stop worrying about the car,' he said. 'The important thing is to find out who did this to you.'

The police seemed to need some kind of explanation to help tie it all up, but Claudia didn't want to re-visit that night. Look back at the darkness, how the wind still howled despite the fact that the thunderstorm had passed. But they looked at her and waited for her to speak.

As she began to remember what happened, the fear returned like a cold flood running through her body. The recollection, that her life had been threatened, shook her to the core. Had she made the right decision? Should she have waited back at Sandy's house? But then there was no way of communicating, everybody would be worried. Justin had never been separated from her for more than a few hours a day. He'd be so fretful and upset.

She had left Sandy's house before the rain had stopped, followed the little, winding lanes that led to the main road. But she had been met with storm damage, a huge branch of a tree blocked the road. A group of men were trying to clear it, but they said it would take some time, especially as the weather was still bad. They pointed out a possible diversion. They called it the top road. It was a narrow but straight stretch along the ridge. It had passing places so she should be OK. She kept her head and turned in a nearby gateway. The ridge stretched ahead, and she left the comfort of the lower road where the hawthorn hedges, either side, helped guide her. She was scared, but she had committed to this detour, and there was no chance of turning around. She slowed right down to get her bearings, as visibility was very different up there. There were no trees or hedges on the skyline. Her headlights seemed to die in the darkness. The car shuddered, as a gust of wind hit it broadside. To her horror, headlights appeared in the distance. There was a pull-in just ahead, so she stopped and waited. The vehicle stopped, and the driver got out and knocked on her window.

'You haven't left me enough room,' he called above the noise of the wind. 'Shove over a bit.'

Appalled by this man's attitude, Claudia lowered her window a couple of inches. 'I'm right on the edge. I can't possibly give you any more.'

'You've got plenty of room. I've got a trailer with livestock in it.'

Claudia lowered the window even more. 'You're moving animals in these terrible conditions?'

'It's none of your bloody business.' When the man leaned closer, Claudia could tell he'd been drinking.

'Then get on with it? You've got plenty of room there. Or we could call the police to come and help us.'

'You won't get a signal up here.'

Claudia knew that, so her threat died a death. 'I don't need a signal. This is a corporate car, and it has a Gallier radio communicator.'

'What the bloody 'ell's one o' them?'

Claudia deliberately hardened her voice. 'I don't have to explain that to you. It's issued to all female executives, in case they get stopped by threatening drivers. If you don't back off and get on your way, I'll use it. Tell the police I'm being threatened by a driver, who's drunk out of his ugly mind. They respond very quickly to woman callers.'

'Well, don't blame me if I scratch your nice, corporate car with my trailer.' He walked away unsteadily. Claudia closed the window, shielding her from the sounds of the wind whipping through the heather.

'Somebody should tell Rowmont that it's still summer,' she muttered.

There was no number plate on the battered vehicle, but when the driver was back in it, Claudia quickly released her seatbelt, reached for her phone, lowered the window, just enough to focus on him, and took several shots. She had no idea what she would do with them, but she was so angry at this point. This thug had delayed her, kept her from her little boy. As the vehicle inched past, she took a quick picture of the trailer that carried a large crate, which appeared to contain two pigs, but it was very dark, and the rain obscured any details of what it was. The trailer rocked, and Claudia's heart was palpitating as it passed and then moved on. She thrust the car into first gear and tried to move forward, but the wheels went into a spin on the drenched, loose grit that had accumulated at the edge of the pull-in. It caused the rear end of the vehicle to slip sideways, Claudia then knew that one of the back wheels was off the edge. When she tried to move forward to rectify her position, she felt the car slide backwards a little. In a panic, she turned the wheel and tried to stop it, but it moved a little more. She feared that she would continue to slide backwards, but trusted that this SUV could cope with climbing back onto the road. All she had to do was make it go forwards and upwards. Her attempts brought the car in line only to find it starting to roll forwards, and she realised she had no control over it. It was going to gather more speed and then plunge right down into the valley. She had no idea how deep it was or what would meet her there when she hit the bottom. Justin flashed into her mind, and she grasped the door handle, ready to bail before the car gathered speed. She pushed the door as wide as she could, concerned that it would hit her and then drag her down with the car. It had to be a big leap, and quick. The car moved faster, and she couldn't see the ground clearly, but trusted that she would land in the thick heather. She had jumped clear of the door, but her momentum took her downward, rolling like a log, for what seemed like an eternity. She had no memory of anything after that, except waking up in hospital.

'Pigs,' DCI Brent said at last. 'That's what he was doing, moving pigs?'

'Yes.'

'He didn't attack you or try to get you out of your vehicle?'

'No, he just wanted me out of his way.'

'What made you think he was drunk?'

'Apart from the smell of him, his speech was slurred, he stumbled about when he got out of his van, and he looked drowsy when he eventually drove past.'

'That's probably why he needed more room.' DS Grant commented. 'He probably had no licence for moving pigs either.'

'So, it was an accident?' DCI Brent said. He seemed surprised.

'Hardly an accident, Guv,' DS Grant complained. 'That low-life, drunken cretin as good as pushed her off the ridge.'

'Your promotion hasn't improved your protocol, has it, Sergeant?'

'Sorry, sir,' she said curtly.

He shook his head. 'I love the way you apologise to me. Sometimes it's almost as if you really mean it.' He turned to Claudia. 'We can return your things now.' He moved to leave but then turned back. 'You mentioned a, what was it, a Gallier radio communicator.'

'There's no such thing. I made it up.'

'Brilliant!' DS Grant said. 'Absolutely brilliant!' She lingered. 'Good luck you two. Have you set a date yet?'

'No,' Fraser said, 'not yet. We'll probably sort it out when Claudia recovers.'

Not knowing how far Fraser had taken this pretence, Claudia smiled and said nothing. She understood why Fraser had made a claim to be her next of kin.

Chapter Twenty-Two

'You look great, Claudia,' Jenny said. 'How does it feel to be out and about again?'

'Fabulous!' Claudia answered. 'I can close my eyes now without seeing all that heather coming up to meet me.' She grimaced and added, 'I still feel really bad about the car though. Tony must think me such an idiot.'

'Tony thinks like the rest of us,' Lizzy assured her. 'He's relieved you survived. And we're glad to see you looking so much better.'

'I hated being an invalid, but you've been brilliant. It's such a comfort staying at Larchwood. What would I have done without you all?' She laughed. 'Fraser still calls me sweetheart and darling like he did in the hospital. I have to remind him that the pretence is over. He said he's got used to it now.'

'He had a really tough time,' Lizzy said. 'We were all shocked, but he was in a bad way.' She smiled and added, 'But, here we are, all back on track.' She poured Claudia's tea and then looked across the table. 'How about you, Jen, are you in a tea mood today?'

'No, I'm in a hot chocolate mood.'

'Not happening!'

'Tea it is then,' Jenny drawled, and then she examined her cake, like a fortune-teller staring into a crystal ball. 'Look at it, just sitting there, reminding me of all the new challenges I face every day.'

'Challenges?'

'How to get out of the bath like a normal human being instead of an overfed penguin. I can't pick things up because my body won't bend where it's supposed to. One day, Will's going to come home and find me stuck in the tub, and the floor littered with all the stuff I've dropped.'

Lizzy stared at her. 'You can see all that in a cream horn?'

Jenny chuckled and looked at it on her plate. 'Don't mind me, it's just a minor rant. I've never actually had one of these before. Is it possible to eat it without getting flaky pastry and jam everywhere?'

'I once held my mother to ransom, with a cream horn.' Claudia said.

Jenny laughed. 'You make it sound like a weapon.'

'That's what it was, a weapon, and it was *so* loaded.'

'Loaded?'

'A beautiful flaky pastry cone, full of lovely, red, squidgy, sticky jam, swirls of cream and coated with crunchy flakes of crystalized sugar.'

'Did you threaten to throw it at her?' Lizzy said.

'No, it was much more tactical than that. We were in a very genteel, big-sorted teashop. We had to kill an hour on our way to an audition. Mother had set her sights on this job and desperately wanted me to get it. She was going for it with everything she'd got. I wore new clothes, with an insane price tag. I had to listen to a running commentary about what to do, what to say. But then, Mother made a big mistake, totally out of character.'

'What did she do?' Jenny urged.

Claudia mimicked her mother. 'Claudie, you should have chosen a plain cake. Get one crumb of that on your clothes, and you're in serious trouble, my girl.'

'Stuck her head right above the parapet,' Jenny suggested.

'She, of all people, should know better than to expose a weakness. I slowly picked up my pastry fork, watched by my mother's narrow, grey eyes as I started to play with my bespoke cake. I pushed it about, made little stabs at it. She thought it was going to burst all over my expensive clothes. It was a rare experience to see my mother on the other end of a threat. I mean, who would give a job to a kid with jam all over her clothes?'

'The feisty little tearaway strikes again,' Jenny said. She shook her head. 'You were such a wicked child.'

'Oh yes, I was very cunning. But she always had a trump card, so my power was short-lived.'

'If only you could find a way to turn the tables on her,' Lizzy suggested. 'Find something that threatens her, instead of her threatening you.'

'And dodge the trump card,' Jenny added. 'If you could do that with a cream horn, what would you do with a really serious threat?'

'Yes,' Claudia said. 'I could probably bring her down with a crash.'

'Anyway, you can forget her for the time being,' Lizzy said. 'You won't need to think about her in Tuscany. It's going to be fabulous. We can have some quality time with the children, picnics, walks, swimming... And we can go to the Flea Market, just the two of us. Justin will have plenty of people to keep him amused.' She laughed and added, 'So there won't be any guilt.'

Claudia grimaced. 'There's going to be plenty of guilt,' she contradicted, 'when I meet Fraser's mom. I won't be very popular, will I?'

'Being the mother of her grandchild doesn't make you her daughter-in-law,' Jenny said. 'If she has issues about it, they're with Fraser, not you.'

'I suppose so. I can't stay long today. Molly's got something on at the farm, I need to get Justin early.'

'That's a pity, I was hoping we could have a chat,' Lizzy said. 'I need to talk to you...before the guys get home. It's really important.'

'I'll come and find you when I get back to Larchwood.' Claudia assumed it was to discuss getting together to sort out her antique textiles.

Lizzy seemed uneasy, 'OK. I'll wait for you. I really do need to talk to you.'

After tea, as Claudia made for the main door, the receptionist called out, 'Miss Hamilton!'

Claudia approached the desk.

'Are you feeling better?' the receptionist asked.

'Yes, thanks. Aches, pains and bruises all moving on.'

'A letter came for you. But it arrived inside another envelope addressed to reception. I opened it thinking it was a booking.' She handed the letter to Claudia. 'Your mother enclosed a note, asking us to give this to you personally.'

'My mother?' Alarm bells rang in Claudia's head. Her mouth dried so swiftly, she could hardly speak as she realised that Elsa Hamilton knew where to find her. How did that happen? The accident had cost valuable time, and not only that, but her apparent carelessness on the road was potential ammunition. Her mother would suggest that Claudia was irresponsible for driving in those conditions. Discredit her for being unfit to be on the road. Claudia needed more information, so she bluffed her way along. 'She wrote to me?'

'I suppose that's because she missed you when she came here.'

Another blow hit Claudia. The woman was here, but nobody had said. 'Yes, I suppose that would be a disappointment.'

'Don't worry, Mr Franklyn and Mr Gallier entertained her. Irena was here, too, so she was well-looked-after.'

Claudia was shocked, but she kept calm. 'I'm sure it was mentioned to me, but I was probably still a bit concussed. I don't like to keep pestering about it. They've been so worried about me, you see.'

'Yes, of course,' the receptionist agreed.

Claudia felt tendrils of foreboding creep through her body, her bones, her heart, but this wasn't a good time to let her guard down. Her mother had breached the walls of her safe haven, and was well ahead of the game now. She wondered how much information she could get from the receptionist, without exposing her own ignorance about the visit. Nobody else seemed to want to tell her, but why? 'My mother's desperate to see me.'

'I booked her in the night before,' the receptionist said. 'Then in the morning she asked to see Mr Franklyn. Mr Gallier was here too.'

'I don't recall anybody telling me that. I must have been very vague.' She was shocked, but she smiled and said, 'It takes a long time to get back to normal.'

The receptionist volunteered more information. Her eyes were clear, her mind open and honest, unaware of the treachery that lay beneath it all. 'Mr Gallier and Mr Franklyn were already here, so they met her in the private lounge. But I'm afraid she had to leave early, she had a migraine.'

'Poor Mummy!'

'It was a really bad one. Mr Gallier and Mr Franklyn helped her though. Irena arranged a flight plan. She went back in the company plane. All three of them went with her to the airfield.'

Claudia's heart ached in the knowledge that Fraser had betrayed her, after promising to be on her side no matter what. She expected better from him.

'When they were waiting for the courtesy car, I heard your mother saying how anxious she was.'

'About what?'

'I don't know. It was only a flying visit, apparently, to pick something up. I'm sure you know all about that.'

'Yes I do.'

The receptionist smiled, and a sympathetic look filled her face. 'I can see that you're shocked, but don't worry. Mr Gallier was very reassuring. He agreed that the rightful owner should have the property, and he would do his best to make that happen.'

Anger began to swamp Claudia's earlier feelings of foreboding. She hated the thought of Fraser comforting her mother, and that she had enlisted him as an ally. That's why he never mentioned the visit—nobody did. Elsa's web was closing in on her, and once more, she had to face it alone. Which part of the lies had he believed, for she would have surely manufactured a whole new truth, one that would be very compelling? It was high time to toughen up. Forget the accident, the injuries, the aches and pains, and move back into her own home where she could reboot her independence.

Molly was in a hurry when Claudia arrived at Heather Brow, so they didn't talk except to allow Justin to wave bye-bye.

While Justin played on the carpet, Claudia opened the letter. She was prepared for treachery, but this was horrendous. Elsa suggested that Fraser had seen sense, and he was going to get the diaries for her to save her returning to the UK. She had a number of people in a new movie about to be released, and she wanted to be there for them. There was a postscript:

A little bird told me about your baby son. He's inherited your curly hair I believe.

Claudia scooped up Justin and held him. Then she went to her spare room to re-pack the diaries and find a safer place for them. She almost shrieked with horror when she saw the empty desk. The shock was debilitating, but she quickly took Justin back downstairs and put him on the carpet to play. Then she perched on the sofa and clamped her hand over her mouth to suppress the sobs. Her promise to Grannie was torn to shreds, her vow to Alyona was meaningless. Her world caved in on her as she watched Justin moving about, his shape just a blur through her silent tears. It was clear that she might just as well have stayed in London.

*****

Fraser had been at Wainford and arrived at Larchwood late in the afternoon. Lizzy met him in the hall. 'Have you heard from Claudia?'

Fraser frowned, and his voice was laced with concern as echoes of Rowmont resounded in his head. 'Not since this morning. Why? What's happened?'

'She left the hotel early to get Justin, but she isn't here yet. We arranged to get together for a chat. I need to talk to her. It's time somebody told her. I hate this secrecy, Fraser.'

'She hasn't been well enough to take it on-board. Don't you think she's got enough to deal with?'

'She hasn't completely recovered, but she's not frail. She's been coping with Elsa Hamilton all her life, she can do it in her sleep. We're her friends…her family, and none of us told her that her mother turned up looking for the diaries. She'll think I was in on it, and I had nothing to do with it.'

'All the same, I'd rather you didn't discuss it with her—not yet.'

'It isn't your call, Fraser, is it? I realise that you had to do something at the hospital, claim that you were in a relationship—engaged even, but this masquerade about being her next of kin is over now. It's insulting not to tell her. I called Heather Brow, but she isn't answering. And her mobile's switched off.'

'I'll go to Heather Brow,' Fraser said, 'she might have called in for something. If she's there, I'll explain everything. And I'll reassure her that you had no part in it.' He wasn't looking forward to telling Claudia about Elsa Hamilton's visit, but Lizzy was right, she needed to be told.

Claudia's car wasn't there. He entered the house and looked around. A couple of Justin's toys were on the carpet, but no special ones…no cat. There was a note on the sofa, and with a glimmer of hope, he reached for it. But that glimmer turned into a dark fear when he realised that Elsa Hamilton had beaten him to it. A fit of rage surged through him. The woman didn't even try and hide her lies and deceit.

The sound of Claudia's car, coming up the drive, drew Fraser to the window. She parked behind his vehicle on the drive. He sighed with relief and went to the door. 'What are you doing, Claudia?' he called to her.

'We needed food. We've been to the supermarket.'

'Why have you come back to Heather Brow?'

'I live here. So does Justin. But he can still spend visitation days with you, at Larchwood, when we've sorted it out.' She seemed unemotional and cold towards him.

'Visitation...?'

'Do you prefer the term access? I don't mind which one you use, just sort out your side of it as soon as possible.' She reached into the car and released Justin from his seat.

Fraser stood by the rules of not having a row in front of Justin, but he had to hold down a lot of anger and frustration. Claudia wasn't likely to listen to his explanation yet.

'I have to get Justin ready for bed,' Claudia told him in a matter of fact way, 'he's exhausted.' She took the child inside, leaving Fraser to do the only thing that was of any use at that moment. He unloaded the shopping and put it in the kitchen, then helped himself to a cold drink. Claudia had obviously been devastated by the letter, what's more she didn't deem him to be innocent. This was going to be hell.

'You can go up and say goodnight now,' Claudia said when she came back downstairs. 'But you'll have to be quick, he's almost asleep.'

Fraser wanted to talk to Justin, stroke his head, but the child was prone to waking suddenly with enough energy to play for another hour or so. This was difficult enough already, so he decided not to stay by the cot for more than a few seconds.

When he returned to Claudia, she stood motionless, as she looked through the window. He said nothing, it seemed better to leave her to speak in her own time.

'When were you going to tell me?' she asked, without turning to face him. She seemed calm, but he knew that her well-practised coping mechanism was holding her together.

'When you recovered.'

She turned from the window, her eyes seemed to burn her anger into him. 'You know me,' she said, 'I recover from situations very quickly. So are you going to tell me about my mother's visit?'

'How did you find out?'

'She mailed a letter to the receptionist, at the hotel, and enclosed one for me to be delivered personally. The receptionist reassured me that you were a perfect gentleman and helped her.'

'Your mother was ill,' Fraser explained. 'Even so, we couldn't get her off the premises quick enough. We put her on the plane, and she went home.' He could see that Claudia felt betrayed, but she remained controlled.

'After all she's done you offered your plane?'

'We were stalling her until we could warn you. In the end, we thought it would be better to get her out of the country, as quickly as possible, and then work out what best to do.'

'Clearly that didn't include telling me.'

'Claudia, not so long ago I thought you were kidnapped or murdered. I even feared that you might not wake up, you might have memory loss, brain damage even. You wouldn't ever know me or Justin again. So forgive me if I've been a little over-protective.'

'I haven't forgotten what you did for me. I appreciate what you say. But how could you…?' Her self-control fled from her grasp. She failed to hold back the tears that surged from her eyes as she cried out, 'How could you be such a cruel, heartless turncoat?'

Fraser was horrified at her suggestion. 'A what!'

'Why did you take the diaries, Fraser, why?' She gulped and pushed the tears from her eyes with the flat of her hand. 'Why did you give them to her? I know she's dangerous, but I was going…' She was unable to continue.

Fraser made a move to comfort her. 'Darling please let…'

Claudia held up her hands to stop him. 'Did you learn nothing from what she's been doing? For goodness sake, are you still on her side?'

'Will you just—'

'I've broken my promise to my grannie, and Alyona. Do you think it's going to keep my mother quiet for the rest of her life?

What about that phantom, Russian jewellery? Did she tell you about that?'

'Yes, she mentioned it.'

'She's going to keep fighting until she's got hold of it.' Claudia shook her head. 'And it doesn't even exist. What will you do about that, buy some and send it out to her?'

Fraser scowled. 'Claudia, for Christ's sake, will you listen to me.' He reached out to her again. She backed off. It was agony. He wanted so much to hold her and comfort her. He knew the pain she must have been feeling these past few hours. He raised his voice in desperation. 'I promise you I didn't give Elsa Hamilton the diaries. I moved them, they're at Larchwood. They were at risk here. After meeting your mother, it wouldn't surprise me if she got somebody to break into this place.'

'But she said you were helping her. She made it clear—'

'And you believe her? Suddenly you can take her word for it? I lied to her to get rid of her, and to get her off your back for a while. Surely, you don't have a problem with that. I certainly don't have any worries about it.'

Claudia looked shaken. 'Where are the diaries now?'

'Joe's got them…locked in the security office, in a safe. If your mother wants them, she'll have to get past Joe. That's not going to happen.'

Claudia expelled a long sigh as she slowly sank down onto the sofa. 'That's what she does, isn't it? She injects suspicion in your mind.'

Fraser sat by her and ventured to put his arm around her. She accepted the gesture. It was a great relief to him. 'Lizzy gave me a hard time for not telling you earlier. She was hoping to talk to you when you got back, refused to leave you in the dark any longer. She also made it quite clear that I'm not really your fiancé, so the pretence has to end.'

'I hope you didn't fall out over it.'

'No, we didn't.'

Claudia looked at him, her eyes full of fear, but her voice steady. 'She knows about Justin. I'm so sorry.'

'Yes, I know, but for the moment, she thinks I'm on her side.' He tightened his arm around her, and she leaned against him. 'She knows about Wainford, too, so I guess that puts me in the firing line along with you. We're in this together now. God knows how she found out so much about us. But there are ways, I suppose.'

'It's hard to imagine who would…' Suddenly she sat upright. 'Oh, no!' she said with a sigh. 'It's obvious now I think of it. Todd! He's been in that alcove, scrubbing away at the paintwork, listening to everything. He knows about Justin, Wainford, the hotel…'

'Todd? Are you sure?'

Mother didn't turn up at Larchwood, did she? Because she knows that Todd's working there. She might still need him in place. She wouldn't risk blowing his cover.'

'Why would he do that? Todd likes you.'

'Not more than his career. Mother's a successful agent, she casts films, theatre, TV drama… He's so hungry for a start in the business. That magazine was a gift from heaven. He obviously managed to make a trade. She might have suggested an interview, a small part in a movie maybe. He'd have no idea that he was being reeled in as part of her plan. She's no doubt done with him now and already spat him out.' She shook her head. 'Poor Todd, he got to play Iago for real.'

Chapter Twenty-Three

Claudia was amazed at how much easier travelling could be when there was a doting father to help. That alone was allowing her to feel more relaxed, so she was able to push the memories of the accident aside and allow them to fade along with the physical bruises. Holiday mood was the order of the day for the family, and it was impossible not to feel the same. It felt good to get off the crazy merry-go-round, that controlled her life, and move on to a more manageable pace for a few days. Fraser now understood the true extent of what she had been up against, and the pat-on-the-head kind of support he previously offered had been replaced by a much more realistic backup. That, at least, eliminated some of their differences.

Fraser had arranged their transport from the airport to Villa Firenze. All she had to do was put Justin in a child's seat in the back of the vehicle.

'Is this your car?' Claudia asked as she fastened her seatbelt.

'No, I hired it.'

'I like it. It's really comfortable…a nice family vehicle.'

'I'll get you one when we go back to—'

'That's not what I meant,' she hastened to say. She turned around to check on Justin, who was in one of the five seats behind her. 'I meant for other people, couples with three or four children.'

Fraser grinned. 'What a happy thought.'

Claudia expelled a brief laugh. 'You can take that look off your face, Fraser Gallier. I'm not filling all these seats with babies just because you've developed a taste for fatherhood.'

Fraser laughed out loud and then started the car.

Claudia smiled to herself. It was good to be on friendly terms, but she still had to put on a casual air, pretend his smile didn't fill her heart with warmth and longing, deny the hunger in her body when he was close by. He still used the terms of endearment that he adopted in the hospital. It seemed he'd grown accustomed to using them and continued to do so. Claudia thought it petty to object, and she had to admit that she enjoyed the sound of Fraser's voice calling her darling or sweetheart. He hadn't mentioned his proposal again, which was just as well because the way she felt sometimes, she would accept that offer with every atom of her being. She would unashamedly take what she could have and worry about the consequences later.

There was still no sign of a permanent arrangement for Justin, both child and father seemed to like it the way it was. Claudia didn't care for their it-ain't-broke-so-don't-fix-it attitude, but as all three of them were going through a time of recovery, she decided to let it lie for a while. She leaned back in her seat, turned her face to the window and gazed out at the unmistakable, Tuscan landscape. The sunflowers had yet to be harvested, and the fields were still yellow and gold where the corn had been cut. Hints of purple flashed before her eyes as the car passed rows of ripening grapes.

'You're very quiet, sweetheart,' Fraser said, as he steered the car along the picturesque, winding roads.

'I've never been here before. The landscape is just...' She sighed.

'Yes, it is, isn't it?'

Claudia loved the way Fraser understood what she meant.

*****

Villa Firenze was large and impressive. It stood in extensive grounds with beautiful colourful gardens and closely cut grass, scorched by the sun. Vehicles arrived in convoy. Porters quietly waited by the entrance steps, but as the vehicles pulled up, they sprang into action, like dancers launching into a well-rehearsed choreography. They knew their parts, some parked the cars and some dealt with luggage. It was so efficient.

Then, Irena greeted them and told Fraser that his parents were already waiting to see him.

Claudia encouraged him to go.

'I should show you the cottage first,' Fraser said.

'Cottage?' Claudia queried.

'It's a smaller villa than this one,' Fraser explained. 'Lizzy said she preferred it when she first came here. She thought you'd feel the same.'

'Sounds lovely.'

'Then we'll stay in the cottage.'

'We?'

'Don't worry, I'll be in another room.'

'If you could just tell me how I get there, or maybe get one of the porters to show me.'

'I will show you,' Irena said.

Fraser looked a little tense but smiled and kissed Justin's head before he dashed off.

Claudia carried Justin as Irena escorted her, from the forecourt of the Villa Firenze, and across the grass towards the pool. It was, as Jenny had told her, kidney-shaped, with steps fanning out in the recess. Several luxury loungers were placed on the paved surround. The water glistened in the sun, it was so still and inviting.

The cottage nestled on the higher ground beyond the pool. A grassy hill rose behind it and led to a patch of woodland. Claudia felt a ripple of excitement as they followed a cobbled footpath through a shrubbery and into a terraced garden. She looked up at the terracotta-roofed villa and then down at the colourful, billowing plants each side of the stone steps that led up to a veranda, where cane chairs were arranged around a table.

'Fowa.' Justin wriggled his fingers at the sight of the blooms.

'Yes,' Claudia said, 'aren't they lovely. We'll come back and see them in a minute.'

Inside, there was a very spacious kitchen diner. The dining area was arranged with a long table and chairs, and there was a staircase against the wall opposite the main door. An archway led to a lounge, with a wide window that looked down on the gardens and the pool. Two long sofas were placed opposite each other, and a low table between.

'The refrigerator is well stocked,' Irena said, 'you can cater for yourself if you wish. Otherwise you can join the family. Most of the time they will probably eat outside, beneath the pergola, but if the weather is not suitable, then it is served in the dining room.'

Irena showed her the upper floor. The smaller of the two bedrooms was light and cheerful. There was a cot and two single beds. In the master bedroom, fitted wardrobes, white and extensive, filled one wall.

Claudia went to the patio doors that closed off the balcony, pulled back the lawn curtains and looked at the view beyond the grounds. Fields of sunflowers stretched towards a stout villa in the distance.

There was a separate bathroom, and Claudia made a mental note to be vigilant when coming out, after a shower or a bath. Not a good time to be bumping into Fraser on the landing.

Justin began to make signals that he wanted a drink, so they went back downstairs. Claudia put him in the high chair at the head of the table. 'He's going to think he's king of the castle sitting here.'

Irena smiled. 'He is a happy child. You have done well. But it is only two weeks since your discharge from hospital. You must tell me if you need anything. I have an office in the reception area.'

'You seem to have an office everywhere you go.'

'As I said before, it is essential to maintain a high level of support. I hope you will remember that if you need anything.'

'Thanks Irena,' Claudia said, 'I will.'

When Irena left, Claudia smiled at Justin. 'Want some juice?' He answered with a chuckle. She opened the fridge. 'Wow! I don't think we'll starve here, Justin.' She got him a drink and cut up some slices of banana, then sat by him. 'I think we're going to have a great holiday,' she said. Justin's eyes were fixed on her, his brow twitched as if he was trying to work out what she was saying. 'Daddy wants to pay all our bills, so I can write my book. What do you think? Should I let him? Maybe I should marry him. Could it work, me being in love, and he still thinking of me as a special friend? What do you think, hmm? Tell your mummy what you think of it all. Come on, give me a sign.'

Justin knocked his beaker off his tray and shrieked with delight to hear it bounce on the hard floor.

'That's a sign?' Claudia shrugged her shoulders. 'Maybe you're right. He's not going to ask again anyway. He won't expose himself to another rejection. Maybe he'll go back to

Natalie.' She smiled at Justin. 'But I'll always have you, so nothing else matters now.'

Chapter Twenty-Four

Fraser and his parents, Diana and Graham, sat at one of the poolside tables. Tension between them was rare, but today the atmosphere was strained. Conversation so far had been about the journey, the impending harvest at their vineyard, and Fraser's business. Nobody seemed to want to broach the subject that was causing the uneasy feeling between them. Fraser wanted to get through this discussion without causing conflict, but the situation didn't look good for an amicable outcome.

After a while, Fraser decided to take control. 'OK, Mom,' he said decisively, 'let's get this over with. Say what you're thinking.'

Diana was silent for a moment and then she said, 'I just don't understand why it's taken this long. I'm not criticising you, Fraser.'

'So you're blaming Claudia?'

'I don't know what to think. But if she didn't tell you…'

'She had good reason. I don't want to talk about who's to blame, we've already worked our way past that. This is about my son and his future relationship with you.'

'Our relationship with a grandson, who is already one year old,' Diana returned.

'Can't you think about all the wonderful years ahead instead of just one that you missed?'

'It's not that easy.'

'You don't have to be part of his life if you don't want to.'

'Of course we want to,' Graham said steadily, 'but we're worried for you. We don't even know this girl.'

'I take it you don't want to.'

'We're not saying that. It just seems odd that, after all this time, his mother decided to contact you—why now?'

Fraser scowled at them. 'You think that beautiful woman back there in the cottage is just after money? That she's suddenly turned up for a handout because she's short of funds?'

'That's not fair, Fraser,' Graham returned. 'We have a right to be concerned.'

A waiter brought a jug of fruit punch. Fraser poured it. He wasn't sure where this was going to lead, or how tolerant he was going to be. His parents were reasonable people, and they had a point. But they hadn't given themselves enough time to become fully aware of the situation. He took a long drink and then said, 'I realise that you have questions, doubts and probably fears, but why can't you trust me to make the right decisions and choices over this?'

'We're not suggesting that she isn't entitled to some support,' Graham said.

Fraser was hard-pressed to overcome the exasperation that was taking hold of his patience. 'If I could get Claudia to take it, I'd be a much happier man,' he said. 'You need to know that she won't take a penny from me. So at least that settles one of your concerns.' He noted a faint reaction in his mother's face but didn't comment on it. 'She won't allow me to repay her costs over the past year or so. They have a nice home, Justin has the best of care.' He paused a moment and added, 'If you think I'm blameless, then you're mistaken.'

'Apart from the obvious, how are you culpable?' Graham said.

Fraser explained that he never hid the fact that he didn't want children in his life. He frequently made it clear—even publicly on occasions. Claudia knew that, even so, she had still tried to let him know. He explained his relationship with a movie star, and that there was a wall of paparazzi around his home and his office. Had they found out about Justin, he would have been chased around and plastered all over the papers and magazines.

'Claudia, quite rightly, protected him from that,' Fraser continued. 'In fact, she protected me too. How long would you expect her to chase me around when she was pregnant? By the time Justin was born, she had far more important things to do.'

'So why did she contact you?' Diana asked.

'She didn't, it was a complete fluke. She could have moved on and said nothing, I'd be none the wiser. But she faced me and told me. Offered me a choice to be involved or not. I gave her a hard time, and I'm not proud of that because she was completely alone through it all. The only thing she's asking is that Justin should know his grandparents. We need to know whether you want to be part of his life or not?'

'Of course we do, he's your son,' Diana said. 'Does Claudia's mother know about him?'

'She's estranged from her mother, and with good reason.' Fraser stood up and said, 'I'll leave you to talk about it. I have photographs and video clips if you want to see them later. I love you, and I respect you, but I won't tolerate any criticism or bad feeling towards Claudia. She doesn't deserve it.'

'We wouldn't do that, Fraser,' Diana said. 'I'm sorry, we were just confused.'

Fraser nodded. 'Yes, that's understandable. I realise it might hurt, it certainly hurt me at first, but he's a wonderful child, and we've been through a really bad experience together. I'll tell you all about that another time. If you'd like to get settled in, I'll see you back here in a couple of hours, and you can meet him.'

'Surely you didn't expect it to be easy, Fraser.' Claudia said, when he arrived back at the cottage. 'Some woman turns up and presents you with a one-year-old son, what were they to think?'

'You're not some woman,' Fraser protested.

'They don't know that. Give them a chance to work through it. They just want to know where your child has been all this time.' Claudia went to him, characteristically slid her arm through his. 'You must help them over the initial period, your mom especially. Justin probably has mannerisms that you had at his age. She'll experience them all again, and she'll know exactly what she's missed. Try and understand that.'

Fraser bowed his head and kissed her hair. Times like that he wanted her to know how he felt. But Tony was right, that clumsy proposal was more like a business deal, so why should she believe he had come to love her so much, realised that he always had. He had to handle it very carefully, bide his time. She was worth the wait. He looked at her face, her eyes were questioning him.

'What's the matter now?' she said.

He smiled. 'I'm so proud of you.' It wasn't what he really wanted to say about his feelings, but it helped to ease the ache in his soul, the longing to hold her, love her.

'That makes you stressed?'

'No, I'm not stressed.' He hugged her, sighed against her hair, 'My…my Claudia, what would I do without you?'

'You don't have to. I'm here, just like before, in the old days…yes?'

Fraser had missed the old days, but now he wanted new days, a future with her and not just an echo of the past. Claudia had once settled for friendship when she wanted a deeper love. He knew that was what he must do, but for how long? Would those feelings she once had for him ever return? He smiled at her. 'Sure,' he said, 'like the old days.'

*****

Claudia was about to take Justin back downstairs after changing his clothes, ready for meeting his grandparents. She stopped when she heard Fraser on his phone. She stepped back not wanting to interrupt him.

'I can't talk now,' he said and clearly thought Claudia was out of earshot. 'I'll get back to you later. I promised I would, but I can't discuss it now.' He lowered his voice, but it still carried up the stairs.

Claudia's heart pounded, her insides twisted. She suppressed a sob in her throat. Just a few minutes ago, she was his Claudia, but now she had to admit that there would always be a Natalie or a Paloma. Was that what marriage would be like? Swinging from moments of affection to moments of reality when he was in touch with his old life?

'This isn't a good time,' Fraser continued. 'I'll call you back later.'

The caller seemed persistent. Claudia was about to go back to the bedroom when she heard Fraser say, 'I know what I said, but I can't possibly do that before I've had a chance to talk to Claudia about it.'

Claudia held Justin tightly as she listened to a strange conversation that included her in some way.

'Of course I'm going to do it,' Fraser said sharply. 'But when we discussed this, I couldn't have anticipated Claudia's accident. She needs to get over it. Damn it, she was almost killed. This isn't going to be easy for her. She doesn't deserve all this, and I won't make a move until she's had this holiday.'

Claudia crept back into the bedroom. She controlled her emotions for Justin's sake, but her mind raged. How could Fraser be so attentive and caring but still retain a part of him for somebody else. Was it a betrayal? Or was it simply none of her business? To her surprise, Fraser came upstairs and called out to them. She very quickly slipped behind her mask.

'Here he is,' she called out, 'all ready now.'

Fraser beamed a smile. Claudia marvelled at his ability to do that as she handed Justin over to him. 'Will you sort out what Justin is going to call your parents?'

'What do you think?'

'It's not what I think, it's what they want. Will you ask them?'

'Yes, I'll ask them. Will you come with us?'

For the first time, Claudia found her convalescence a handy excuse for wanting to be alone. 'If you don't mind, I'd rather stay here. I thought I'd get some rest while I've got the chance.'

There was no argument.

Later on, she persuaded Fraser to dine with the family while she got Justin to bed and then have a light supper in the cottage. Relieved that Justin slept after his busy time with his new grandparents, she lay on the bed, with the balcony doors open, and listened to the distant sounds of the family at dinner together.

The phone call returned to her mind and stabbed her heart. Then anger suddenly pushed aside her pain, and she got to her feet and paced about the room. She hated the fact that this person was untouchable because of her anonymity. She went to see Justin, he was sleeping peacefully. 'I'm not going to let people trample on our life like this, Justin,' she whispered. 'I won't play this game. I'm not going to hang around to find out where we fit in with all these crazy things going on around us. I'll smile through this holiday, play happy families in our cottage with flowers around the steps. But when it's over…'

Chapter Twenty-Five

Fraser met Tony, for morning coffee. They sat by the pool, enjoying the sunshine. Grace and Charlie occupied another table close by. Charlie was playing a small-world game with Stephanie, who put the tiny people involved carefully in place. She told her uncle what was happening as the scene played out. Charlie punctuated her running commentary with brief comments about where the people were going, and what they were doing.

'So, you and Justin are roomies?' Tony commented.

'Claudia suggested I stay in Firenze, she was concerned that I wouldn't be comfortable. But I'm fine, except that I find myself listening to him breathe.'

'You've come a long way in a short time, that was one hell of a crash course in being a parent.'

Fraser nodded. 'It's overwhelming sometimes. Not the work or the responsibility but the emotional part. Justin has to do so little to melt me down. A chuckle, a smile, that little frown he has when he's working something out.'

Tony glanced over to Stephanie and smiled. 'Welcome to the club.'

Fraser shook his head, and his fingers drummed on the table. 'I was a complete stereotypical fool when I first found out about Justin,' he said. 'I laid the blame squarely at Claudia's door. How old-fashioned is that?'

'Don't try and make sense of it. Whatever happened, Justin's none the worse for it.'

Grace laughed. 'The thing that bugs you guys is that women can manage very well on their own.'

Fraser laughed. 'Is that right, Gracie? Did you learn that at med school?'

'It's the way it is now,' Grace said. 'But that doesn't mean we don't need you.'

'That's a comfort,' Tony said. He topped up his coffee. 'Have you seen your mom and dad this morning, Fraser?'

'Not yet.'

'I assume they're pleased about their new grandchild.'

Fraser scowled. 'He's not so new, and that's still a bit of a problem with Mom, even though she says she's OK with it. They think he's wonderful.'

'So they should, he's amazing.'

'I'm going with them, to Florence, to get a belated birthday present for him. I'm afraid the word belated landed a bit heavy.'

Lizzy and Claudia approached from the direction of the cottage, they were dressed in beachwear.

'Is it any wonder that it bugs us?' Tony said as he watched them. 'They've each got a child in one arm, and a great big bag slung over their shoulder, which incidentally is a totally separate limb because it holds the bag on. But they still walk effortlessly. And what's more, they can hold a conversation at the same time.'

Lizzy and Claudia made for the loungers where, with one swift move, they offloaded the bags without stopping. Then their free hands gestured as they chatted on their way to the pool steps where they stopped and encouraged the children to call, 'Hi, Daddy!'

'You see,' Tony continued, 'look how they can juggle it all. They can open the boot of the car, haul a buggy out of it, have it unfolded in seconds and still not drop the baby. Lizzy does that before I can get a car park ticket.' He frowned and slowly shook his head. 'Can you imagine trying to manufacture a gadget that did all that?' He slapped Fraser on the shoulder, leaned closer and lowered his voice. 'Stop worrying about payback. Just love her.'

'I do.'

'Then tell her. Take a risk.'

'I can't, not yet. Two weeks ago, she came out of hospital. I have to give her time. She's got so much on her plate right now. Besides, she's already turned me down. She'll think I'm putting on an act to get her to change her mind.'

They watched and laughed as their little sons enjoyed the water. After a while, Lizzy made for the steps. Tony got to his feet, laughed and said, 'OK, so the love of my life can do this all by herself, but I'm going to help her anyway because I'm the daddy.'

Fraser's eyes fixed on Claudia as she played with Justin. Her hair was tied back, but it was springing up into wet, shining spirals. She then held Justin, so he could put his feet on the steps and climb out of the water. He shrieked and chuckled each time his foot met with solid ground. Then Claudia found a dry stretch of paving slabs and held his hands so he could walk and make wet footprints. Fraser was impressed. Would he have thought of that, or would he just have thrown him in the air to make him giggle? Such simple things, and yet he couldn't take his eyes off them.

He heard Claudia and Justin's voices counting up to three and then starting again until they made their way to the lounger. He followed Tony's example and met them. He wrapped a towel around Justin, so that Claudia could rub her hair and put on a terry robe.

'What time are you going to Florence?' Claudia asked as they dressed Justin.

'As soon as my folks turn up. Will you come with us?'

'I think you'll all enjoy it better if I don't.'

Diana and Graham arrived and stopped to speak to Grace. Fraser picked up Justin.

'Off you go, you guys,' Claudia said cheerfully. 'There's his kit bag. Don't forget his hat. He keeps taking it off, but you must insist.'

'How?'

Claudia laughed. 'You work it out, you're the daddy.'

'I wish you'd come with us.'

'Why, because he won't keep his hat on?'

Fraser laughed. 'You guessed.'

'I'll come and say hello.'

Fraser was about to introduce Claudia to Diana and Graham, but she smiled and reached her hand towards Diana. 'Hello, Mrs Gallier, I'm Claudia.'

'Diana…please.'

'I'm Graham,' Fraser's father said.

Claudia shook his hand. 'I'm thrilled that Justin's going to know you. Grandparents are so important, aren't they?'

'Yes,' Graham agreed, 'they are.'

'And I love the names you've chosen. He's very quick to learn, and his words are really coming on. He'll soon get the hang of them.' She turned to Fraser. 'Won't he?'

Fraser found himself watching Claudia again. He was glad of her ability to approach the occasion without seeming nervous or uncomfortable. He could see that she had charmed his parents, and any doubts they still had were fading. Within a few minutes they were chatting, and Diana was telling Claudia about Fraser when he was the same age as Justin.

Claudia looked at Justin. 'You have a Nana and a Poppa, isn't that brilliant?' She clapped her hands to urge him to follow. Justin clapped and smiled.

Fraser looked at the light in Claudia's eyes. She was genuine in her wish for Justin, and she was dealing with this brilliantly. His parents were completely won over, and it was clear that they felt blessed.

Chapter Twenty-Six

Claudia returned to the cottage, showered away the pool water and dressed in shorts and a T-shirt. She was determined to make good use of this free time and decided to focus on a plan to ward off her mother. With the smell of freshly brewed coffee drifting in the air, she put her laptop on the table, a notepad and pen beside it, and her mug of coffee within reach. She took a deep breath to focus her mind, and then stared at the screen. Where to start? It had to be a good plan, so she knew it wouldn't come easy. The simple solution would be to hand over the diaries, but that wasn't just a case of giving up a pile of journals and notebooks, to give in to her mother would be to condone all that the woman had ever done. These things seemed much worse since she had witnessed how other families lived. Felt the love and consideration they had for one another. A catalogue of all the battles, rows, standoffs, defeats ran through her mind, page by page—the threats her mother had made, the ones she had coldly and callously carried out, and the ones she was poised to make now. This was the last stand. To lose now would mean that Alyona would have no voice, nor would that feisty, little tearaway who deserved some kind of payback. And for Lennie, she would do it for him too. Claudia had to win for all of them. The odds against her were stacked high, she wasn't going to threaten her mother with a freshly baked cream horn this time. But at least that day in the smart tea shop confirmed that if Elsa Hamilton had a chink in her armour, that is exactly where it would be, in her work, her precious agency and her image. By lunchtime, a blank screen and pages of useless notes, adorned with flowery doodles, had come to nothing. She had explored every angle except…

A harrowing memory, long since imprisoned and locked down tightly at the back of Claudia's mind, presented itself as a possibility, a very strong one that would silence her mother once and for all. But could she equal Elsa Hamilton's guile? Fight dirty like she did? Use blackmail with such cold precision that would bring her mother tumbling down, along with one other objectionable person. Could she carry it out, coldly, unemotionally and still live with herself afterwards? Her body shivered at the prospect, and she couldn't even bring herself to make a note on her pad. She gritted her teeth and thrust the ugly matter back into its cerebral prison, then locked it down again. There was no plan A, no plan B, and plan zero wasn't even brought to the table. She could almost hear Elsa Hamilton's voice, feel her closing in. A blast of intense anxiety hit Claudia's lungs, and a bitter concoction of fear, anger and frustration suddenly pumped through her veins. She leapt from her chair and paced about the kitchen, clamped her hands to her chest. Flashes of memory from her accident began to gang up on her, and she re-lived that moment she took a leap of faith from Tony's car as it began to roll down the Rowmont Ridge. The doctors warned her she might have reactions like this, but knowing that it was normal was no comfort at all. She left the cottage, ran down the steps, along the cobbled path and on towards the pool. There she stopped. Nobody was around to see her in this terrible state. The pool looked calm and soothing, she dived in. The sound, as she entered the water, rushed past her ears, like a gust of wind, and then it was silent as she glided for a few perfectly peaceful moments, eyes closed, so that no sensations distracted her from the feeling of being far away from the world. All she could feel was the caress of the water on her flesh. Then with a burst of energy, she emerged, and her arms reached ahead, each in turn, to propel her body and push her frustration into her wake. The urge to swim faster overcame her, and her limbs worked harder. After several laps, she felt the tug on her lungs and the pain in her abdomen. She clutched her stomach, coughed and choked out the water that lapped into her mouth. She used her free hand to scull to the side of the pool.

A strong hand gripped her arm, then slid around her back and carried her to the steps, where she sat down. For some time, she continued to gasp and cough. At last it passed, and she was calm.

'That was impressive,' Eliot said as he sat by her side.

a groaned. 'Stupid more like, I haven't done anything
since before I had Justin.' She grimaced at the pain
red in her abdomen. 'You won't tell on me, will you?'
rse not. It's not as if I plunged in fully clothed to help
you. At least I'm dressed for it.'

Claudia looked at his naked shoulders, 'That's more than I
can say.'

'So…what was that all about?'

'You're way too perceptive.' She paused a moment and then
said, 'I felt overwhelmed. My thoughts got a bit crazy.'

'Reaction from the accident,' Eliot said. 'You'll still get that.
When's Fraser coming back?'

'I don't know.'

'He's frustrated as hell.'

'About what?'

'He wants to support you so you can write your book. He
believes you deserve it. Hasn't he spoken to you about it?'

'Kind of but…'

'There's no shame in being sponsored, particularly by the
wealthy father of your child.' Eliot continued tentatively. 'Your
accident shook him. It hit all of us, but Fraser was in a bad way.
He was very controlled when he was with Justin, but you could
see it was taking everything he'd got. He was even making plans
to take care of you for good.'

'Care for me? What do you mean?'

'He thought you might have suffered permanent damage, at
the very least, some kind of memory loss. It happened to me, so
it was natural he'd think about it. He was scared, really scared.
Thought you wouldn't know him or Justin. But you'd still need
him, and he was going to be there for you. He even asked me to
help him find a house.'

'I didn't know that,' Claudia said, and a wave of guilt came
over her.

'I'm not saying you should do him any favours, but don't be
afraid to accept what he can give you. It's not about money or
control, it's about creating opportunities for you to explore who
you are, use your talent because he can do that for you. That's
why Tony's getting rid of the relics at last, to give Lizzy
something way more valuable than expensive gifts. That studio
will enhance her life and give her some space, an opportunity to

be who she wants to be—who she *should* be.' He expelled a affectionate laugh, 'That guy has got so much love in him for Lizzy.'

'I know. Don't you have somebody?'

'How could I get involved with a Lizzy or a Claudia, when I don't know what happened in Cape Town?'

'It was an accident, wasn't it?'

'I don't know. Maybe I leapt from a runaway car, like you did. Goodness knows why it only took three weeks out of my life, but I'm thankful that's all it was. Can you imagine a life of married bliss suddenly being wrenched apart by the discovery of something really terrible? What if I'd hurt somebody?'

'Oh, come on! You wouldn't do anything really bad. You can't deny yourself love or marriage because of it.'

Eliot put his arm around her shoulders. 'Thanks for that. I'm the only one of the cousins who looked forward to family life.'

Claudia leapt to her feet and said, 'I can hear voices. I don't want to be caught out in these wet clothes.'

Eliot got up, stepped into the water and then turned back. 'You could accept Fraser's offer, write your book and spend more time with Justin. What's not to like about that?' He plunged into the pool.

Claudia's conversation with Eliot surprised her. Fraser had never discussed the accident at all, let alone the plan he had to care for her, even though she wouldn't recognise him. Her mind tossed around the idea that she had jumped to conclusions about the phone call. Why should she assume that it was a woman? It could have been about a house, Eliot said he was looking. Fraser was keeping it from her at this stage so he would have been secretive about it. It could have been the police, called to ask more questions about what happened at Rowmont.

Claudia showered again, put on a robe and flopped on the bed. She wasn't given to napping in the daytime and was very surprised when she woke up to find that she had slept for four hours. Not so long ago that was a whole night's sleep. It was quiet downstairs, so she took her time over getting ready for dinner. Having chosen a maxi skirt, she considered a simple top, only to find that her shoulder was still bruised. If Fraser really had a bad time over her accident, she didn't want to worry him by the lingering evidence of it. A silky tunic blouse with sleeves seemed a better option. Makeup was called for, especially as she had time to apply it carefully. A silver pendant that Lennie gave her, before he left the series, seemed a perfect addition.

The anticipation of seeing Fraser made her feel happy, and she began to behave like a woman expecting her man home.

At the top of the stairs, Claudia suddenly stopped, transfixed at the sight of Fraser, where he stood in the open doorway. He held a long, gold box in the crook of his arm, Champagne. A small gift bag hung over his wrist, and he wore a full beam of a smile.

The sight of him plunged her back in time, to one of those evenings when he had just turned up out of the blue.

She had answered his familiar rap at the door, fixed her bluffing mechanism in place, composed herself and smiled at him.

'No date tonight then?' she said lightly, as she stood back to let him in.

'I didn't want a date, I wanted to see you. I brought Champagne.'

'So I see. How did you know I'd be home?'

He pressed a careless kiss on her cheek and said, 'You're always home.'

'One day I won't be,' she warned as she went to the kitchen. She returned with a napkin, two glasses and put them on the coffee table. 'What will you do then, hmm?'

'Sit on your doorstep and get rolling drunk to drown my bitter disappointment.'

'No, you wouldn't. I'm sure one bottle wouldn't do it anyway.' She fixed her eyes on him as he eased the cork from the bottle. 'You're all pumped up and fizzy,' she said.

Fraser frowned as if she had insulted him. 'Pumped up and fizzy?'

'I suppose you've pulled off one of your risky punts.' She often did that, levelled him with honesty when he got too big-sorted.

'Risky punts?'

'Stop repeating what I say. And don't look at me like that. You know what I mean. You've brought very expensive Champagne, so you must be celebrating.'

There was a muffled pop beneath the napkin. 'Trust you to discover my guilty pleasure,' Fraser said.

'Taking wild business risks?'

'No, just playing a little dangerously with money, a very small amount that I keep for the purpose.' He shrugged. 'It's just a game.'

'What's the point of it?'

He grinned. 'To fly, like Icarus, and not get burnt.'

'You get burnt?' she scoffed, as if it was a ridiculous idea. 'If you got too close to the sun, a whole bunch of lady guardian angels would catch you. Then they'd gently set you back on your feet—totally unsinged.' She shook her head, but her eyes smiled at him.

He pretended to be affronted. 'Are you saying I live a charmed life?'

'You certainly do,' she told him. 'But I have to admit that you've worked hard for it and against the grain.'

He put down the bottle and stared at her. 'What do you mean, against the grain? Come on, out with it.'

Claudia regarded him, affectionately, 'It isn't in your heart, is it? You're good at it. You have to be, but it just isn't who you are.'

'Go on.'

'You wriggle around, unable to find the right place to be. It seems to me that you play this game to put some excitement into it because you don't really care for it.'

'My father started that business. It was only right I should join him.'

'But it's nothing like your father's business anymore, is it? You've taken Gallier and Co and turned it into a corporation so big, it's just referred to as Gallier.'

'What was I supposed to do?'

'Whatever you wanted. You once told me that you wanted to open a restaurant.'

'Stop nagging and drink your Champagne.' He handed her a glass, she raised it a little and looked as the bubbles rose. Then, savouring the moment, she reverently took a sip. It tasted good, and it brought her wonderful memories. She found Fraser staring at her. 'What?'

'Are we going to drink a toast?'

196

She had smiled at him, and they had raised their glasses as Claudia said, 'To your guilty pleasure.'

'You're standing up there as if you're about to make a big speech,' Fraser called to Claudia.

She was still poised on the stairs, looking down at him and asking herself why she had turned this man down. She always said that she had no chance compared to the likes of Paloma Cardini or Natalie, but where were they now? Fraser was here, and the way he looked at her was different. She felt a change had suddenly come over them, a warm, promising feeling of a new kind of relationship, and it was going to begin right here and now. 'You startled me.'

'Did you think I was a ghost come to haunt you?' Fraser said.

'Ghosts don't wear black polo shirts,' she said.

'I showered and changed at Firenze.'

His smile and the look in his eyes made Claudia's heart cry out, 'Ask me! Ask me again because at this moment I'll say yes.' But she couldn't bring herself to speak those words aloud. Instead, she smiled and continued to walk down the stairs. She looked at the gold box and stepped into her comfort zone of friendship. 'I doubt you've had time to pull off one of your Icarus deals, so what's this all about?'

Fraser laughed as he went back to close the door. 'I haven't done one of those for a long time.'

'So what are you celebrating?' Claudia shook her head. 'Did I forget your birthday?'

Fraser smiled. 'No, it seems you forgot yours. Happy birthday, sweetheart!'

Claudia was drawn by the smile and warmth of the moment. 'I don't usually celebrate my birthday.'

'You do now.'

Claudia put her arms around his neck and ventured to press a kiss on his cheek. 'It's a lovely surprise, thank you.'

'Hold on,' Fraser said. 'You have me at a disadvantage.' He put the box and the gift bag on the table, rested his hands on her face and pressed a soft but lingering kiss on her mouth. The taste of his lips was delicious, it tormented her hunger, and she drank in this blissful moment with unashamed pleasure as she took another step towards a different set of rules in their relationship. He seemed happy, almost elated.

'I'll get some glasses,' Claudia said. She stepped back and willed her cheeks not to blush any more than they were already. She set the glasses on the table.

Fraser gestured to the box.

Claudia carefully laid it down and reverently opened the lid. The Champagne bottle was swathed in gold cellophane it crinkled and squeaked a little as she unwrapped it. 'This is lovely,' she said, 'but you didn't swop it for the baby, did you?'

Fraser laughed. 'Aren't grandparents wonderful? They took him shopping, and now they're looking after him while we share this little celebration. They even bought a travel cot, so they can babysit during the holiday.'

Claudia watched as he opened the bottle, recounting his adventures of going into toyshops with a small child. 'The children are going to have dinner with the grown-ups this evening. Stephanie's beside herself with excitement. Little Eddy's going to be there. We wanted to be sure that you were too.' He poured the sparkling drinks, handed her a glass and said, 'But for now, it's just you and me…happy birthday to my…my darling Claudia.'

Claudia took a sip and then nodded her approval.

Fraser's brow puckered momentarily. 'You don't do it anymore.' He seemed disappointed. 'I love that ritual that you do.'

'I know what you mean. But that ritual, as you call it, belongs in the past.'

The warmth in Fraser's eyes chilled a little. 'In the past with Mathew?'

'Yes, back there with Mathew, and that's where it's going to stay. So leave it alone…please.'

'But I can see that it hurt you to lose him.'

'I'm not denying that.' Claudia hesitated for a few seconds, and then she drew a sharp breath. 'He'd known me since I was a kid, and sometimes he still treated me like one, like somebody who hadn't experienced much of real life. I hadn't, I suppose. He used to say that you shouldn't rush past the good things in life, likened it to your first glass of Champagne, at a party. Said it was foolish to squander it…assume there was an unlimited supply.' She looked him in the eye. 'I had to learn to let him go five years ago, so why don't you? I thought this was supposed to be my birthday celebration.'

Fraser frowned. 'You're right. I'm sorry.' Then he smiled and said, 'I have something for you. I hope you don't think it's a cliché giving you something in a velvet box. But I promise you I searched for it, gave it a great deal of thought and chose it carefully.'

Claudia opened the chunky red box and stared at the beautiful wristwatch. She gasped. 'I'm...'

'Speechless, I know, but please don't tell me you're trying to find a polite way of rejecting it.'

'I'll do no such thing. This is stunning. I just didn't know what to say, how to say...' She put her arms around his neck. 'It's perfect. Thank you.' She kissed his face. Fraser responded by tightening his arms around her and for a while they remained in the embrace. Claudia could have happily remained there, but she broke away. 'Shouldn't we go and join the family?'

When they arrived at the pergola, Claudia was greeted with a chorus of birthday wishes. This was another big surprise, a short while ago, she didn't even know what date it was, let alone what it meant. Now here she was, being treated like a fully paid-up member of the Franklyn-Gallier clan. Claudia and Fraser sat down, like guests of honour.

It was dinner in true wine-country style, babies, parents, grandparents sitting around a long table beneath a gnarled, woody vine that weaved its branches and lobed leaves into a canopy overhead. She watched Justin pointing up at the trusses of grapes that hung down like purple lanterns. He sat in a high chair, betwixt his grandparents and was completely at home. This is what Claudia wanted for him, to know the love and protection from his family.

'Poor Claudia,' Diana said, sympathetically, as she helped Justin break up a piece of bread. 'Hope we haven't embarrassed you.'

'Don't you worry about our birthday girl,' Eliot said. 'She knows how to make an entrance at a party. She had lessons, right Claudia?'

'Absolutely, lessons for everything.' She became aware that something was afoot, as Stephanie was hanging her head. 'Is something wrong?' she prompted softly.

Grace explained that Stephanie was going to play postman and give Claudia her presents, but she changed her mind and got upset about it.

Claudia got up and moved around the table to Stephanie, picked her up and hugged her tightly. Stephanie clung to her with all four of her limbs. 'It's OK, darling,' she said. 'You can change your mind. You're just a little girl. You don't have to do it if you don't want to.' It felt so good to feel the child's response, the little arms squeezing around her neck.

'We put them in a bag for her,' Lizzy whispered and handed it to Claudia. Then she smiled and mouthed the words, 'Thank you.'

Claudia set Stephanie back on her feet, took her hand and asked, 'Will you sit with me and help me?'

Stephanie nodded.

Claudia sat the child on her lap, and they opened the birthday presents together. Stephanie found her courage again and explained about the gifts, all wrapped in colourful paper and dressed with ribbons in decorative shapes. Claudia said a few words of thanks, then she turned to Fraser and smiled. He winked at her. It was such a private gesture. It warmed her heart, but heated her blood.

Later on, when Justin and Eddy had fallen asleep, and Stephanie's eyes were closing, even though she tried not to let them, Diana and Graham insisted on taking Justin to their suite, so the party could continue. Nathan and Ruth took Stephanie and Eddie.

It was such fun to be with grown-ups for a whole evening, even if the subject of conversation returned to Claudia's career in the ranch.

Earlier in the day, Grace had been on-line to search for it and had watched two episodes. Everybody listened to her account of it. She described a 14-year-old Claudie, with her wild, curly hair, her Stetson hat raised as she pulled up her horse and waved.

'Mathew Jay!' Grace expelled a sigh of lust, which attracted everybody's attention. 'Now I know what Paige was talking about. When he rode up with that herd of horses... Wow!' She hardly had time to catch a breath before she continued. 'That scene when he was covered in dust from the trail, and he stood in the stream, fully clothed, and washed it off.'

'Well, at least he didn't take his clothes off,' Eliot said.

'He didn't need to,' Grace answered with a laugh, 'I did that for him.'

Claudia realised that Fraser hadn't told them about her relationship with Mathew. She said nothing, it would be too embarrassing for Grace if she told them now.

Tony looked at his sister in surprise. 'Who spiked Grace's wine?' he said. 'She hasn't lusted over a movie star since she was 15.'

'It's not the wine,' Charlie spoke up, like a preacher in the pulpit. 'It's the snug jeans, the fancy, leather boots, and the way his sinful butt sits in the saddle that leads to temptation.'

Lizzy laughed. 'So you saw it too, Charlie?'

'I certainly did.' He pretended to be stern. 'A man's got to keep a check on his wife's fantasies about men, fresh off the trail and washing the dust off in the stream.'

Claudia felt Fraser draw in a sharp breath and decided that he was tired of hearing about Mathew Jay.

Chapter Twenty-Seven

Claudia looked at the mellow, amber lighting that spilled around the pool. 'Doesn't it look tranquil at night? It has a calming effect on you. Or maybe it's the wine. I don't normally drink that much.'

'You didn't drink much this evening either,' Fraser said. 'You're over-cautious because of Justin.' He slipped his arm around Claudia's back as they walked towards the cottage.

'Do you think he'll be OK?' Claudia said.

'They said they'd call if he needed us.'

'It feels strange. I've had a whole day without responsibility and now a whole night. Your family's amazing. You're all so close.'

'We're not saints, we have our moments. You've been adopted now, there's no getting away. You've certainly charmed my parents.'

'They needed a bit of reassurance, that's all.'

At the cottage, they hovered in the dining area. Claudia noticed the Champagne was still on the table. 'Oh no,' she sighed, disappointment rang in her voice. 'I didn't put a stopper in the bottle.'

'Don't worry about it.'

'But it's a bottle of Cristal, and it's almost full.'

'That doesn't matter now.'

'Of course it matters.'

Fraser's voice raised a little. 'It's served its purpose. It was just to wish you happy birthday.'

'It was a very generous gesture, and I appreciated it, so I won't discard it as if it was nothing.' She put a stopper in the bottle.

Fraser then became irritated. 'This is the beautiful Mathew talking? I'm beginning to recognise his influence on you.'

'Why shouldn't I be influenced by somebody's wisdom?'

Fraser looked at her, his eyes lost the warmth she had enjoyed during the evening. 'But you reflect his angle on life, as if you're determined to hold onto him. You're never going to forget him, are you?'

'No, I'm not. Why would I?'

'Because he left you,' Fraser said bluntly. 'Now you keep the flame burning in the hope that you'll get him back. You've probably got a picture of him in your pendant.'

Claudia glared at him, her heart was twisting as she defended a man she once loved dearly against a man who was the love of her life. 'Mathew doesn't need to be in my locket, he already has a place to stay.'

Fraser's jaw tightened, and he seemed agitated. 'Sure he does, deep down in your heart, no doubt.' His words were streaked with jealousy. 'No wonder you turned me down. He set the bar too high for anybody else. Who can compete with a guy you remember every time you look at a damn pinecone?'

Claudia stared in surprise. Jealousy wasn't an emotion she had ever seen in Fraser. 'How do you know about that?'

'I watched you, that first day we met in the park. You picked up a pinecone and ran it down your cheek. It was obvious that it meant—'

'Everything!' Claudia bit back. 'That memory meant everything. But what do you know about love? What makes you entitled to know all about my one past relationship?'

Fraser seemed to emerge from his jealousy as if he had mentally checked his attitude. He drew a long breath that enabled him to speak quietly. 'Forgive me, I've spoken out of turn.'

There was a chilled silence, but Claudia was offended and decided to make something clear to Fraser. 'I'll just tell you a couple of things about Mathew, and then perhaps you can leave my personal memories where they are.'

'Claudia, no, it's OK…'

'I'd rather tell you,' Claudia insisted, 'even if you think it's ridiculous. Mathew used to tell me I was like a pinecone in winter, tightly curled up, afraid of being warm enough to open up and trust people. His analogy made me understand.' She gulped down a lump that suddenly gripped her throat, and then she continued. 'And so did the Champagne thing. He wanted to help me understand that life wasn't a work in progress. He was being too kind. He should have just told me outright. My beautiful man was…was trying to say goodbye…he was trying to tell me that he was dying.' She saw the shock in Fraser's face but continued. 'The terrible irony was that his big, kind, warm heart was failing him. I wanted to stay with him, take care of him. He was very determined and even got angry with me for trying to change his mind. He checked into a nursing home and asked me to say goodbye while he was still on his feet. I clung to him, I couldn't let him go, but he made me leave, didn't want me to witness him fading away. I was devastated. I loved him so much.' Tears blurred her vision, but she remained strong. 'I had lessons to teach me how to make an entrance, nobody taught me how to make an exit like that.' She blinked away the tears and stared at Fraser's face, he'd become pale. 'All your shallow relationships together couldn't measure up to what we shared. So don't you dare mock my time with him…don't you dare.' Fraser was visibly shaken, but he made no attempt to speak or move, he seemed stunned, stared at the floor, his shoulders lifting and dropping as he drew breath. Claudia was still angry with him for bringing jealousy and conflict into their relationship. They had made wonderful progress, and he had snatched it away. 'You talk to me about being second best? Well, I know how that feels. Movie stars and all the tall, beautiful celebrities you've known. Compare them to me—it's a no brainer.'

Fraser's eyes suddenly came alive. 'That's not true! I'd never offer another woman your place in my life—never.'

'Of course not, I'm the Prima Donna now. I gave you a son. That put me on the A-list. Until then my love for you wasn't enough, I had to bring much more to the table than that.'

'You have no idea how I feel,' Fraser said in a quiet, controlled voice. 'How I felt sitting by your hospital bed, not knowing what…what to expect.'

'Of course I've no idea, you've never told me. I didn't know you felt jealous of Mathew either, I had to find out during a fight. Is this what marriage would be like for us? Bitter arguments, jealous fights, kiss and make up and then off to bed? I'm not ready for that.'

Fraser was grave, his face pale as he said quietly, 'I'm truly sorry about Mathew. I'm mortified that I insulted his memory. I admit I was jealous of him. I don't recall feelings like that before. But I envied a successful, good-looking, heroic man who was still alive and well. A guy who could snap his fingers and get you back any time he wanted. I had no idea what had actually happened. I hope, one day, I can make amends.' He stared at her for a few moments, then he turned swiftly and made for the door. 'Forgive me... Goodnight!'

Claudia willed him to change his mind, turn back and hold her. Suddenly, the kiss and make up idea seemed good. They had both been cruel and bitter, they had never quarrelled before, sharp banter was the closest they had ever come to it. She desperately wanted him back, but as she stared at the door, it was clear that he was gone. She paced about for some time, and then wearily climbed the stairs up to her room.

She changed out of her eveningwear and put on a short, cool nightdress. It had thin straps, so she could feel as cool as possible. She lay on top of the covers.

For a long time she tossed about, but there was no hope of sleep to pass a night of torment. Her eyes were dry as if she had no tears left. She got up and went to the balcony. Few lights burned in the villa. Was one of them Fraser's? He was obviously not staying here tonight. Then she saw him. He was out there, slumped in a chair by the pool. His dark clothes hardly visible in the mellow light, but his face was lit. She could just make out his hand beating up and down on the table. She stood for a long time, unable to turn from him. Then, at last, he glanced up. She raised her hand in a feeble wave. 'Please come back,' she whispered, as if the balmy night air would carry her message. 'Please come back. I love you.'

It was as if he heard. He got up and walked towards the cottage. For several seconds he went from her sight. Was he coming to see her? She couldn't tell. Then she saw his face in the shadows beneath her, now lit by the moon.

'I should serenade you,' he said, 'but I don't know any Russian songs, so what am I to do?'

'A guy who can fly like Icarus, and not get burnt, should be able to work something out.'

'You'd think so.' He was silent for a moment and then he said, 'It's a risky punt, but if I come back, will you kick me out, or can I stay awhile? I've behaved like a coward, allowed my own possessive feelings to get out of hand. I hid behind the trauma of your accident when I should become stronger because of it. I know how you hate to fight,' he paused a moment and then added, 'and I'm truly sorry. If you'll forgive me, I'll be able to get some sleep, and maybe you will too. Otherwise, you'll be tired for your trip with Lizzy tomorrow.'

'I told you before, I only need three hours. Why don't you come back, and we can talk some more? Don't forget I rescued the Champagne, and it's still my birthday.'

Claudia opened the bedroom door, but Fraser was standing there holding the bottle of Cristal. He had two upturned glasses between the fingers of his other hand. The anger had gone from his eyes, but he still seemed tense. 'Mathew's absolutely right,' he said. 'We shouldn't assume there's an unlimited supply.' He set down the glasses on the dressing table, poured the sparkling drinks and then offered a glass to Claudia. 'I should know that already,' he said. 'I thought I'd always have my friend, right there in her apartment where I could find her when I needed her. And then, in the hospital when I sat with Justin, I thought we'd lost you. That's what he meant, isn't it?' He smiled, and his eyes lit with affection. 'You know, Paloma Cardini used to get really hacked off when I talked about you.'

Claudia expelled a gentle laugh. 'Quite right too. A girl doesn't want to hear a guy talking about other women.'

They sat on the bed and sipped their drink as they talked, mainly about old times, sometimes about Justin, a little about daffodils. When their glasses were empty, Fraser put them onto the bedside table. 'Am I forgiven—just a little?'

'Yes,' Claudia said. 'I know my accident caused you a lot of worry, and I can't bear to think how it must have hurt you to see Justin so upset. But why didn't you talk to me about it? You've been sharing your troubles with me for a long time, why give up now?'

Fraser drew a long breath as if he didn't know how to begin. He turned to her and looked directly into her eyes. 'God, Claudia, I thought you'd gone, your body was there, but it was so cold.' His voice was laced with panic, Claudia had never witnessed this kind of emotion in him before. 'You didn't know me. Your eyes just stared. I couldn't deal with it…my Claudia, not to know me,

206

not to know Justin. It was hell, and I'm still trying to deal with it.'

Times like this Claudia would link her arm in his and say something cheery or supportive, but instead she made the move she always wanted to make. Put her arms around his shoulders, reached her face into the hollow of his neck, then pressed her lips softly onto his flesh. Such a gentle kiss, but she felt Fraser's body shiver, and a groan juddered through his chest as he put his arms around her.

'We're supposed to be talking.' His voice was hoarse and restrained as he whispered against her head.

'We didn't agree on the language,' she told him. 'I like this better.'

'I hope you understand what's being said?' Fraser pulled her closer to him and pressed his mouth to her naked shoulder. Her flesh shivered, and she suppressed a sigh against his bowed head. The balmy scent of the Tuscan evening drifted into the room, fanned by the flimsy, lawn curtains that fluttered, twisted and danced. Fraser kissed her neck, her jaw and then her mouth. She could feel how his solid body trembled with restraint as she slid her hands beneath his polo shirt and eased it upwards, over his chest. Then there was no more talk, save for the secret dialogue shared by their bodies, a potent, arousing language clearly understood by both. Claudia had so much love for him and had kept it carefully hidden, but now it fled from her control, and she no longer questioned what was in his heart. His body loved her, adored her, worshipped every inch of her, his touch told her so, until it appeased her inflamed senses.

In the stillness of sated peace, Claudia rested her hand on Fraser's chest, he clasped her fingers, turned his head and smiled at her. He had uttered fevered words of love, a feast for a heart that had hungered for them for so long. If this was the only time he could say them, when he was on fire for the want of her, then she would embrace it. She smiled as she looked up to the ceiling where the shadow curtains danced, voyeurs entwined in a ghostly *pas de deux*, as if to mimic what they had witnessed beneath them.

Chapter Twenty-Eight

Claudia felt ten feet tall when she spotted Fraser, he was sitting by the pool, watching a game—Justin and Eliot versus Tony and little Eddy. The baby cousins were shrieking and laughing as they pushed a large, coloured ball about.

Claudia's loose tunic top rippled gently in the breeze, her colourful skirt fluttered about her legs as she walked. Fraser waved and smiled, and when she arrived, he kissed her and held her for several fabulous seconds.

'Hi, sweetheart,' he said, against her cheek. The tone of his voice, the warmth of the kiss, made her feel so special, like she was loved and cherished. Last time she made love with Fraser, she got a note. This time, he was there in the morning, with a kiss and hug. She didn't allow herself to question it. Today she was number one. The only woman ever to get a proposal of marriage, and that offer was still open.

'Why don't you look tired?' Fraser said.

'I'm bluffing. Besides, you did the early morning shift while I stayed in bed.'

'You look beautiful,' Fraser said, 'artistic.'

'If I'm going to be admiring the Fountain of Neptune, or perhaps David, then I should dress accordingly, don't you think?' She looked at the pool and smiled. 'Didn't you feel like swimming?'

'It wasn't planned, Eliot turned up and invited Justin to join him.'

'Justin loves his new family.'

'It's your family too.' Fraser clasped her hand. 'Claudia…' he hesitated for a moment as if he found the words difficult to say. Then he continued. 'That child has completed my life. I had no idea what a great void there was until I saw him. I'm beginning to understand what you went through. I only had to care for him for a short while by comparison, and I had a lot of help. I didn't want to leave that unsaid any longer. I wanted to put things right before you went today.'

Claudia smiled, a verbal response wouldn't seem right.

'We'll miss you today,' Fraser said.

'Oh, don't! I feel so guilty going off for the whole day. I know you must be tired too.'

Fraser laughed. 'Justin's bound to crash out for at least an hour after this, so maybe I'll catch up then. We're having lunch with Mom and Dad, and then I thought we could walk along the footpath behind the cottage. There's a stream, and it's very pleasant up there among the trees. So don't rush back. Go…glean through the Flea Market, but try and leave something for everybody else.'

The sound of a car horn made them turn back to the Villa Firenze. Lizzy was waiting in a beautiful, dark blue convertible.

'She means to drive you in style,' Fraser commented.

Claudia waved to her, slung her bag over her shoulder and said, 'Call me if…' She stopped as Fraser pressed a credit card in her hand. 'Fraser, don't,' Claudia protested. 'I can't take it.'

'Please…' Fraser gently closed her fingers around the card. 'You must, at some stage, learn to accept what I can give you. Do some shopping, anything you want… Humour me.'

*****

Claudia sighed, closed her eyes and tilted her head back. Curls or no curls, she allowed her hair to blow about. 'This is ridiculous,' she said with a laugh.

'What is?'

'Us…cruising along the Tuscan roads, in a Bentley Continental. For goodness sake, we're going to the Flea Market.'

'Well, we're going to do some posh shopping,' Lizzy reasoned.

'Hmm! Swanning around with Fraser's credit card in my bag.'

Lizzy was swift to reassure her. 'It's no shame to let him buy you something.'

'It's a rite of passage,' Claudia complained.

'What is?'

'Allowing a man to buy your clothes. I've earned my own living all my life. For goodness sake, I even paid for my own baby cereal.'

'Well you can decide when we get there. Shall we do the Flea Market first? Then hit the shops until lunchtime?'

The Flea Market was bustling and colourful, Claudia and Lizzy scoured the stalls to find interesting trinkets and trimmings. They admired the beautiful and laughed at the grotesque.

They moved on to the fabulous shops and boutiques, where they discussed the design of the clothes, the quality of the fabrics used. Claudia shopped but couldn't bring herself to use Fraser's card. It remained in a small pocket in her bag. She was aware of what she spent but not in the least bit worried, her expenses had been very low recently, and this trip, with Lizzy, wasn't a time for counting the housekeeping money.

They had a spring in their step as they walked along the Via del Parione, shopping carriers swinging back and to as they moved.

Lizzy glanced at her watch, 'Lunch?' she suggested.

Although there were plenty of seats outside, they decided to sit indoors. As they walked into the restaurant, Claudia snatched her breath and whispered, 'They've got a whole display counter for chocolate.'

'It's just as well Jenny's not here,' Lizzy said. 'This would be too cruel.'

It was a spacious, genteel restaurant, with a high ceiling and large, old paintings on the walls.

Lizzy looked around and laughed. 'Do you think they'd like Silas hanging up here?'

'Perhaps not, the staff might cuss at him and upset the punters.'

They chatted and laughed through lunch, talked about their plans to work together.

Claudia sighed and said, 'I haven't relaxed like this for…a long time. I feel lazy.'

'Tired you mean,' Lizzy teased.

'Yes, tired,' Claudia admitted.

'It's worth it though, yes? You two actually got your act together.'

'Oh no, does everybody know that?'

'Course not.' Lizzy reached across the table and clasped Claudia's hand. 'I know you have doubts, but Fraser wouldn't spend the night with you if he didn't love you. He wouldn't just be with you for sex, he respects you way too much.'

'I'm sure you're right. I should have more faith, shouldn't I?' She reached for her bag. 'We'd better do the sights?'

'You don't sound very enthusiastic.'

'My brain is but my body won't back it up.' She drew a deep breath and said, 'Come on, let's do it.'

'Why don't we call it a day? We can go back, chill out by the pool, doze on a lounger…swim even.'

'Are you kidding?'

'I wasn't suggesting we swim to Dover, just float about.'

'But this is Florence. It seems irreverent to leave before we've admired the art. Catherine of Bologna might come back and haunt us for ignoring them.'

'David isn't short of admirers, and Hercules is big enough to take care of himself. They won't miss us,' Lizzy said decisively. 'Let's go! Want to drive?'

'No way! I've already wrecked one of Tony's cars. That's quite enough for the time being?'

Chapter Twenty-Nine

They arrived back at the villa, mid-afternoon. Lizzy went to find Tony and the children, Claudia went to the cottage. There was nobody there, she presumed that Fraser had taken Justin for a walk to the stream. She decided to go and catch them up. Anticipation made her heart beat faster as she made her way through the garden and on to the footpath that rose upward towards the trees. The thought of an embrace and kiss from Fraser, made her walk faster, even though she was tired and out of breath. As she followed the path through the woods, Justin's voice echoed through the trees, they were close by. Her feet trod carefully, the snap of a broken twig would spoil the surprise.

As she reached the curve of the path she saw them—all three of them. Shock exploded in her head, her stomach felt sick but she had the presence of mind to dodge behind a tree. Breathlessly, she leaned against it and clamped her hand tightly over her lips so that the screams in her soul wouldn't escape through her mouth.

She willed herself to look again. Fraser was strolling casually with Natalie. He was carrying Justin, and Natalie was holding the child's hand and talking to him. When did this tall, beautiful, woman become so interested in children? Claudia's heart ripped apart, her limbs grew weak. She had been here before, watching Fraser and his beautiful girlfriend walking together beneath the trees in the park, only now there were no daffodils. Her decision, that day, to back off and raise her child alone was no longer hers to make. Fraser had rights. Was this why he wanted to set the record straight before she left for Florence? Was it just a loose end to tie up?

Almost blinded by shock, she ran back to the cottage, snatched up her bag and made for the villa. The pool area was busy, so she weaved her way behind the bushes, past the Firenze kitchen. She ran up the steps, across the reception area and hammered on Irena's office door.

Irena was characteristically calm, and she helped Claudia to a chair. 'What has happened? Has there been an accident?'

Claudia shook her head, frantically trying to speak. 'It's Fraser,' she gasped, 'he's with Natalie.'

'When you say, with…?'

'Walking, I saw them,' she made a limp gesture to indicate the direction, 'behind the cottage.'

'I cannot understand that. Natalie was invited earlier in the year, but, since the break-up, it was assumed that she would not be here. No arrangements have been made for her.' Irena retained her calm, practical attitude in contrast to Claudia's angst. 'It is not what I would expect of Mr Gallier.'

'Neither would I, but it's happening right now.' Claudia's voice became bitter as the shock turned to anger. 'She's there, laughing and chatting, playing happy families with my baby. Maybe they didn't break up after all. He spent some time in London, didn't he? He asked me to marry him, a few weeks ago, but what if he wanted the best of both worlds? He could have a secure family home for his son and a girlfriend for his London life.'

'That does not sound true. You are too upset to try and understand what is happening. We should find out, and then you can confront him.'

'And what right do I have to do that? Nothing's official between us. Nobody's made any promises.' Claudia described the secret phone call that she overheard, relayed Fraser's words. 'It all fits now…everything fits. And he made a point of telling me not rush back.' She could no longer trust that Fraser wouldn't cheat on her, there would always be a beautiful woman to tempt him. The vision of a happy life, raising their child together, began to crumble into bitter particles.

Irena put a glass of water in her hand and instructed her to drink it. As the water moistened her dry throat, Claudia began to think more clearly and knew exactly what she had to do to get hold of her own life once again.

'Claudia?' Irena's voice pierced her thoughts. 'Are you all right?'

'Yes.' Claudia braced herself and added, 'Yes, I've got this.'

'Got what?'

Claudia's determination didn't prevent the tears that spilled as her voice wheezed through her throat. 'I've faced this one before. I know exactly what I'm going to do.'

'Please tell me how I can help you.'

'I'll be fine. Fraser's cosy little walk with Natalie was a shock, but at least it's helped me make up my mind. I'm done with casual, amicable arrangements. Fraser will have to apply for access.'

'I will help you. What do you want to do? I could arrange accommodation for you in Florence if you wish to be alone to think.'

'Thank you, Irena, but I'm going to LA, and I'm going now.'

'You think your mother can help you through this?'

'No, but I have a long, overdue showdown with her. I'm tired of waiting for a dignified solution. Life isn't dignified, it's just plain cruel and callous, so that's what I must learn to be. I'm going to get my life in order. I'm going to hit my mother with plan zero.'

'I do not understand, what is that?'

Claudia raised her head high and looked at Irena. 'The answer,' she said bitterly, 'the one thing I can use to silence my mother once and for all, but it needs to be delivered her way—her cold, calculating way.'

'You are too upset to make a decision about this. You must rest.'

'I'm leaving now,' Claudia insisted, 'before they get back. I don't care how long I have to stay in the airport, I just want to get out of here. Fraser will take care of Justin, and he's surrounded by people to help him. I won't be away long. I only need a short time to do this.'

'You sound very sure.'

'I was poleaxed back there in the woods, but I know what to do now. I don't mean for you to be disloyal, but I really could use your help to get me on a flight. And I need a taxi to get away. I must do it quickly, please, Irena.'

'I was instructed, by Mr Gallier, to do all I could to help with your problems concerning Elsa Hamilton. He said that I should not wait for permission to do that. So I will arrange a flight plan for the company plane.'

Claudia shook her head in protest. 'Don't risk it, Irena. It's against their policy to use it for only one passenger?'

'It is allowed in a family emergency. Go quickly to the cottage and pack a few overnight things. Then come back here. But I must tell somebody what is happening.'

'Tell Lizzy and Tony, but please, nobody else.'

Claudia was hyperventilating as she dashed back to grab an overnight bag. It made her light-headed. Natalie disliked walking, so Claudia couldn't imagine they would be much longer. It took several minutes, but it felt like hours.

When she returned to the office, Irena was talking to Lizzy, who was brimming with tears.

'Claudia,' Lizzy hugged her. 'I can't believe this. What does he think he's doing? I spoke to Tony, he's terribly shocked. He thinks there should be some explanation…Fraser isn't normally sneaky like that. Come to our suite, Claudia, we'll try and find out what it's all about.'

'It is uncharacteristic,' Irena said, 'but it is happening.'

'I'll be gone very soon, so that should take some of the embarrassment out of it,' Claudia said.

Lizzy's breath jerked in her lungs. 'But we had no idea she was coming. Nobody invited her.'

'I guess we weren't supposed to know,' Claudia said. 'I have to stop myself getting jerked around. I need to take control…starting with my mother.' Her throat choked up, but she continued. 'I was so afraid I'd turn out like her. I didn't want to do things her way, but it's my only option now. If she wants to fight dirty, so will I.'

'Oh no,' Lizzy sighed and put her arms around her again. 'This isn't your way of dealing with things.'

'It is now. It's time I showed her what she's taught me over the years. Don't worry, Lizzy, I know exactly what I'm going to do. I've had the speech in my head since I was 14 years old.' She braced herself and added, 'I'm going to nail my mother to the wall. And then I'm taking my baby back to our peaceful life in London. Fraser will just have to sort out his access through a lawyer. Of course his legal backup will be better than mine, but I'm an actress, if necessary, I can hold myself together in court. I'll match any move he can make on me.' She picked up her bag and then hugged Lizzy once more. 'This won't change anything between you and me. I'll finish my work at Larchwood, of course. And we can still work together…yes?'

Lizzy nodded.

'People are going to ask questions,' Irena said. 'You can tell them the truth that Claudia needs to visit her mother urgently. And I have gone to accompany her.'

'Irena,' Claudia gasped, 'I can't let you do that. I'll be fine.'

'I have leave to use any means at my disposal. I will come with you.'

*****

Fraser sighed heavily as he parked the car. Life was certainly giving him a hard time. He needed to talk this over with Claudia. When he arrived at the cottage, he called out, 'Claudia, sorry I'm late, darling, I had to deal with something. Claudia, are you there?' She was nowhere to be found in the cottage, so he made his way to the villa.

Tony was hovering in the main entrance, his angry glare aimed at Fraser. 'Board meeting,' he said brusquely, 'Irena's office.'

Fraser was concerned about the possibility of a problem at Wainford, but he wasn't in the right frame of mind to deal with it now. 'What's this all about?' he said as Tony closed the door behind them. 'Will it take long? I need to find Claudia.'

'Where the hell have you been? You left Justin with Diana and Graham, and never even told them where you were going.'

'I needed some time to deal with something.' He glanced at his watch. 'I really ought to go and get Justin.'

'There's no need. They've prepared for him to spend the night, he's asleep now.' Tony looked wounded. 'So are you going to tell me what's been going on this afternoon?'

Fraser's heartrate increased. 'I see what you're getting at now. I couldn't avoid it, Tony. I had to deal with it.'

'Yes, we know. We kept it on a strictly need-to-know basis.'

Fraser was taken aback when he realised that he had been seen with Natalie. 'Somebody saw us?'

'Just one.'

'Well, that's a blessing.' He looked at his cousin and the definite sign of pain in his eyes. 'Tony, I'll discuss this with you, but I really should talk to Claudia first. It's a very difficult thing to explain.'

'Explain what? That all men are tempted sometimes?'

'Just let me find Claudia.'

'She was the one person that saw you walking with Natalie, in the woods.'

Fraser gasped as a sharp dart of shock pieced his insides. 'Oh, God!'

'You might well pray, Fraser.'

'I must find her, make her understand.'

'She's already formed an opinion. You're in big trouble.' Tony paced about, his exasperation showed clearly in his body language. 'You bloody idiot. You could have had it all. Claudia wasn't going to give you a hard time over access, but now you've blown it, it's visitations for you now. She's gone!'

'What? Gone? Gone where?'

'To LA, to nail her mother to the wall. And that's Claudia's terminology, not mine.'

'Claudia said that?'

'Yes. Needless to say, she's devastated but very determined. She's going to deal with Elsa Hamilton, once and for all. Irena's gone with her, she'll take care of her. They're already airborne. They'll be gone for three days, tops.'

Chapter Thirty

'Jet lag is not going to interfere with your schedule,' Irena said to Claudia. There was no emotion in her tone. She behaved like a coach who was preparing an athlete for a big event. 'Drink some coffee and then take a shower. That will wake you up. As for your love life, it does not exist until you get back to Italy.'

Claudia sighed and sipped her coffee. She felt lethargic and unmotivated. 'You're being very bossy.'

'I am from Ukraine, I do not see things from a British angle.'

'I know, if there's a job to be done, you go straight for it with no hesitation. Lizzy told me.' She frowned. 'You're amazing—it annoys me.'

'Hmm!' Irena shrugged. 'When you have changed, we will take a stroll along the boulevard and find Elsa Hamilton's agency.'

'Now?'

'It is just a recce, so we can go directly to it tomorrow. That way you will not be frustrated and stressed. Call it a rehearsal if you wish.'

The way Irena told her about the schedule reminded her of her childhood, when Elsa would relay the day's events to her. But Irena wasn't doing all this for her own sake, as her mother had done. 'Yes, you're right…good idea. I should have thought of it myself, shouldn't I?'

'I will take care of the schedule. Your job is to do what you came here to do. When we have located the Elsa Hamilton Agency, we will visit Lennie.'

Claudia looked more alert. 'Lennie?'

'He owns a ranch-style diner now, it is not far away.' She raised her brow. 'I am surprised you did not already know this. He is your special friend, is he not?'

'I haven't seen him since I was 14. It's kind of you to think of it. I'd love to see Lennie.' She stared at Irena. 'You've been busy.'

'It is all part of the plan to keep you focused. Today, you also have to go shopping.'

Claudia scowled, 'Shopping for what?'

Irena raised her palms toward her. 'Please do not be angry with me. I am not your mother.'

'I'm so sorry. That was awful.'

'Do you think you are going to defeat her looking like that? She will squash your self-esteem into the floor at the first opportunity. It is important that you wear smart things to show her that you are formidable and successful, also high-heeled shoes to give you more height. Your mother is taller than you.'

'I can't afford to go shopping here. I already spent a fortune in Florence. Lizzy's right, I should have used Fraser's card.'

'Do you still have it?'

'Yes.'

'Then you must use it today.'

Claudia looked horrified. 'This is my fight, not his.'

'You must do whatever it takes. You cannot afford to be too proud to let Mr Gallier pay for this.'

'It's not pride, it's—'

'Then I must pay,' Irena declared.

'OK, OK, I'll use the wretched card.'

'Will you please go and change into whatever you have, and we can go shopping.'

Claudia showered and dressed in jeans and a cotton blouse, and in an attempt to shake off some of the shock and pain, she lifted the tone of her voice when she returned to Irena. 'Do you think Lennie will let me into his diner dressed like this?'

'You look much better.'

The improvement in Claudia's mood was small, but Sunset Boulevard defied her to be morose. 'This place is so alive.' She gazed at the skyline ahead where beautiful, pale-toned properties nestled on the high ground and looked down over the billowing, green, leafy escarpment at the boulevard below. It reached every sense in her body. Her eyes drank in the contrasting colour tones between the pale, sunlit buildings and the splashes of vibrant hues from flowering plants. Despite the energy and the activity of the boulevard, Claudia felt calm and unrushed.

'It is very busy, and a little crazy I think,' Irena said.

'But it's not like London, it's more of a relaxed kind of busy.'

'That is a very confusing comment.'

Claudia pointed up to a placard on the top of a building. 'That film looks good. I'll have to look for it when it comes to the UK.'

'Your mother would be pleased. She has some of her actors in it.'

'You're incredible, Irena, your ability to research…' Claudia stopped and looked at her. 'You met her, didn't you?'

'Yes, when she came to the hotel. You were expecting her to make a move, and that was it.'

'But did she threaten Fraser?'

'It could be argued that she was just making conversation, but it was clear that she had enough information to do a great deal of damage to the family. We realised that she was being manipulative, even lying. The idea was to discredit you, so that they would give her the diaries for safekeeping. I took notes. Do you want to see them?'

'No, I know her patter.' Claudia was unmoved for her own part, but angry that Elsa had drawn Tony and Fraser into it. 'But can you take notes of my meeting with her, as many as you like.'

'Good idea, then you will have some proof of what actually transpires. Perhaps an audio account would be more convincing.' She smiled, 'It could be entertaining to hear you… nailing your mother to the wall.' She walked on. 'Come, you have shopping to do before we go to see Lennie.'

The instant they walked into Lennie's diner, Claudia heard his loud cry of, 'Claudeee!'

'Lennie!' She threw her arms around him. Lennie had always been such a rock, and right now it felt so good to be with somebody so reliable and loyal. 'Oh my God, Lennie, it's so good to see you.'

Lennie looked at her and smiled. 'What happened? I used to be taller than you.'

Claudia smiled at him fondly, then looked around. 'You always said you'd get a place, Lennie. I love it.'

Lennie smiled at her. 'You're beautiful, Claudie,' he shook his head, 'just beautiful.'

Claudia introduced Irena and they all sat together at a table. Claudia explained why she was there.

'So, at last, little Claudie's gonna kick her momma's badass, huh?'

'Which is it going to be?' Irena said. 'Nailing her to the wall or kicking her bad ass?'

'From my experience of Elsa Hamilton,' Lennie said, 'it'll take both. Need any help, Claudie?'

'No, Lennie, you helped a long time ago and suffered for it.'

'Nah! It was worth it. That arrogant young bastard's nose crunched a lot harder than my knuckles.'

Lennie stayed with them while they had a meal, and the conversation continued to flow like torrents. They talked about everything, a nostalgic pastiche of memories intertwined with news.

Lennie regarded Claudia affectionately and said, 'So you're a momma now? Are ya gonna marry his dad?'

Claudia was caught on the hop. 'Ah! Well…he proposed and left me to think about it.'

'Does he love the little guy?'

'Crazy about him! He's a great dad.'

Lennie squeezed her hands. 'Do you love him, Claudie?'

Claudia felt her heart twist painfully, and she faltered a moment. Then she looked at Lennie, tears rushed to her eyes. 'All around the ranch and back, Lennie…all around the ranch and back.'

'Aw! Ya miss him?'

She wouldn't share the details of recent events. Lennie so wanted her to be happy. She wrinkled her nose and nodded.

'When's the big shootout, huh?'

'Tomorrow.'

Lennie squeezed her hand and said, 'Will ya be OK, Claudie?'

'You bet, Lennie,' Claudia said with a determined look in her eyes. 'Tomorrow, I'll be the one calling the shots.'

*****

Irena approached the table where Claudia sat with her morning coffee. 'I did not realise you had come outside. How are you feeling?'

'I know where I am, what I'm doing here, and what I still have to do, but my perception of the world is out of shape.'

'Jetlag, is not just a matter of changing sleep patterns.' Irena put some papers on the table. 'For you,' she said, and then sat down. 'Your estimated earnings during your childhood. I thought it might come in useful.'

'How on earth did you…?'

'You do not need to know that, you just need to see the figures. I assume that she did not leave much of it in your trust fund, otherwise, you would still have a large proportion of it. You are not the kind of person to spend it all recklessly.'

'This is great. Thank you.' Irena looked so cool, composed and very smart, Claudia felt secure in her stalwart company. 'I didn't expect you to come and prop me up, but I'm so glad you're here.'

Irena rested her hand on Claudia's arm. 'What you are going to do will take a great deal of courage. You have that, be sure to use it.'

'I suspect that's your thing, bailing women out, when they get in a pickle.'

'The memory of my own pickle, as you call it, is still very clear. I picked up my children and moved from Ukraine, without hesitation. Mr Franklyn gave me a job and made the move a positive one.' She looked Claudia in the eye. 'I can organise your travel and accommodation, I can also support you as a friend, but I cannot ease your pain. That, you must do for yourself.'

Claudia nodded. 'Yes, I know.' A gush of air snatched at her lungs, and a sob escaped her control. 'Dear God! Did I do something so bad to deserve all this?'

'It does not matter whether you did or not,' Irena said steadily. 'The task is still the same. Do not look to your anger to help you. Today, you will need concentration not anger. Gain control of the meeting at the very first opportunity, and do not let it go.'

Claudia knew she was right. She hated the thought, but it had to be done. She sipped her coffee and looked around at the flamboyant Bougainvillea plants in the courtyard, red, orange and pink, like flames around the walls. They spilled over large planters, wrapped their tendrils around pillars and looked down between the bars of the pergola overhead. Their sumptuous bracts almost hid their tiny, dainty white flowers, too small to compete with such a show of colour. Yet, beneath all that blazing beauty, sharp thorns lay in wait, spikes to prick your fingers should you get too close. It was like the beautiful life she reached for, only to find the hidden barbs too late.

'You should have breakfast,' Irena said, 'then you can get ready. I made a call, remained anonymous and established that Elsa Hamilton was there. You do not want to ruin the plan by missing her.'

Irena's phone rang. She answered it and then looked at Claudia. 'Mr Gallier wishes to speak to you.'

Claudia's body quaked. She shook her head, and then listened to Irena trying to convince him.

'Mr Gallier insists that it is very important?'

Claudia couldn't expect Irena to argue with him. It might even be Justin who needed her. She took the phone, her lungs tightened, she tried to take a deep breath but was denied it. 'Is Justin all right?'

'Yes, he's fine. He's having a fabulous time. Claudia...'

'Not now, Fraser.'

'Darling, please...this is killing me.'

'Do you want it all ways, Fraser? You want what you want and for me to make it easy?'

'If you'd just listen...talk to me. I love you. I love you so much.'

He whispered those words in the night, when it was easy to express emotions. This was the first time she'd heard them in the light of day. They were like heavy blows to her body, apologetic terms of endearment to try and excuse what had happened. She brought her voice under control, it was flat, emotionless, void of the nuances of friendship or love. 'I love you too, Fraser, I always have. But you must remember that I've lived with these feelings for a long time. And I'm tired of carrying them around like useless baggage.'

'Of course they're not useless. Please, my love, let me explain—'

'Another time. Take care of Justin, that's all I care about at the moment. Can you remember the bedtime song? If not, I can text the words…' Her voice faded into silence.

'I can remember them now,' Fraser murmured.

'Please don't call me again.'

'I'll do as you ask if you promise that we can talk when you get back.'

'I have to talk to you, Fraser, packing up my life and moving on isn't so straightforward anymore. I can't just take Justin away from his family.'

'I told you, it's your family too.'

'I have to go. Bye, Fraser.'

'No, no, don't hang up, please…'

'I'm sorry I can only face one demon at a time.' She ended the call and sat in silence for a moment. Then she said, softly, 'Of all the times for him to say "I love you", he had to choose now. Is that how they do it, Irena? Is that how they keep a woman in tow? When they're losing her they say "I love you" and start making new promises, until the next time?'

Chapter Thirty-One

'My God, how much has she spent on this place?' Claudia whispered as they approached the sprawling reception desk at The Elsa Hamilton Agency.

'Good morning. May I help you?' The receptionist asked.

'I'm here to see Elsa Hamilton,' Claudia said clearly, with her head high the way her mother taught her.

'Do you have an appointment?'

'I don't need one,' Claudia spoke boldly.

'I'm afraid you do,' the woman said, in a patronising tone. 'Mrs Hamilton is a very busy woman. If you'd like to leave your details—photographs and resume…'

Claudia pointed to an enormous picture on the wall behind the reception desk, the one where her horse was rearing, she was smiling and raising her Stetson hat in the air. 'There's my photograph, it launched this agency, and I don't need an appointment to see my mother.'

The receptionist gasped and reached for the phone. Irena calmly pressed her hand on top of hers. 'Miss Hamilton would like it to be a surprise.'

'She doesn't like surprises. Anyway, she wanted to know immediately if you made contact.' The receptionist seemed nervous.

'I'm sure she did,' Claudia said and moved towards the office door. 'She'll get over it.' She stopped a moment as she heard Elsa's voice, but it wasn't coming from the office, it was breathing against the back of her neck, a memory that was as welcome as a persistent hornet buzzing in her ear.

So often she had stood like this while Mother had issued instructions. 'Come now, Claudie, head up. They're looking for somebody with courage and spirit, not a wilting wimp. Don't forget to tell them you can ride and swim very well. I'll count to three, and then you'll open that door and walk in, confident and cheerful but not too precocious. Do you understand? One…two…' Claudia mouthed the countdown and then burst through the door.

Elsa Hamilton sat at her enormous desk in a cavernous, luxurious room, like a dictator in a fictitious land. Her brow lifted in surprise, but she wasn't thrown off balance.

The receptionist tried to make a hasty apology. Claudia approached her and spoke in a low voice. 'I don't want to be interrupted, otherwise, I'll scream at my mother, and then she'll scream at you.'

'But what if somebody…'

'They wait—understand? And no phone calls.'

'I should check with Mrs Ham—'

'You shouldn't ignore my request, otherwise, a virus will hit your computer within seconds. You won't be able to find your clients' records.'

The receptionist's eyes stared in fear. 'You can't do that?'

'No,' Claudia said in a cool tone, 'but *she* can.' She quietly spoke a few words, in Russian, to Irena.

Irena responded, also in Russian. Then, cool and silent, she sat down on one of the chairs against the wall and laid her case on the next seat.

'Got it?' Claudia said with a lift of her brow.

The receptionist's eyes rounded, and she glanced again towards Elsa Hamilton who waved her away.

'What's this—Mother's Day?' Elsa drawled. 'Or has my daughter come to her senses at last.'

'You guessed.' Claudia assumed a dignified demeanour as she crossed the plush, carpeted floor towards the vast desk. She looked at Elsa's cold eyes, the expression she wore when she was expecting an explanation. Claudia showed no emotion. She would explain when she was good and ready. This was where the old rules ended, and the new ones would be printed indelibly on Elsa Hamilton's mind. Claudia raised her head and made her first move, one she knew would irritate her mother. 'Hello Ma!'

Elsa's nostrils twitched. 'Don't call me that, it's so undignified.'

'I know, that's why I came up with the idea a long time ago. It annoyed you intensely. Small consolation, but it helped me survive.'

'Have you brought my diaries?'

'Patience, Ma,' Claudia said. 'I thought we'd have a chat.'

'You came all the way out here for a *tête-à-tête*?' Elsa said.

Claudia moved to the edge of the desk. 'I understand that you did the same thing. You went to Merevale, had a chat with my boss.'

'You've fallen on your feet. It's the oldest trick in the book to have a rich man's brat. Nice watch, by the way, you got yourself a fine bread ticket.'

'You married a poor man and made a bread ticket out of your child.' She stared into Elsa's cold eyes. 'I'm not here with the diaries.'

Elsa's lips tightened. 'Then what?'

'A dual,' Claudia said. 'There's obviously no point in hoping for an amicable, round-the-table discussion, so it has to be movie-style. A fully blown, once and for all, "High Noon" shootout. I'm calling you out, Ma.'

'You think because you burst in unannounced, you've gained ground?' Elsa suddenly laughed. Not the kind of musical sound that one normally makes with laughter, but a fabricated, metronomic burst of sounds designed to taunt and insult.

Claudia shook her head. 'There's no need to use the old, let's-demoralise-Claudia routine, because it won't work anymore.'

'You shouldn't be too sure of that.'

'Well, I'm fresh out of bunny rabbits and fluffy kittens, you sold my horse from under me, long ago. So what's to lose? And before you can threaten to use my child for your power games, you should be warned.'

'Of what?' Elsa scoffed. 'Get to the point. I've got important people to see.'

A flash of anger burned in Claudia's eyes, but she remained cool. 'More little working babies?'

'They're up for it.'

'Not all of them. There'll be one or two like I was. Little earners, playing out Mummy's dreams.' Claudia spoke in a cool tone, she couldn't allow her mother to gain ground. 'So,' she continued, 'here's the deal, Ma. You're going to get out of my life for good, and stop turning up unannounced to threaten me and my family…understand?'

'We've already established that, once the diaries are handed over. I don't even want the bloody things, just the translation will do. You can have the useless bits of paper and the dogeared notebooks.'

'You don't understand,' Claudia said, unruffled by Elsa's arrogance. 'You're not getting the diaries or the translations.'

'Then you're bringing nothing to the table, you silly girl. What are you going to do, sue me? See where that gets you.'

'Sue you, Ma?' Claudia said boldly. 'What kind of an ungrateful daughter would do that? No, I'm playing this your way.'

'My…?'

Claudia stared down at her mother and said, 'This is not a good time to upset me…'

Irena suddenly coughed.

Claudia realised that it was a warning, her control was wavering. She got back on track and spoke in a determined but steady voice, 'Your rules…one dirty, low-down trick for another.'

'You're bluffing. You can't play it that way. All you can do is run away.'

'This is a one-off special.'

Elsa sniggered. 'Go on then, you silly girl, deliver your first…blow.' She remained seated as if she wielded more power from there.

'You always told me that my earnings were in a trust fund, and when I was 18, I could access it. You gave me papers and everything, but they were just a prop to keep me quiet. When I turned up for my college fees, there was no such thing as a trust fund.'

'What are you going to do, give me slap on the wrist?'

'I'm preparing an article about it for your local press. My mother made me work for over ten years and then stole my trust fund, leaving me penniless. I think they'll print that.'

'I think not. If you're going to play that worn out card around here, you need to get in the queue with all the other disgruntled child stars. I submitted accounts. It was all perfectly legal. By the time we paid all those expensive personal coaches—'

'Three million dollars-worth, *my* three million dollars.' She glared at Elsa. 'They'll print that, especially if I throw in the box set fraud. Nobody said you could do that?'

'So, is that it?' Elsa shrugged her angular shoulders. 'Is that your scary threat that's going to settle this? You'll have to do better than that.'

'Well, we're playing my game but with your rules, so I guess my threat wasn't dirty enough. Each one has to be worse than last—right? So try this one. A different story, a follow-up to that little spread you arranged in the magazine. Except that it will be in a nice glossy one, more local to you.'

'What can you have to say that the public want to read?'

Claudia strolled about the office, 'Imagine it? I met with my estranged mother. She was so delighted to hear about my little son, that she couldn't wait to use him to steal my inheritance bequeathed to me by my dear grandmother.'

Elsa's cool slipped. 'I never used your son.'

'Oh, but you did, Ma. You stood on my doorstep and said you would look for my weakness. By the time you'd traced me, to Larchwood, there it was…my baby boy. Then every step you took was leading to him. You knew exactly what was happening in my life. Did you think I wouldn't realise that it was Todd, spoon-feeding you all that information? A hungry actor, desperate for a start in his career, a guy who wouldn't do panto, but he sang like a little bird for you, didn't he? What did you promise him, a green card? Movies? Work on Broadway? American TV…?'

Elsa got up from her chair and strolled around the desk towards Claudia. 'I couldn't have been better informed if I'd bugged that banqueting room where you work. He contacted me when he saw the magazine. Then got over confident and held me to ransom with information about your son. I actually paid him for it. Poor fool, thought he could make it here, but he's just a snappy talker with a good body. I could round up any number of guys like that, waiting tables in the restaurants along the boulevard.' She stared at Claudia for a moment, then sighed and returned to her desk, as if to deny her daughter any kind of victory. 'Will you get on with it I've already told you, I have appointments?'

'They'll wait,' Claudia said. 'Of course they will, they need work, and you're the great provider.' She closed in on the desk. 'By the way, I met Lennie yesterday. You remember him?'

'That little jockey? Why would I be interested in him?'

'Do you remember he got sacked for punching Joel Nixon's nose, when we were shooting the final series of the ranch? They had to write an extra scene in it to explain the bruises. Don't you remember?'

'For goodness sake,' Elsa muttered impatiently.

'Do you really believe that everybody has a weak spot?'

'I most certainly do.'

'Even you?' Claudia felt herself gaining ground as Elsa's eyes flickered. She planted her palms on the desk and leaned over. 'Think back, Ma, why did Lennie punch Joel's face?'

'How should I know that?'

'Because you were supposed to chaperone me. I told you how Joel wouldn't stop picking on me. I begged you to stay with me, but you were always somewhere else…schmoozing.'

'You weren't my only actor, I had my agency to run. He was just a big kid, jealous because you had the lead, and he only got bits here and there. You'd been in the business long enough to put up with a bit of ribbing.'

'That despicable, arrogant bastard made my life a misery, constantly mocking me, dripping sly, quiet comments. It went on for months. Every day's shooting was the same, even when we were on set, he couldn't resist leaning over and saying something about my stupid curly hair, or my fanciful, English accent. He became more and more threatening. I had to drag my self-esteem off the ground every day he was on set. But what did you do about it…a big, fat nothing. Was it any wonder I became a feisty little tearaway?'

'He was only three years older than you. You were quite capable of putting him in his place.'

'He was over a foot taller than me, had no morals or a conscience. I wouldn't stand a chance.'

'With what?' Elsa scoffed. 'He had no talent. He came off the football field. He was only there for his brawn and his youth.'

'That brawny youth threatened me. Said he'd put me in my place, and he'd do it on the next night shoot, the one where the barn catches fire. That night we were waiting to be called. We weren't needed yet. When the fire kicked in, and everybody ran around shouting, he started to nudge me towards the stable door. Said he knew what to do with feisty little Brit bitches. I yelled for him to back off, but there was too much noise. He laughed and said nobody would hear me—they wouldn't believe me either. They wouldn't take my word against his. I was terrified. I looked for Mathew, but he was already filming. By then Joel had pushed me right into the stable. I even screamed, but there was nobody. Then Lennie turned up. Joel laughed, but Lennie lunged up at him and punched him in the face. He got into serious trouble for hitting a six foot, two hundred pound teenager, who was behaving like a dirty, old man.' She paused a moment and then added, 'I was entitled to your protection. After all, you had all the money.'

'And you're dragging all this up, because…?'

'It's another story for the magazine.'

Elsa Hamilton shrugged her shoulders. 'Am I supposed to be afraid?'

'Yes, Ma.' Claudia spoke coldly. 'You're about to threaten my baby, so I have to stop you.' She strolled to look at the picture gallery on the wall and stopped at the largest one. It was in a frame, a little girl with curly hair and a faraway look. There was also a display of current, successful, professional children. 'Once I was your only one, but now you've got a whole collection of babies, princesses, cute little boys. They all want to be movie stars, do commercials, TV dramas and kid's shows…the whole glitzy enchilada. And look at these pretty ingénues, ready to burst onto the screen as young, wide-eyed adults.' She paused a moment and then looked at a large picture of an adult male, handsome, slender, tall, in his prime. 'Look who's all grown up. So, you kept him on your books, ignored what he threatened to do to your own 14-year-old daughter.'

'It's just business.'

'Yes, your business, your precious business. I had lessons for almost everything, but the most valuable one, right now, is the one I learned from you…how to find somebody's weakness and use it.'

'To do what?' Elsa Hamilton scoffed.

Claudia didn't answer, she gestured to the gallery. 'Beautiful, aren't they? Elsa Hamilton's precious little adorable pets, each one a bunny rabbit, a fluffy kitten, a pony…'

'What on earth are you talking about?'

'You took away my little pets, so I'm going to take yours. I can do that to you now, I'm not hampered by integrity. I'll clear your agency of all your little baby actors. No child's mother, pushy or otherwise, is going to entrust her valuable little girl or boy to you. You turned a blind eye when your own teenage daughter was being seriously threatened by Joel Nixon. Look at him now. The handsome, heartthrob doctor in that new series, a great hit I believe. He's a big star. Much higher up the fame ladder than when I knew him, but just think how much further he'll fall these days. I'm going to bring you down, Ma, and he's going down with you. He can say goodbye to his fans, and you can say goodbye to your babies.'

'You haven't got it in you.' Elsa Hamilton's face showed her fear.

'Once mud gets slung around here, it flies everywhere, and it's going to stick all over your agency. The scandal would be huge. It would grow and spread, like a virus, through the media, the social media, too, gathering extra details that may or may not be true. Maybe even bring more victims into the open. I might not have been the only one. Other girls wouldn't have had Lennie to protect them. The story will last long enough to ruin you and Joel Nixon. You'll be lucky to manage a list of walk-ons and extras. You'll probably even call Todd back.' She stared at Elsa and knew she had beaten her. It wasn't a glorious victory, it hurt her deeply.

Elsa sat motionless for a few seconds, and then she said, 'I suppose if this was a movie, I'd start applauding very slowly.'

'I wasn't acting, Ma. I was very serious.'

Elsa Hamilton sighed irritably. 'All right, just give me the jewellery, and we'll call it a day.'

'This isn't your day, it's mine,' Claudia scoffed. 'I've already told you, there's no jewellery. Maybe Grannie sold it. Good for her. This has been quite a shoot-out, and I can see that it's hit you right in the reputation, which will remain intact at my pleasure. I'll contact you with an address, and you are going to redirect any repeat royalties you receive to me. And that includes the box set. I'll get my lawyers to draw up an agreement.'

'And if I don't?'

'Then you can add fraud to your ruined reputation, I'm not afraid to take you to court anymore. Think of all those nasty rumours. Even your walk-ons and extras list will end up in the trash. They can't afford to be ripped off. And, oh boy, how some of them gossip and complain. And think how many of them work in restaurants. By all means, take your commission. Shall we say ten percent?'

'Twenty.'

'Don't push it. You can have 15.'

'So you've struck a deal,' Elsa said. 'Did it all by yourself. Being a mother suits you, it's taught you how to fight. All your actions, the move from London, the effort to keep me away, it was all for your son.' She sighed. 'Imagine that. You've cost me a fortune, you know that? The diaries were going to be made into a movie. I took a front-end payment.'

'That was obvious,' Claudia said. 'Even you wouldn't have pushed so hard otherwise. You took a big risk, it was illegal.' Claudia turned from her and made for the door.

'Wait!' Elsa got up and approached. She stared for a few moments, then rested her hands on Claudia's cheeks. 'Come back, Claudie.' The words came in a husky whisper. Claudia felt nothing, she just stared, silent and numb as the plea came again. 'Come back! Work with me.'

Claudia was suspicious. She thought it was all over. But Elsa Hamilton never made affectionate gestures, certainly not to her. What was going to happen now? Was she grasping at straws? Was this an overture to a much bigger gesture? Claudia decided to have faith in her conquest over her lifelong bane. She remained calm and cold. 'It's over, Ma. Deal with it.'

Elsa dropped her hands to her sides, turned and walked away. Then suddenly, she whipped around and cried out as if she was grieving. 'You could have been up there on those billboards.' She thrust her hand towards the window. 'I could have made a great star out of you.' She pointed up to the picture of when Claudia was a Russian princess. 'Look at her! Look at that child...that incredible child.'

'I can see her, Ma. But look at her eyes, that isn't acting, she didn't want to be there. Maybe all these other kids do, but *she* didn't. She just wanted her kitten back.' Claudia stared for several seconds, then looked, for the last time, at the cold, grey eyes, 'Goodbye Mother.'

Claudia made her exit as boldly as she had entered. As she walked along the boulevard, she felt high. She had won, for Justin, for Alyona, and for that little curly haired princess on Elsa Hamilton's wall.

Chapter Thirty-Two

Claudia stood on the balcony. The cottage was quiet and still, so she knew she was alone. Her hair was still damp from her shower, and she wore a simple sundress. She could vaguely remember Fraser meeting them from the plane, Grace and Lizzy helping her to bed, but she had no idea when that was. Grace and Charlie were swimming with Lizzy. Laughter filled the air as they splashed about playing with the coloured ball brought for the children. Ruth and Nathan sat at a table. Life was going on, just as before. They made it look so easy.

She went downstairs, there was a note on the table, addressed to Claudia darling, and she sighed. Even now he used these terms of endearment. The note was to let her know that Justin had gone with Diana and Graham, to a children's playpark in Florence. Claudia was disappointed, she longed to see him, to put her arms around his little warm body. He was safe now.

There was a large space in Claudia's mind where her feud with her mother had dwelled for so long. It was like a dark, empty room, and she had no idea how to put some light into it to exorcise the abiding bitterness there.

She went out onto the veranda, sat down on the steps and looked at the flowers leaning over them. Her heart was breaking, and she desperately needed to find a way to get through what was left of the holiday, don her motley once again. Fraser would have the support of his cousins, no matter what he'd done, but they wouldn't give him an easy time.

'Claudia!'

Claudia's heart leapt with surprise.

'Sorry, darling, I didn't mean to startle you.'

Claudia said the first thing that came to her mind. 'Is Justin back? I haven't seen him yet.'

'Not yet... Can we talk?'

'About Natalie?'

'Yes.'

'Then don't bother. It's none of my business.'

'Of course it is. And we need to talk about it.'

'What do you want from me, Fraser? Have you come to tell me that we're going to live by the old rules again? The ones where I stay home and wait for your random visits, turn the other cheek and pretend that your love life doesn't hurt like hell?'

'You *are* my love life,' Fraser protested.

'So what does that make Natalie?'

Fraser scowled. 'Do you think I'd keep seeing two of you? Does that sound like me?'

'No,' Claudia admitted softly.

Before Claudia could protest, Fraser sat by her side on the steps. 'I don't want Natalie. If you'd just listen for—'

'Please don't talk about her. I just want to wait for Justin.'

'We'll wait together. I know I handled this badly, and I'm deeply sorry. But you must let me tell you what happened. She's done enough damage, don't let her do any more. We're not together anymore. She just turned up.'

'And you felt the need to take her for a walk?'

'Yes, to get her out of sight. She needed my help, she was desperate.'

Claudia scoffed. 'Desperate?'

'Natalie's not like you and Lizzy. When life hits out at her, she can't hit it back...she reaches for some guy to help her out. She remembered that I'd be here because she was originally invited to this holiday.'

'I'm expected to believe that she travelled all this way? That you were the only man on earth that could help her?'

'She was already staying in Verona, with a guy called Damien. They were celebrating their engagement, even making wedding plans. They were having lunch, drinking lots of wine when Natalie made a confession. It was a big mistake. She should have kept it to herself. Damien's very jealous, but she'd had quite a lot to drink.'

'What were you supposed to do about it?'

Fraser paused a moment and then said, 'She told him about the time when I was in London, a few weeks ago, and she'd turned up at my apartment. She'd had a row with Damien, at a party. My place was nearer than hers, and she assumed I'd let her stay, but I refused and made her leave. I was angry that she still had a key, and she'd let herself in.'

'So what was her problem?'

'Damien didn't believe that nothing happened that night, he threatened to break the engagement, stormed off back to the hotel. Natalie thought of ringing me and then remembered about the family holiday. She'd had too much wine to drive, so in her panic, she jumped on a bus to Florence and then got a taxi out here. I was furious, tried to hide her, afraid you'd see and get the wrong idea.'

'You got that right.'

'I drove her back to Verona, by then, I was just as angry as Damien. I confirmed Natalie's claim that nothing happened, told them to get on with it. By the time I got back here, you'd gone, and I was the one in trouble.'

Claudia felt dizzy from being pulled from one emotion to another. She looked down at her hands, they were clenched on her lap. 'But the phone call.'

'What phone call?'

'I was upstairs, dressing Justin, ready to meet your parents. I overheard it. You were being very secretive.'

'That wasn't Natalie, it was your mother. She still thought we were cooperating with her and wanted an update. I didn't want to tell you. I was overprotective after your accident.'

Claudia sighed heavily. 'She's still…'

Fraser put his arm around her shoulders. 'No darling, she's gone, you've seen to that. I heard the recording.'

'Good performance, hmm?'

'You were amazing.'

'I'm not proud of it.'

'But I'm very proud of you. All this talk about Natalie and her damn boyfriend is just information. Something you needed to know. But what a terrible waste of time it is. The holiday's nearly over. Why spend it talking about them when we could be talking about us?'

After a few moments silence, Claudia began to breathe deeply, for the first time in weeks. The flowers suddenly looked more vibrant, the sky more blue. She hardly dare believe that Fraser had no intention of meeting up with Natalie. He even had an opportunity that night in his apartment, but he hadn't taken it. She turned to him. 'I really jumped to conclusions, didn't I? I'm so sorry.'

'It was understandable, sweetheart. I was an idiot. I should have kept it in the open, nobody would have questioned it. I was so afraid to lose you again.'

A sob caught in Claudia's throat. She had been privileged to spend a little of her life with a beautiful man, and now she was blessed with another. She thrust her arms around his neck and felt the strength in his embrace. They kissed, with unashamed hunger, healing the conflict, doubts and the pain of too much time apart.

Fraser looked at her, 'I adored you as my special friend. I needed you. I had to know you'd always be there when I knocked on your door. It was so selfish. I should have admitted that I was in love with you.'

'But the love doesn't cancel out the friendship, we'll still have that, won't we?'

'Yes, darling, we will.'

She smiled. 'So is your offer still on the table? Both of us under one roof? No daddy days and mummy days, just one family together...?'

'That was a terrible proposal. Let me make you a better one...please. It would make me feel a lot better.'

'OK.' She expelled a gentle laugh. 'Anything to make you happy.'

Fraser enclosed her hands in his, looked into her eyes and said, 'I want to make the commitment, the vows, the promises... Will you meet me somewhere? Perhaps on a sunny beach, a snowy day in church, a fabulous hotel in the mountains, a spring day standing in a sea of daffodils... Will you do that, my love? Will you marry me?'

Claudia looked at him through misted eyes and answered, 'Yes...to both of your proposals.'

They sealed the bargain with a lingering, loving, warm kiss. Then Fraser smiled and said, 'I really do love you.'

Tears spilled from Claudia's eyes and her mouth trembled as she asked, 'All around the ranch and back?'

'All around the ranch and back,' he confirmed. 'So, about this one roof we're going to share.'

'What about it?' Claudia said as she brushed her tears away.

'We need a house. One with a nice garden, with flowers, Justin will like that.' His eyes were alight as he said, 'And we'll need a cat.'

Claudia suddenly laughed at the way he talked of flowers and a cat, and the way, after so much worry and conflict, they were able to dream like any other couple. 'Yes,' she agreed, 'we must have a cat.'

'We also need a bit of land,' Fraser said.

'Why?'

'For the horse.'

Claudia's brow puckered. 'Horse?'

Fraser smiled. 'A man can't marry a girl who can ride like a Texas Ranger unless he's going to buy her a horse.'

Chapter Thirty-Three

The July sunshine flooded through the drawing room windows at Larchwood. The round tables, previously immaculately laid with shining cutlery, sparkling glasses and crisp, skilfully folded napkins were now in disarray with empty coffee cups and glasses. The candles were burnt down.

Fraser kissed Claudia's face and whispered, 'I love you,' very privately in her ear. He had no idea whether she was nervous or not, there had been no signs of it on her face or in her mannerisms since his first sight of her in church. She walked tall, looked relaxed and confident dressed in her beautiful gown, designed by Lizzy. Eliot was the nervous one as he escorted the lovely bride, but honoured to be the one chosen to give her away.

Fraser stood up to make his speech. He cleared his throat and began. He told the guests about that frosty day in the park, when he first saw that girl with Peter Pan hair. When they sat and leaned against a tree and discussed the theory of daffodils.

'I'll never stop thanking her for our beautiful son.' Emotion snatched at his voice, and he paused to clear his throat again. 'What an incredible journey it's been for me to get to know Claudia. The time she spoke Russian to Yuri. And when she danced the tango at a party, Grace called her an Argentinian gypsy. The time I found her in the sugar room, boiling heather she'd gathered from the brow to dye some yarn. But those of you who saw the finished tapestry would know that she was absolutely right. And now I'm proud to say that a few days ago, Claudia received an offer for her book.' He paused and allowed the guest to applaud, some cheered. 'Her dream to give her great-grandaunt a voice, after all these years, burned brightly. Her determination was inspiring.' He took a small envelope from his pocket and eased a folded note from it. 'I have permission to read something to you. It's one of Alyona's letters, from Richard. He

240

wrote it when he was staying in London, in 1921. It's always been Claudia's favourite. It celebrates a man's deep and unconditional love for a woman… as I celebrate mine today.' He reverently unfolded the letter and read it out.

'My Dearest Alyona,

What a delight your sweet letter was tonight, forwarded to me from the Geological Society. It was not there when I went to dinner. After waiting 15 minutes for a table, I went to the desk, and there was your letter alone in its glory – but it filled such a gap, such a want, such a desire, and gave me great joy. Oh how your words do go home deep down into my very heart and soul. I could not wait for the end of the letter, so I ran to the telephone, and in some 20 minutes came your voice. Oh how I was delighted. It is late, but I would not wish to retire without writing a word to you. What hopes rise bright in my mind as I think of you! Is it right? Why not? You have been in my mind every moment since I met you, since it was revealed to my eyes, to my mind, to my heart and soul a personality for which I have so longed to know and find and appreciate. It is all as a dream of sweet reality.

Good night – *au revoir* – *à bientôt.*
Richard.'

THE END